The Land of Bliss

a fairy story

by

KEITH BRAZIL

Books by Keith Brazil

The Anthology of Joy:

The Land of Bliss
An Alchemist's Wedding
In Consideration of Cats
The Chameleon's Last Dance

The Yin-Yang Experiment:

The Wilderness Diary
Popcorn, Parasites, Precious & Pearls

DEDICATION

To Michael and the Pyjama Army – with love,

Keep on marching.

To Kassie – with thanks for her patience and insights.

To my Mother, Angela, and my Father, George.

To my Brothers, Stephen and Andrew.

To my Nans Edith and Esther,

And to my aunts: Bubbles, Mary, Ollie and Godmother Tilly

And Goddaughters, Hannah and Zara.

To my Stepmother, Tanya.

To Ben – our friend.

To all the Mothers, Fathers and Guardians making it up in bedtime stories

Keep it going

To the Magdalena – for divine inspiration.

To the International Council of Thirteen Indigenous Grandmothers

and to Grandmothers everywhere…

In peace, in love, in prayer.

With a big thank you to Hathor, the Moon and all her people.

CONTENTS

Acknowledgments   i

Cast of Characters

1   The Land of Bliss – a fairy story   1

"If you're a mushroom, jump in the basket…"
(Russian saying)

ACKNOWLEDGMENTS

Developmental Editor: Kitty Malone

Dramaturge: Michael Brazil

Cover Concept & Design: Keith Brazil & Jason Tanner

Rose Illustration: Colin Francolino-Scott

Special thanks to: Kitty, Michael, Jason, Stephen Pucci, Nick &
Brendan Sweet-Rogers, Colin, Rachel, Zara, John Damer, Teresa &
Paul, Mike & Tom, Mark & Jim, Pearl & Kitty, and to everyone at
LSBU for their help and support.

A Rose Pink Production

KEITH BRAZIL

Cast of Characters

Anders the Bard & Little Milk (pet goat).

Magnus Skovgaard – The Headmaster
(aka Mathmagician & former Mayor).

Mr Janus Woolfe
(aka School Caretaker & Lone Silver Wolf – brother to the Huntingsman).

Eirik the Huntingsman
(brother to Janus Woolfe & father of Rose Pink).

The Family Rose:
Mother Rose & Father Rose; their son Jack; their four daughters: Rose Red
& Rose White (twin sisters), Rose Pink & Snow Rose.

Jack Rose
(aka Flash Jack, muddled-headed Peter, Peter Bear, Mayor Bear).

Miss Beret/Miss Berry
(aka Wild Rose, Rose Pink).

The Family Littlesøn:
Grandmother May Littlesøn, Mr Littlesøn, Mrs Littlesøn,
& Raoulf Littlesøn.

The Golden-haired Singing Princess
(aka the Lovely Lady, Beltane Belter, daughter to the King and Queen of
Awe, & stepdaughter to the Witch Queen).

Fairy Godmother
(aka Waltzing Matilda of the long silk stockings/Silly Tilly).

Cast of Characters contd.

Witch Queen
(aka Enchantress, Giant Witch, Shadow Witch & Wicked Stepmother).

Grandmothers of Awe:
Able Mable, Mable Fable, Ninny Nanny, Grinny Granny, Nanny Nine
Toes, Ninny Goat Griff, & Nanny Goat Gruff.

The Cloud Littles:
Mr & Mrs Little, and their five daughters:
Little Pearl, Little Star, Little Seed, Little Spark & Little Bliss.

The Town Statue
(the Philosopher-Prince).

Brethren Brothers of Olde & Iberian Sisters.

Screech Witches, Giants (frost, cloud and land), Trembling Fears, Goblins,
Pixies, Wolves (including Big Bad), Fairies, Air Angels & Trolls.

Gunnbjorn the Gruff
(aka Park Keeper and Head Game Hunter).

Sundry Townsfolk:
The spell-infected turning wolves & gunmen, Old man Joseph, Cartwheel
Charlie and his Grandpa, Billy Goat Plum, & the Sky Monks.

Various Talking Trees, Speaking Birds and Hungry Grasses.

The Land of Bliss

a fairy story

Honour your Mother and Father

Honour your Mother-Father God.

And so it was that Anders the Bard laughed as his beloved goat, Little Milk, wandered to a nearby grassy bank and chewed away at the sweet-headed daisies, bleating contentedly. They were tired and thirsty having travelled across the notorious Hook Heath to the beggars' town of Strange Stone. Wishing to rest his weary bones, Anders pulled up a barstool and ordered a flagon of ale from Less-than-Jolly Roger – a particularly grizzled, patched-eyed, pirate-looking landlord of the grim "Peg Leg and Hook" inn.

Having quenched his thirst, the Bard slowly took from out of his pocket rolls of parchment and two tail feather quills (one light, one dark), given to him in his youth by a flock of migrating Swallows. Slowly, he began to compose his straying thoughts. Peddling poesy and love sonnets along the wandering way had meant a very meagre living and life was proving tough. Only one of his stories – the notorious retelling of "Goat's Beard" – had found any success as the last flummoxing entry in a compendium of grisly children's tales. It was rumoured that the Daisy Fairies had told the story to the goat as white as milk, who had in turn tickle-whispered it into her master's ear whilst he slept.

Now, tying up his precious goat for the evening, Anders scratched his head and tugged upon Little Milk's beard for fresh inspiration. Far away in his mind "The Chronicle of Ages" began to gather – a distant, drifting tale, as curious as the speech of clouds and children, but the scribbling Bard had no recollection of its true beginning. Perhaps it was inspired by the sudden flight of twilight birds swirling overhead; perhaps it was the garrulous, growling, chin-wagging clientele who were eagerly licking their lips as they hankered after the delicious-looking goat. Not since their infamous chase after the Wishing Pigs, which had ended in such hilarious calamity, had the wolf-tufted regulars been so hungry and desirous of food.

Anders mused... Uncertain times required unlikely heroes and heroines to redress the balance, and history required geography to help set the scene. Slowly a map began to unscroll before his eyes...

Once, in Europa's northern most territories, there lay a Jutted Land called Awe. Surrounded on three sides by water, Awe was separated from its northerly neighbours – the Lands of Ore, Yester Yore and East Scandavia – by the perilous Slippery Sea. The remnants of a fallen Giant turned to granite in the war against Witches formed a hazardous link to Awe's rocky coasts and wind-swept dunes – a broken causeway called Buckle Belt Bridge. Further away to the Polar North West, floating Ice Islands signalled the frontier of the Old Hawk Land and the beginning of the harsh snow plains of the Frozen Kingdom. Here, at the top of the world, the few remaining ancient creatures – Fire Dragons, Frost Giants, Screech Witches, Banshees and Wolf Men – all still lived.

Looming tall on the inhospitable, sea-beaten shore of Ore stood Two Towers, one dark, one light, which shone their probing eyes like lighthouses as they searched the heavens and disfigured the sky's natural aurora. Caught in the Towers' rotating oppositional rays, the residents of Awe, Ore and Yester Yore were unwittingly swayed as they struggled with age-old issues of blood-prejudice, feuding blindness and partial wise-sight. Most served one Tower or the other, but only the Mathmagicians and Brethren Brothers of Olde knew there could be no winning in their constant churning and tug-of-war – only deeper reckoning.

Awe's pleasant southern territories were full of plentiful pastures and rich grassland that rolled gently down to the Basin Wetlands and on into Europa. In the North there rose a semi-circular range of ferocious mountains called Fang Ridge. High up in the peaks, where stone met cloud, loomed a cloistered monastery called Sky City. It was a misty place rarely visited, partly due to its precarious heights and partly because its one point of entry, a high-arch bridge, was guarded by a band of Hungry Trolls; grumpy, stunted Giants left trapped on the Earth Lands from the toppling of beanstalks in the gruelling Hundred Year Axe Feud that had raged so many centuries before. At the foot of the mountains, sheltered by Fang Ridge, flourished the Forests of Fir, Fur, First and Thirst. Yet in reality they were all one wooded tree-mass divided only by a mapmaker's mishearing and the mischievous misspelling of names.

On the edge of the four Forests, not a million miles from the human settlements of Down Town Cow and Old Salt Lick, nestled a town called Town, which resided not far from Slow, in the West, by the side of the sea. Town was twice twinned with the curmudgeonly villages of Wife and Mid-Witch, but no-one really liked to talk about that for it had been a fierce political manoeuvre of obfuscation and obvious self-benefit by the presiding Mayor – Peter Bear. However, the inhabitants of Town were an unusual assortment; a mixture of ordinary lost souls plus a particular brand of old-style Fairy Folk and enchanted Ne'er-do-wells – denizens of a fast-disappearing magical age. They resided behind everyday fences, walls, and gardens where, thanks to resident Pixies and Fairies, vegetables grew oversized and washing hung out on the line dried quickly, if not completely blown away by Zephyrs or stolen by passing midnight marauders.

Cartographically, Town's central market place was adorned with pretty shops, a small canal and several winding streets, which were all connected to a long, horse-shoe shaped road that rolled down from the mountain monastery. This road wound its way through the Forest fringes, the wild fields and the outskirts of Town to a small flint church where it swerved back on itself and became a meandering, tree-lined avenue. This avenue headed back toward a park, some allotments and a once well-meaning, but now Witch-misguided, wood before branching off to neighbouring villages and swooping back into the depths of the frightening Forest of Fur.

On one side of this long, looping road nestled a small Folkeskole with a Statue of the Philosopher-Prince standing on a plinth within the confines of its playground. A Swallow circled lazily overhead in the afternoon sky, whilst inside one of the School's classrooms a young teacher read to the children their customary end-of-day tale.

'*…and they all lived happily there, then and in the ever, ever after…*

So it was, inadvertently, through love and best wishes that another Land of Bliss was formed – a floating Nimbus Cumulous Collectus cloud of rounded edges where the whats and whichevers looked after themselves. The Cloud Land was divided into six arching branches – three right and three left, in the shape of a presently upside-down palm-tree with a central connecting trunk. It was a drifting cloud by nature so was not always to be seen this way up, although its shape remained the same. The branching kingdoms were known as Upper, Middle and Lower Bliss, with Upper Bliss located at the bottom of the cloud, Lower Bliss at the top, and Middle Bliss was…'

Miss Beret paused from her reading. 'Well children!' she quizzed. 'Can you guess where on the map that might be?'

'Oh! Oh! Oh! In the middle, Miss Berry,' exclaimed Raoulf Littlesøn eagerly as he waved his hand in the air. 'In the middle…'

'Yes, that's right, Raoulf,' Miss Beret replied kindly, 'in the middle.'

The large, illustrated "New Book of Joy" – subtitled, "Fairy Stories for Estranged Children" – was currently on loan again to the

School. The book was embossed with a circular Town Hall stamp stating, 'Property of the Mayor', but it did not belong to him. Miss Beret lowered the heavy book into her lap as she gazed out of the window. A Swallow swooped by, dropping down to perch on the Statue to converse with the Philosopher-Prince. Momentarily Miss Beret grew reflective and the children, accustomed to her drifting story-telling ways, grew silent. They looked at each other, rolled their eyes, and politely waited until she was ready to return – which she invariably did. The wait was always worth it.

The "New Book of Joy" seemed oddly familiar to Miss Beret, but she did not know why. It was as though she could recall the stories from her own childhood – a distant and transfixing voice returning to recount chilling tales of trials and tribulations, magic, mischief and love. But to whom did these faraway dulcet tones she could hear in her mind belong? She had little recollection, yet was sure the book had a different name back then: "Tall Tales from Yester Yore". Was that it? She could not be certain, but sitting in front of the sea of attentive faces none of that mattered now. Lifting up the enthralling tome, Miss Beret gathered herself together, turned back to the children and the telling of extremely tall tales…

'Located on the right middle branch of the drifting cloud was Inner Bliss, a homely cloud-hamlet where perched the towns of Haven't Woe, Woe Haven't and Care-Not-I. Care-Not-I lay on a point that, when viewed from below, completed the upward triangle of towns. The place of Care-Not-I was different from the Land of Not Care – a habitat hard, brutal and oft devoid of love – which resided on a dark cloud and belonged to an entirely different story altogether. However, situated on the left middle branch of the palm-tree shaped cloud were the towns Top Notch, Top Bottom and Town-How-Pretty, which formed a downward triangle. When Fate dictated, and the vagaries of the wind blew in a certain direction, the cloud branches were pressed back in such a manner that the cloud seemed to have swan-like wings and the two triangles of towns overlapped

and clustered together. That was when a rare star shape could be seen to twinkle. It was happily rumoured that under this star, if you wished the right wish and your heart was pure, dreams of joy could come true.

Inner Bliss was a pleasant place where residents lived on such streets as Strawberry Sunset Strip, Blueberry Burst Boulevard, and Raspberry Ripple Row. Everything was smooth and ran in a fashion that can only be called tickety-boo, for life was fine in Bliss, mighty fine actually, for that was how the Creators had intended it to be. Little did they expect the entwining fate of fairy tales to befall, when one day…'

Suddenly, a harmonious pealing of bells signalled the end of the School day. The children stood smartly, collected their coats from the pegs at the back of the classroom wall and formed a straight line in astrological order by the door. Tall, know-it-all Virgos stood at the front, whilst diminutive, sensitive Cancerians and wilful Leos shuffled along messily at the rear. Raoulf, being the youngest and smallest of all the children, was standing at the end of the cockleshell row holding his new strawberry-red coat in his arms.

As they stood in line, a beam of sunlight stretched through the large windows and fell across the classroom. The brass Door Knob glinted menacingly and the children's upside-down shadows reflected within it, creating a curious, murky, yet sparkling world. The Door Knob was rumoured to have come from a Giant child's bed that had enchanted travelling properties, which could snatch you away to 'Who-Knows-Where?' in the blink of an eye. These Inner Realms of Light and Dark were inhabited by all manner of Fairies, Goblins and Sprite-like creatures that lived on hope, fear and the many different kinds of childish dreams and disappointments.

Miss Beret, who was aware of, yet somehow immune to such things, opened the classroom door and the children slowly made their way out one by one, trying to ignore the brightly polished Door

Knob that flashed at them with a blinding wink. However, as the children marched out of the room they could not help but be intrigued, each peering sideways into the Globe-of-Brass longing to see that their reflection was safe, yet at the same time also longing for the taste of strange adventure. They wondered if they were interesting enough to be stolen away.

No-one was sure of how or why the recently reawakened Door Knob had started operating again. In fact, ever since the inexplicable disappearance of Cartwheel Charlie and his Grandpa, no child had dared touch the Door Knob for it could lead to uninvited adventure and was considered somewhat dangerous. Although it was rumoured that the Globe-of-Brass could whisk you away to the bestest dream-place ever, the children were warned that it might also take you somewhere dark, somewhere worstest, somewhere terrible in the Land of Grim. In this foreboding place, you had to be brave and overcome nightmares to return home – a place from which some had not made it back at all.

After leaving parents' evening late one night Charlie and his Grandpa had touched the Door Knob at the exact same time. Their wishes for adventure and a new life thus entwined, but the differing dreams of the young and the old collided disastrously, sending them off to an Impossible Place in the Giant Cloud Lands. No-one had seen them since. Still within the elder children's memory, Charlie's disappearance flickered amongst them like a chill of creeping fear. When knees were scraped and elbows grazed in mysterious playground incidents, parents could always be heard cursing the missing boy and his errant Grandpa. Forbidden by their parents and guardians to talk about them at home, they had become a legend lost to hopscotch chants and grisly skipping-rope songs:

'Charlie Cartwheel – where are you?

I'm caught in a cloud with a misty view.

Is it true, did you touch the door?

That's why we're not there anymore.

Did you suffer a Fairy fate?

No dungeon door or palace gate.

Did a fearsome Giant snuff your wicks?

Blown in a breeze, we were snatched like sticks.

Tell us fair, tell us true – were you boiled in a Witch's brew?

Hansel and Gretel we are not –

Trapped in a place that Time forgot.'

Poor Charlie and his Grandpa had been left to fall through the hazy veil to become occasional ghosts for playground tales. In the months when usually invisible breath turned to mist, the children would huddle together and stare into the curling autumnal vapours. In the cold playtimes some said they could still see Charlie doing cartwheels around the schoolyard like a spirit lost in the fog. They said if you turned around, touched the ground and then pointed your mitten at him whilst calling his name, Charlie would come and whisper things you did not wish to hear. He was not being cruel; he was just trapped in an Inbetween Land – caught struggling in a nightmare cloud from which he and his Grandpa could not escape.

Back in the classroom, each passing child's disquiet doubt called out loudly to those dwelling within the Door Knob. Every Trembling Fear, Travelling Goblin and Sprite-of-Dread sprung awake wringing their hands and licking their lips. They knew that it was a child's un-chaperoned entrance or exit that afforded most opportunity to be spirited away. So it was that the Demons-of-Darkness were prepared to roll out at a moment's notice.

'Young'uns leaving,' muttered the Trembling Fears amongst themselves, 'how tasty!'

Yet the Guardians-of-Good stood equally ready as the Fairies raised their lanterns in ever-watchful protection. The Door Knob did not mind whose soul it took captive for all were invited to take its marvellous travelling test; a carriage to distant countries, remote seas and far away skies as well as a ticket to the Lands of Illusion, Dark Dream and Light Adventure. For the inhabitants of the inner realms it was a war; a duty of Fairy care against a duty of Goblin dare…

'Just one touch and we'll take you there,' promised the squabbling voices echoing from within the shiny Globe-of-Brass.

'Trick or treat? Hands or feet? Fetch me a fork and a child to eat,' cackled a haggard, hungry Shadow Witch.

'Goodnight children.' Miss Beret spoke loudly over the departing children's excited din and the hubbub of on-gathering voices in the classroom. She paused, briefly defeated, and then added brightly, 'Remember to bring an empty yoghurt pot, two tin cans and some string to School tomorrow…'

As the children slowly filed out through the classroom door, they instantly forgot what she had asked, for they already knew far too well the art of eavesdropping, listening through walls and those crafty ways of communicating that led to getting their own way. Home time meant so many different things – but a rare chance for adventure seemed to some an opportunity too good to be missed. However, as the children passed by the ominous, yet alluring Door

Knob they kept their thumbs and fingers firmly tucked away, crossing their arms and putting their hands safely in their pockets.

'Goodnight Miss Berry,' chorused the children.

'The little darlings!' Miss Beret mused.

Strange, that was the same name Miss Beret called the small blue pills she took to help calm her failing nerves. At least they meant a few hours of decent sleep in her Battle of the Somnia that had carried on these past few years ever since she had returned to her childhood home. Once finally asleep she would often find herself walking through the mist of dreams, which ended in rapid explosions, a sense of falling and a sudden sharp tap on the head. On half-awakening, she had a disturbed feeling of confusion as a voice called out to her,

'Where are you, my child?'

Miss Beret could not reply because she did not know where she was or to whom the voice belonged. Smoke billowed and screams echoed all around as she was pulled away from something very important, then nothing but plummeting fear as she fought her way out of her thwarting world of uneasy slumber. Now, shaking herself free from the troubling dream recall once more, Miss Beret quickly re-orientated herself, smiling and waving as the last of the children left the room.

'Goodnight children…'

Miss Beret always smiled and waved; it was her preferred, professional reaction, yet it still faintly annoyed her that the children did not quite pronounce her name correctly. This thorny confusion over her last name frustrated her, but what was she to do? Continue with them an ongoing war of enunciation? She had decided upon her surname sojourning in the illuminating City of Kites on her journey back home to the Jutted Land. It was Beret – silent 't' – not Berry. It was jaunty and modern, not fruit-laden and full… or so she chose to believe, whereas the children in their innocence somehow thought she was from the hip of the rose; a secret fruit of Nature's most beautiful blossoming bush.

Yet it was not so much the children's mispronunciation and their wilful inability to correct it, but more the fact that Miss Beret did not know her real name that secretly perplexed her. The fragments of her family history and of her origin she had gleaned from the Headmaster's opaque insights only held her back. Issues of identity haunted her, but what was in a name anyway except over-identification in the World-of-Things? She had no sense of belonging to the categories of the collected, collated and similarly called.

The Headmaster, on first hearing his ward's choice of name, had smiled warmly and blessed her. Then again, he had blessed anything and everything she had wanted on her return. It was as though in her early, tragic loss he believed she was owed so much – far more than her magically bedazzled mind suspected and her shielded memory had managed to retain. Fortuitously, it was the fact that Miss Beret did not know her true identity that kept her safeguarded from the kidnapping Fears and Goblins. They were aware of her presence, but they could not capture her body or soul if her charmed fingerprint immediately cloaked who she was, which it did.

Miss Beret presented an intriguing challenge for the rogue inhabitants of the Door Knob as they repeatedly tried, and failed, to steal her away. Was that why the Headmaster had opened up the previously abandoned classroom in the knowledge that she could teach and remain shielded? Or was it because that a part of her soul was already missing?

The Fairy Folk living within the Realms of Light and Dark laughed out loud at Miss Beret's rambling thoughts and self-deception. She who had been brought up on autumnal leaves and forest brambles was not the third of three children, as she believed, but the fourth of five. This much they had gleaned. Miss Beret had one brother and three sisters – all of whom were born from the womb of the same mother, but there a gene differed between them. In fact, the mistiness of her memory could be in some way attributed to her terrible family fall; a local story of beauty, sin and reckoning attributed to the tale of two fathers, one who might not have been all that he seemed.

However, if Miss Beret did not remember any of this, she did sometimes half-guess at the orbiting truth, for she had more than her fair share of dreams and hunches on which to ponder. Even now as she tried to take her memory by surprise, pushing against her mind's brick wall in an attempt to recall, a 'Spell of Forgetfulness' fell over her like a gentle rain protecting her secret. Yet who could hold Miss Beret's hand and help undo that particular enchantment? It would take wondrous, powerful magic and a tiger-sized portion of bravery, daring and love. And it would mean, once more, the tackling of Fears, Goblins and Witches.

So the mists of Miss Beret's hazy past swirled about her like an ever-changing twirl of twilight birds. How often in her dreams would she reach out to touch the faces of her two most famous elder twin sisters – Rose Red and Rose White? It haunted her; they were so lovely, yet so faint and far away now, so out of all adult grasp. They who had been so universally loved and adored were so unlike her own wild, wooded, wilful ways and barefooted childhood roaming.

Thus, in a daze and distant dream, Miss Beret wandered around the classroom sighing, turning the children's chalked slates over one by one and wiping them clean. She smiled to herself as she viewed their innocent scribbling of life on a farm. Raoulf's picture of a wiggly, talkative worm with a suspended word-bubble saying 'Woof' particularly amused her. A hungry squawk hen holding her flapping wings over her ears in dismay accompanied the worm, as if offended by the worm's unexpected remark. Really, what was Raoulf's drawing actually about? Then, a last, lone, lingering voice took her by surprise.

'Goodnight Miss Berry.'

It was Raoulf Littlesøn standing by the door, holding his strawberry-red coat in his arms and looking up at her as she struggled with her inner turmoil. He could feel her being pulled away from his side of life and the important plight of children's grazed knees. He knew it because he had seen the same distraction in his mother's eyes these past two years. Miss Beret helped Raoulf on with his coat.

'Goodnight Raoulf,' she said, and then added gently, 'do take care and remember to wait at the gates.'

Miss Beret watched as Raoulf's fingers gingerly held onto his coat sleeve and tried to pull the door shut by the smooth and shiny brass Door Knob. As he daringly looked within he saw both of their upside-down reflections in the golden gleam; not only theirs, but also the faces of the tricked, the trapped and the recently damned. Cartwheel Charlie and his Grandpa waved. Distracted, Raoulf waved back. As he pulled the door closed behind him his fingers slipped from beneath his strawberry sleeve. Did he merely rub against the air or did he put his thumbprint there? The featherweight faintness of a single print was all the Fears and Goblins required in tracking down a child before stealing them away.

Miss Beret could not refute the fact that all of the children's hopes and all of the School's good luck had gone awry since the sudden disappearance of Cartwheel Charlie and his Grandpa. Even now an impending announcement that would unfortunately affect the fate of them all was beginning to gather like a storm cloud in the Headmaster's office. Meanwhile behind her, in snake-like waves and marching lines, the Fears and Goblins came parading into the classroom like a mercenary army, feeding on greed, dread, and a pack of echoing lies.

'Step on a crack?' bellowed the singing Goblin Captain.

'The Trolls will attack,' answered the grinning Goblin platoon as they trudged across the room.

'Take a purse?'

'And catch a curse,' replied the accumulating Fears.

'Make amends?'

'Or fortune ends,' spat a particularly spiteful bunch of malevolent Sprites swinging on chairs and laughing.

'And an apple a day keeps you well on The Way,' countered Miss Beret, as she turned to confront the amassing army. Tongue-twisting limericks, protective lilts and optimistic lullabies rapidly ran through her fear-rebuffing mind. 'For Life is but a bowl of very many merry cherries...'

Numerous marauding Fears and sinister Goblins were now floating around the classroom, creeping out of the cupboards and over the children's desks. A small, grey cloud hung outside blocking the light. The room fell cold and gloomy. In the dingy over-shadowing she could feel an old distrust of strangers-at-the-door rising: crones and criminals, giants and gypsies, witches and wolves – professional fairy tale distractions all.

Now that the children had disappeared, including the lingering Raoulf Littlesøn who had been watching her closely through the windows of the door, Miss Beret took a deep breath and rolled up her sleeves. Ready for action, she raised her arms and spun swiftly around the room.

'Be helpful and sound or get thee Hell-bound,' Miss Beret commanded waving her arms about furiously.

Out of her graceful, gesticulating hands flew a flurry of 'Classroom Binding for the Sake of the Light Spells', which secured the ceilings, walls, and floors of the classroom for the Realm-of-Good. In neat, horizontal rows the desk lids rapidly opened and snapped shut. In so doing, they emptied themselves of any lingering childhood doubts and leftover nasties. Now demanding that anything dark should disperse, for her sake if not for the sake of their own survival, Miss Beret bound them together alongside some miserable Goblins and cowering, corner-lurking Fears. She then cast them all out through the open window in the direction of the Statue. Obligingly, the Goblins and Trembling Fears gathered together and speedily left. Yet this was not because Miss Beret had commanded them to do so, but simply that it was not her they were after.

'There,' she thought, as she brought the bright-blue, crackling electricity back in through her smouldering fingertips, 'that ought to do the trick.'

Yet even simple protection spells exhausted the novice Miss Beret. Breathing heavier, but feeling somewhat safer now she was once more in command of the classroom, she sat down at her desk and opened up her patchwork 'Exceptionally Useful Bag'. She pulled out her enchanted compact case that had originally belonged to her mother, but which had been given to her by the Headmaster as a treasured gift when she had returned home. Flipping open the lid she peered into the mirror, whilst her slender fingers made smoothing facial adjustments with her powder puff.

'But how do you feel?' asked the Genie coughing for so much dust.

'I'm quite fine,' Miss Beret lied. As she moved her head from side to side she momentarily tucked her hair behind her ears to admire their large, good-fortune gypsy rings. 'So no tricks or tests from you today, please. I am not in the mood.'

'Only asking,' retorted the Genie sulkily, 'I thought you could do with my assistance, that's all. That 'Fear Removing Spell' must have been hard work.'

Engrossed in her regular end of day beauty regime, Miss Beret smoothed her face as white as snow, pinched her cheeks as pink as blossom, and pressed together her lips as red as cherries into a plump Cupid's Bow. With her dextrous fingers, she teased her hair as black as ravens into an under-curl bob. Perfect... a flawless façade for the turmoil of feelings frothing beneath.

'Yes,' she eventually replied, 'it's getting into the furthermost corners that I find most trying, but I'll ask for your help when I need it.' She snapped the compact case shut and placed it back inside her 'Exceptionally Useful Bag'.

Outwardly Miss Beret looked scrumptious, as delicious as an apple-fluff delight, but then again that was the nature of the mirror's enchantment. Feel-good façades were an established necessity of the fairy tale game; surfaces, illusions and delusions were tricks of one of the oldest of trades and most wayward of professions. How you looked and how you felt about the way you looked might be a simple 'Spell of Superficiality' to some, but you never knew who was there admiring or judging. Faces, fates and fortunes were all for the seizing by discerning mirrors suspended on walls and beleaguered-looking glasses hanging in halls as they were asked the eternal, vain-glorious question,

'Mirror, Mirror, on the wall, if I am fairest of them all, why do I not dance at the Prince's ball?'

There was no chance of Miss Beret falling for such shallow issues of beauty and age now, but she knew that Dark Oculists were always looking for a way to gain entrance into the world of a hesitant soul. Mirror Magic was an ancient and somewhat tricky craft, but she had grown to believe that no-one was as innocent or horrible, beautiful or ugly, as they first appeared.

So, once again, Miss Beret had managed to pull herself together, outmanoeuvring her troubling insecurities and successfully stepping through another difficult day. As she gathered her belongings to leave she looked out of the classroom window and noticed Raoulf walking slowly across the schoolyard. She watched him struggle half-heartedly with the toggles of his strawberry-red coat whilst playing with his elasticated mittens. Feeling her watchful eye, Raoulf ducked behind the Statue pretending to tie his shoelaces. He was stalling for time, which could only mean one thing.

Miss Beret waited as the minutes ticked noisily by on the Old Norse grandfather clock that stood in the corner. It was one of four classroom clocks twinned with one housed in the Headmaster's office that acted as the School's magical barometer. With its strange numerals and moving decorative images carved upon its large, luminous, moonlike face, the ornate clock baffled the children. Only the tutors could interpret the clocks' mystery through the angle of the hands, which made elaborate patterns, and the pendulums' charming, bell-like chiming sequences. To the initiated, these were in fact reading runes and audible alarms. By such means tutors could inform the Headmaster of any arising difficult classroom situations and he could notify them of important announcements.

Looking back out across the playground, Miss Beret noticed that Raoulf, bright as a red-breasted Robin, was now swinging on the black iron gates. She would wait another few minutes and if he had not been collected by then she would phone his home – either his father or his Grandmother should be there to pick him up. She prayed that he would not stand there on his own again, crying into the twilight like that evening months ago when she had found him forgotten, sobbing his heart out.

Raoulf had been very open in telling the story of his family home situation, unintentionally disclosing the fact that the draconian Doctors had taken his mother away. Miss Beret had felt sorry for the boy, for she tacitly understood the daily struggle for the return of something lost – that much of sorrow, personal circumstance and facial glyphs she could read and empathise with. Now, standing in the classroom recalling the memory of that night, her aura diminished slightly as though a thin veil had been placed over her. Suddenly, Miss Beret felt overwhelmingly sad.

Far away a Huntingsman's horn sounded in the late September air. The weirs creaked. In the nearby woods, the Hungry Grasses quivered with excitement as they hastily flogged and flayed a lost harvest mouse – a tasty snack of sweet bright blood and marrow-filled bones. After a dry Summer the ravenous Grasses were on the prowl again, crawling their way from Black Bog into the midst of the Forest of Thirst. Birds cried out as they beat their wings and took to the sky, while Herons trailed their long legs across the misting, murky waters of Obsidian Lake. Miss Beret shivered as she picked up her belongings and left the classroom. Another five minutes had passed. Raoulf was still waiting alone at the gates and she was perturbed. Somewhere close, small dark clouds began to gather.

Taking a much-needed quaff from his flagon of ale, Anders paused to reflect. Then, slowly unscrolling a new sheet of parchment, he gradually began to roll back the story-telling years…

Jack Rose, only son of the Family Rose, sat at the top of the world, legs dangling over the edge of a beanstalk leaf. He peered down proudly at his newly acquired, overly large, shiny Seven League Boots. The Boots had once belonged to a Witch Queen who had cut them off the legs of a well-travelled, but impertinent, genie. Wind-borne Zephyrs and Air Fairies – some of whom still secretly assisted the Screech Witch clans – now served the Boots. Jack was delighted with his recent acquisition, for jumping, skipping and flying were so much quicker and easier than walking and climbing.

From on high, Jack was the purveyor of several lands – cloud and earth alike. As he turned his gaze further below he glimpsed the distant mountainside with its broken horizontal top. Some called it Hangman's Drop, others called it Lover's Leap or Broken Tooth, last chipped cliff of the snarling Fang Ridge Range. Only Jack knew, courtesy of his first theft – a Giant's ancient map of territories past – that it had been originally called Angel's Landing and was the main alighting and embarkation point for the Air Elementals of Awe.

The broken mountaintop had been one of Jack's earliest expeditions for it was one of the last remaining enchanted territories that met the human Earth Lands. There, the sky inhabitants could roll down upon drifting clouds before shooting the thermal breezes and flying up high to further adventure. The Zephyrs, Fairies, Air Angels, Hill Hawks and Aeronautic Spiders were fast friends with the owner of such magical Boots, which had helped plodding Jack Rose become Jack Flash, conqueror of Giant Cloud Kingdoms.

Now, with his burgeoning swag-bag slung over his shoulder, Jack felt like a king. The bag contained not only the charmed bracelet of the Fairy Queen that usefully allowed you to open any door without being seen, but also the Witch Sticks of the northern Screech Clan that could make inanimate objects like beds, brooms and bicycles soar through the sky. Nestling alongside these items was the terrifying silver Hand-Mirror of Truth, the only enchanted Bed Knob made by the Persian Flying Carpet Company, and the most recently acquired prize – the "New Book of Joy" written by Ghouls, Elves and Fairies to discipline unruly Sprogs and Sprites.

Jack had already procured and hidden such treasures as the melodious Golden Lyre (that when strummed forced the listener to speak true), the miraculous Turtle Egg Tide Turner (that turned back time for one complete Moon-cycle before it sent the novice time-traveller mad), and a rare Dragon Star-Compass (that not only contained a celestial map to safely navigate the Night Skies, but also allowed access to the regenerating force of the Winged Ones' cosmic fire, which could ignite stars and destroy burnt-out suns). Mercifully, Jack did not know how to use the Star-Compass and would remain forever ignorant to its unpredictable ways, but there were many who were interested in such a powerful object.

All these wondrous items had been purloined with the aid of Jack's most important and fortuitous first find – the Seven League Boots – which he found tossed aside in a crumbling turret hidden deep within the Forest. Then, after a visit to Angel's Landing, the

Frost Fairies had shown Jack where to find a magic mirror. Carved from sheet ice and forged using Moon-rock, Mo-snow, and stolen Dragon tears – ores and jewels all smelted together in isothermic heat then plunged into ice-cold water – the mirror had been cast by the Mathmagicians before they abandoned the Dawn School of Eda. Few had access to its true power but, once glimpsed, the fascinating mirror could be used to 'Future See' into other times and lands.

Since the containment of Witches, the craft of Mirror Magic was rarely used, but the trained observer could use any crystalline surface to view the different realms of earth, ice and air. A peripheral dip into any shimmering Looking Glass could lead to observing the wonder of another world or else damn the watcher to eternal entrapment. Infinity Mirrors could be used to check several places at once, but few survived the reflecting insanity effect. In the hands of the impotent, the innocent and the naïve, little trouble could be caused by a mirror's accidental supernatural use – only the possible haunting by past ghosts or ghouls with personal grievances. However, held by the amateur in wilful cleverness for personal gain, all kinds of cloud catastrophe would accumulate.

Yet duplicity belonged to the cunning and disingenuous, and that was not the nature of the youthful Jack. In his early pursuit of wealth and adventure he was not bad, just slightly misguided. He simply wished to help out his struggling parents, who had nothing but roses to sell. So it was that Jack sat on top of the world, figuring out his next audacious heist – the one that would never be. He did not realise the trail of devastation and resentment he had left behind in the Giant Cloud Lands, nor did he perceive the brewing Witch storm that would cause such harm and change his life forever. Sitting carefree in the clouds, things did not bode well for Jack Rose and his family. Regrettably, through his misdeeds, they were all most wanted.

The passing shadow of a cloud – Nimbus Cumulous Collectus – strayed across the Statue of the Philosopher-Prince standing atop a shoulder high plinth. Many years ago the Statue had been moved from the Old Town Square and placed within the confines of the schoolyard. What was hitherto a celebrated silver-skinned, gold-coated Statue of Undemocratic Princeliness was now just a part of the everyday playground landscape – an unadorned forlorn figure, with empty black eyes where sapphires of brightest blue had once been set. The Statue had one arm bent, fist on hip, whilst the other arm and hand was outstretched, with fingers reaching to the sky; a rapier, attached to a belt, ran diagonally backwards. The hilt had once housed a ruby as red as a flaming sunset.

The Statue was unremarkable apart from two facts: one, that it had survived at all, having been rescued from crushing and melting as iron scrap. And two, however impossible it seemed, the Statue always appeared to be looking, listening and thinking. This was in fact due to magic imbued by its Mathmagician makers over a century before, when the Prince was cast in volcanic fire. The Statue's iron had been especially extracted from sacred lava rocks found in the Old Hawk Land and covered in gold and silver leaf procured from the Fire Dragons. The Townsfolk knew him simply as the 'Philosopher-Prince'.

The Statue remained alone except for one stalwart Swallow who had stayed behind to complete a special mission. His regiment, the 'Reverberation of the Hearts of Lonely Writers', was carrying songs essential to artists around the world. They contained a message of truth – that beauty through joy, not suffering, was part of the new way. The rest of his flock flew overhead on the start of their long journey to Maleth-Malat. Mutterings of ancient massacre fluttered from their softly beating wings. Not all was as it seemed as they flew across the Forest to the warmth and supposed safety of Europa's South.

Many months ago, whilst listening in to the quarter-winds of the mariner's compass Rose-lines, the Philosopher-Prince had overheard a whispered conversation between the friendly Zephyrs of the Westerly Wind and the Mountain Monks of Sky City. Speaking through the skyline, they confirmed that all over the world a fairy change was afoot and the Statue, with the help of the birds, had agreed to oversee a part of the Sky Monk's unfolding Dream-plan. It heralded change – both good and sad. So now, in the last sultry days of the Summer sunset larking, the migrating birds had swung the concluding parts of the Sky Monk's plan into operation. Only one last undertaking was asked of the Prince and remaining Swallow.

'The sapphires and silver-leaf have all been safely delivered,' confirmed the Swallow to the Prince.

'Then it is time, my friend,' replied the Statue. 'Take the hidden ruby and the final pieces of my coat's golden splendour to the widow who lives alone and pray that our timing is right. We need all the help we can gather.'

With heaving wings and a beak full of finest Dragon gold the Swallow swerved away, but immediately collided with the Fears and Goblins so recently expelled from Miss Beret's classroom window. On impact, the Swallow veered upwards and the gold tore through the edge of the Cumulous Cloud at a precarious angle. In the collision there was a terrible splitting sound, a grumble of thunder, and a tug on the bird's fluttering heart. The Trembling Fears and Travelling Goblins had been drifting by on a passing breeze heading towards Raoulf Littlesøn, for they possessed a missing print from his thumb. Now redirected by the broadside of a bird, the Fears and Goblins hurtled towards the caretaker's office instead.

Out on a wing and a prayer the Swallow struggled on, flying away on his last mission, though behind him all was confusion. Not daring to stop at the rumbling sound of chaos and cloud tearing, the bird turned upon the buffeting wind to find the right compass direction. That was how, unwittingly, a branch of the palm-shaped Cloud Land was perforated and one of the Kingdoms of Bliss came to be pierced.

In the Land of Bliss, pandemonium and drama ensued after the conjunction of unfortunate mishaps had hit the drifting cloud. Peculiar silver light flashed and extended into every corner, whilst fiery rays of Dragon-gold and sparkling unusualness penetrated the misty vapour and descended upon the several towns. There were rumbles of thunder and the marauding inhabitants of a passing dark cloud were cottoning on that defences were down in Bliss. Viking sky-boats were made ready to set sail. Meanwhile, the 'School for Exceptionally Brave Souls' had taken a direct hit from Miss Beret's recently expelled Fears and Goblins, whilst slicing gold leaf had torn through a corner of the cloud. Several of the Little children were missing. Disaster!

'Mrs Little?' called the now frantic schoolteacher down the telephonic device, 'I'm afraid there's been an accident. I know accidents don't exist... never happened before, by the look of it I think it was a spell back-firing... and a bird was involved... and some wayward Fears, Goblins and Dragon-gold... I'm so terribly sorry... Little Bliss is fine, still here, but at present we cannot account for Little Pearl, Little Star, Little Seed and Little Spark... I'm sure they'll all be found very soon... Yes, others are missing as well... Yes... Mmh-hmm... Certain Silences and Celestials can't be found... and some of the Saints and

Sacreds have disappeared too... I know, I know, loose canons everywhere... What if they descend? Why, Heaven help the Wilderness and the remaining Fairy Folk if they've cloud-jumped early and incarnated into the twentieth century... Oh, I know... Their last lesson? They were learning from the lost Book of Love... They were studying the letter 'P'... Oh, I know, I know, the potions and potency... Yes, we're contacting the Cloud Elders and setting up a Rainbow Rescue Circle right away... The number to call? I have it right here... All mothers will be asked to re-emit their original beams... No, not to re-call, far too late for that I'm afraid, quite impossible, but to boost any descending souls lost in the chaos and the crossfire... Additional sonic frequencies and the master polychromatic rays? Yes, we'll be stabilising them soon, through Venus and the light side of the Moon...'

Mrs Little was distraught. 'Were the children ready for such an adventure?'

'Are any of us ever ready? Of course there is a price to pay for any misuse of the master rays, but the planetary alignment is right again... Remember? Of course I remember. We were some of the first so-called troublemakers in the Paradise firing line... the original wayward sinners jumping so wilfully in and out of Time. Cloud bandits, I think they called us! Oh I agree, it was a riot, so much mischief and fun, but what can we do? What can any of us do except have faith and courage? Helping hands in the slipstream of life... To the world with love, Mrs Little, send the brave handfuls off to the world with love...'

So, as Anders the Bard pondered and Little Milk imagined, a new chapter began to unfold – entwining ribbons from timelines across the ages as though birds were words spanning the pages...

There once was a Lady, a lovely Lady, who possessed long flaxen hair as gold as the colour of sun-kissed corn. She lived, imprisoned, in a turret in the midst of a Forest and every morning she greeted the dawn, conversing with the birds as they swept high above into the warming blue.

'Swallows,' she called out enthusiastically, 'where are you going?'

'Maleth-Malat,' they replied. 'You too must get out.'

The Lady prayed for the safe passage of the winged pilgrim souls and bird arch-mariners as she turned back to her tunes and her spinning wheel. She spun her everyday hums into harpsichord songs, into sums and whirligigs and misery chords and oh so much 'mmh – yes!' that was just uncontainable.

'Hmmm,' she thought, 'the birds are right. I must let joy in… but how to get out?'

Although the Lady had taken time in her turret confinement to explore her artistic gifts, she knew now that Life in all its seeming complexity was simply for the living. So she turned to peer into her Persian Mirror, twisting her long flaxen locks into curls with her fingers as she looked at the door over her shoulder in reflection. Slowly, she turned to face the imposing wooden door.

Perhaps she could crawl like a caterpillar through the keyhole or drift under the door's edge as invisible as a misty wisp? Or maybe climb out of the window, scaling heights with the length of her considerable hair? Her hair might be beautiful and fine, but when wound together it possessed the strength of steel. She looked at the one-eyed opening of the turreted wall where she had practised her daily scales and archery. It was not terribly wide, but she who had come to believe in enchantment could do so many impossible things. Time had taught her that; extraordinary decades of passing time alongside marvellous mishap and muddling mischief – all courtesy of a forgotten ability to create make-believe Wish Magic.

Nearby, a faint click belied the quick closing of cupboards; the prying spirit of someone else was present, but the lovely Lady with sharp senses was onto them. She knew that the Evil Eye was everywhere, trips and traps enough to bring anyone tumbling down, for long shadows still stretched over the fallen castle and First Forest of Awe. She did not want to disturb the marauding malevolent or the unwelcomed wicked, so she quickly closed the double doors that housed her mirror. She knew that either side of the duelling divide could use looking glasses to spy, even good ones.

'A journey into the outer regions, then,' she mused, smiling.

'Not by me without a key,' said the door defiantly. Fixed Witch Magic had compelled the door and it was not in the mood for budging, especially from those trapped on the inside.

'Thank you for the reminder,' said the Lady gratefully to the begrudging door, 'but please be quiet and let me think.'

Bringing attention to her escape was the last thing the Lady desired, so flying out on a charmed bed or an anointed broom was definitely out of the question. Sinister, spying Bird Wardens were everywhere. Some were still under the service of her wicked Witch-Stepmother who, unbeknownst to the incarcerated Lady, had been dead these many years past. However, it was rumoured that the Witch's shadow was just one of numerous Shades still inhabiting the Forest, smothering all that she encountered and mouldering the woodland floor.

On the other side of the door, the Lady could hear the ghostly groans of old governors, gaolers and guards stirring, as though still snoring and rattling their bones even in their long death sleep. Paid in false promises, they had endlessly replaced each other, destined to die at any overt display of goodness towards the shuttered girl. Yet even for the heartless, it was difficult not to be caring towards their child prisoner, for she was so gentle and kind to them. So the constant change of guards, the pile-up of corpulent bodies and the fact that they often dropped dead in front of her, made the growing girl aware of the impossibility of escaping her situation. Something else also lay behind her odd confined circumstance, but what it was remained unfathomed. She was in fact the Princess of Awe, fortunately not the fairest in the land, but pretty and very enchanting.

Over the passing years the Princess had built up a special relationship with her keepers, who had fed her and seen her grow from a child into an unpredictable and unruly youngster. It was they who, on the advice of the birds, had given her the False Unicorn herb when she had turned thirteen and her inner lunar clock had started to flow. The young Princess with the long golden hair had been the only kind person the guards had encountered in their damnable work under her Stepmother's service. Would their imprisoned ghosts believe that the lovely Lady on reaching her twenty-first birthday was now deserving of freedom?

Oblivious, the Princess did not know that centuries had passed, although she half-guessed that her experience of Time was somehow not quite the same as for others. This was in part due to a rather curious artefact – a Turtle Egg Tide Turner – that she used to time her singing practice, and partly because she was lost in a 'Time Spell' of her own creation. Consequently, with the exception of two remaining turrets, her father's great marble-white Palace had collapsed into ruin – covered over with Bear-briars, Wolf-thorns and pernicious woodland green. Forests had grown, families had fallen and memories had become misshapen – so much so that the Land of Awe's true history was distorted and erased. Now the Palace of the Old Kingdom lay long forgotten, even by those who lived close by.

The Lady's current gaolers were now simply Shadow Slaves, trapped ghosts haunting the winding corridors, yet still bound by a 'Spell of Soul Restriction' – the incarcerating last orders given by the maniacal, age-ravaged Witch. However, whilst trapped in the turret the souls of the guards would never be released. In death, as in life, their feeble minds and corruptible wills were still controlled by her omnipotent witchcraft. Perhaps the Lady should ask the good white mice to steal the turret keys from off the Master Gaoler's belt. They could tie the jangling bunch of keys to the end of her hair, which she could then pull back under the door. Yet she did not wish to place the mice into danger again, for the Witch had previously blinded some with briars, whilst others had lost their tails to her slicing wand.

Laughing, the Lady tossed back her head, gathered her hair, then threw it all forward until it touched the floor and surrounded her. Kneeling inside the tent of her hair she drew a chalk circle upon the stone floor and thought about the repercussions of making herself invisible. Using certain golden glyphs and musical keys she unlocked the door of her world, for the harmony of her humming could do that. She decided to peddle her grace, her wares and her considerable charms on the fascinating path of minstrelsy. She would sound out The Way, her way, with earth chants and poetry, songs of joy about the birds, the dawn light and the birth of a boy. Her songs would also entwine tales and stories so old that their mysteries were locked in a box with their meaning felt, but almost forgotten.

Here, the nearby Casket-of-Dark-Secrets winked its inky keyhole at the Princess. Bursting with untold treasure never to be sold, the Casket was filled with terrible deeds and haunting things best left buried and forgotten; murderous thoughts of the living and greedy, and pained feelings of souls seeking heart-ripping revenge from beyond the grave. In-and-of-itself the Casket was not intentionally cruel, but clever the child who had secured it. Suddenly, there was the sound of scissors on split ends and the quick, whirring purr of a spinning wheel spinning.

On the Loom of Life, with her spare hair, the lovely Lady made herself a loose Cloak of Faith, the size of a round carpet. Pricking her finger, she called with fresh beads of blood to the helpful birds and bats, kind rats and cats, who stole through the night to carry the carpet away so she would believe in her innocence that she was flying. In reality her leaving the turret was in fact all down to the benediction of her winged Fairy Godmother, Waltzing Matilda of the long silk stockings – former pageant beauty and lover of the ballroom dance. It was she who was responsible for the Lady's enchanted ability that expressed itself through charm and luck, for it had been Matilda who had bequeathed a thousand fortunate magical wishes at her goddaughter's birth as an all-abiding first blessing.

After the death of her mother, the Gracious Queen, and before the arrival of the Witch, the young Princess had simply wished to make the King happy in his despair. She needed to show her father, as well as herself, a way out of grief. When the Princess had wished her hundredth earnest wish, she sorrowfully learnt that she could not make the dead return. However, she could mesmerise others for the delight of good and so she turned to playing with the other children of the court. Oh! The spirited hi-jinxes they got themselves into. But one day, an accidental misfiring of a simple 'Memory Loss Spell', aimed at an annoying boy she had already turned into a toad several times that day, caused much confusion.

Alas, the spell rebounded off the courtyard's porphyry Well of Tears and Good Wishes and a part of her mind was bedazzled. Not being naturally magical herself, the Princess no longer recalled the fact that she had been bequeathed the power of Wish Craft. Nor did she recollect how many fortunate wishes she had left. Usefully, they had multiplied into the millions triggered through the accidental misapplication of an exponential summoning spell. That was why the lovely Lady, now with short, frizzy golden hair, remembered hardly any part of her former royal life. As a young girl, she had been the beloved daughter of a devoted King and Queen, and adored by the courtiers living in the Palace within the Forest of Awe.

However, her Witch-Stepmother, Second Queen, had confined the Princess so early on that circular turret living was all she knew. It was this small slice of imprisoned life that she had got used to; all she had grown to expect and accept. The loathed Witch, on becoming Queen, ensured that no courtier escaped her clutches by growing a thicket of Wolf-thorn and Bear-briar all around the Palace, whilst within her reign of ice descended. Any courtiers wishing to serve her were kept alive. The rest were imprisoned, put to sleep or killed.

Slowly, the Witch Queen turned the surviving members of court into statues – freezing in pain where once they had danced. To assuage her daily passing whims, she crumbled the statues to dust and destroyed the castle's central courtyard including the Well, which housed the thousand different ways of crying, purification and replenishing hope. Now broken and forgotten, the Well's natural spring began to dry up, and the Princess's daily sobbing only added grief to the growing of Nature's surrounding greenery. That was how the Forest had become tinged with an unnatural aura of sadness.

Through the Witch's enchantment on the Palace, and her later use of death-evading Shadow Magic, an all-pervading sickness spread throughout the land. Ominous, twisted trees sprung up. Devoid of water from the Well, the Forest of Thirst was created – a creeping place of Hungry Grasses, blood-sucking beetles and devouring greedy ghosts. Then, up toward the mountain ridge, the Forest of Firs became known as the Forest of Furs – where accursed local hunters, stricken by the thrill of the kill, would slaughter and hang out the pelts of their innocent, misshapen prey: spell-diseased humans turned into wolves. Once a month, the Forest was a place of ritual lust and rabid ecstasy – the Full Moon legacy of the Witch Queen who could not find love.

Apart from the captive Princess only one other had survived the passing of time and the Witch's spreading shadow crime – and that was Matilda, Fairy-Godmother and magical courtier, trapped in a cell and tied by leg irons so she could not escape and fly away.

Anders the Bard paused to reflect as he whittled away at his quills. In his thoughts, and against his better wishes, "The Chronicle of Ages" grew like a gloomy storm cloud. He bought another flagon of ale to stem the pain as the despair of a much-hated Witch heart spread through his blood like a Winter's chill. Not only in the far off time of Yester-Yore, but here and now in the Land of Awe. Something pervaded the earth and air like the far-reaching stench of no-good.

Up above, through the drifting swan-wings of a passing cloud, a star momentarily shone before being immersed into the thickening dull grey-blue of a bruised sunset. Encouraged by the glimpse of the evening star, Little Milk, the goat of purest white, gently head-butted her master's leg, nudging him on to continue the story. Anders smiled as he gently stroked the goat's beard. Then he dipped his dark Swallowtail feather deeper into the swirling black ink…

Formerly, the Witch had been a terrifying Enchantress descended from a race of Giants, who had grown large and powerful when once the Moon had been temporarily stolen by Fire Dragons and lost to the orbit of the Earth. The Giants then were an elongated race, blue-blooded, ice-veined and whiter than snow. They kept Wolf-Men as pets and coveted power so much that they turned to storm fury with the warm Gods of the East. Years of brutal battle ensued, but eventually the Giant tribes and Witch clans had fallen.

The few survivors were banished by the Gods of the East to the remote Northern Places and Ice Islands to live out their days in cold isolation away from the growing community of man. The Eastern Gods, not wanting to exterminate a race, agreed to spare their lives on one condition – that the Giants were to remain barren. They were believed to be the last of their kind and would one day simply die out, even if it took several hundred years, for Giants lived long.

In the face of defeat and confinement, the Witch escaped from the Frozen Kingdoms of the Far North across the Ice Sea, through the Nor Land snow plains to East Scandavia. She then headed South to White Bear Peninsular, striding across the Slippery Sea's treacherous broken causeway to the Jutted Land. Carrion Crows brought the fleeing Witch good news of her two surviving sisters whose flesh they failed to find and eat.

As the Witch crossed Fang Ridge Mountains, she shrank herself to a more human size with a 'Spell of Essential Survival' until finally she came to a place where the northerly denizens of the Land of Awe resided. The Witch found good fortune when she stumbled upon a rich court where a just King, recently bereft of a wonderful Queen, ruled. A daughter, a much-beloved young Princess with long golden hair, was left to run unchecked amongst the Palace grounds.

The Witch spied upon the court with Crows hired from Black Nest – a mortifying bird pit, hewn into the rocks and trees of the Petrified Forest, located near the deadly, shimmering Obsidian Lake. Through 'False Tear Scrying' and Mirror Magic she realised that the key to winning the King's lamenting heart was through the Princess.

Eventually, after months of preparation and rehearsal, the Witch presented herself to the court as a Temple Traveller – a High Priestess from the far-off Land of Northern Lights – who was gathering fairy stories, legends and folklore to enhance their vast crystal Snow Library. To the King she was a beguiling, learned, beautiful stranger who was a marvellous conjuror and a wise advisor.

Over the coming months the Witch convinced the court of her loyalty when she spun a wondrous 'Invisible Shield Spell' – where no harm 'to the hair-or-head of the Princess' could ever befall. There was no sword strong enough, or grain of sand small enough, that could penetrate the protective layer that now surrounded the child, regretfully not even the Witch's own hand. However, and much to her annoyance, she could not undo the original thousand blessings of the Princess's 'away-with-the-fairies' godmother, Waltzing Matilda of the long silk stockings. Yet bringing up the fair-haired brat would be a small price to pay for such a queenly victory. Soon the Witch was married to the King, and a long, slow poisoning by Dragon's blood to his ear ensued.

Now ruler-of-nothing and all she surveyed, the Witch Queen craftily dedicated each turret to the most ancient and fabulous of creatures – the Fire Dragons; four winged brothers who dwelt in the subterranean caves of the Old Hawk Land waiting to devour the World at the End-of-All-Time. As Planetary Igniters, it was they who had first set the Golden Star alight, and on four separate occasions had stolen the Snow Moon – twice for themselves, once willingly for the Mathmagicians, and once coerced by the Giants who had stolen a rare Star-Compass given to the Dragons at the Dawn-of-Time by the Celestial Creator.

Acting without the Dragon's permission, the Witch Queen believed she could invoke and control their Fire Magic once more through the use of the Star-Compass. The Dragons were displeased to have their power drawn upon in this manner, as it opposed the way of transition and natural law. Disrespectfully, she manipulated their regenerating energy by pulling sparks from their volcanic source, yet something inside her soul began to splinter as thin as a hairline crack within ice.

Using Crows from the Carrion Pit as messengers, the Witch Queen invited her two sisters to stay. They blew in upon an ill Polar wind; a gust so cold that part of the Forest of Firs was further petrified and the few folk who lived there were instantly frozen. At first the visiting sisters were mildly amused by the subservience of the surviving Palace courtiers and the unwanted, yet spell-protected, golden-haired child. However, living up high in the North and South turrets they soon felt isolated and imprisoned, which was in part caused by the Dragons' cunning and far-reaching fire power.

The sisters did not enjoy the same protection bestowed on the Witch Queen by the stolen Star-Compass, and were thus unprepared when an unexpected cascade of burning ash and amber sparks descended. Glaring at each other across the castle courtyard the visiting sisters erupted into discord and heated dispute – quarrelling angrily over their former position, glamour and popularity. Newly inflamed, they fell into ferocious family fury, cursing each other whilst mindlessly blasting the turrets to smithereens. A graveyard quickly formed beneath as crumbling towers and tumbling sarsens crushed the few remaining Palace denizens.

Matilda, the Princess's incarcerated Fairy Godmother, awoke that day under much din and devastation. Opportunity presented itself as the walls of her gaol blew open and the chains of her leg-iron were fortuitously shattered. Unfortunately her wings were grazed, so she used her glass slippers to glide away, slipping through the Wolf-thorns and Bear-briars that surrounded the Palace. The good Sprites and woodland creatures of the Forest recognised Matilda and, seeing her earthbound, helped protect her.

Many years later, her wings withered due to lack of use, Matilda was found wandering down the mountain road with amnesia and tall tales about being hit by a brick in the War of the Witches. No-one in the towns of Wife or Mid-Witch believed her and she was sent to rest in a retirement home in neighbouring Town. There, sat in a chair, she waited forgotten as generations of old folk and their helpers died and passed her by.

After that violent day of feuding and the untimely deaths of the two sisters, the Princess had been incarcerated in the eastern turret. The Witch Queen, ignoring any remaining responsibilities of her guardianship, lived on in the western turret. After the North and South turrets had fallen, the remaining dualities of East and West subdued into a begrudging peace. Only these two turrets remained visible to those wandering the woods, their un-flagged, crenulated spires peaking above the canopy of ever-growing trees.

Mist-like shades – wraiths of courtiers, ghostly gaolers and shadow slaves – arose from the unconsecrated Palace ground, cold and clammy with fear, keeping guard over secrets too grisly to mention and sucking dry the warmth from any inquisitive passer-by. Later, there were sightings of rabid, spell-cursed men – some who turned into wolves and others who turned into gung-ho hunters. There were rumours of peculiar Full Moon rituals where gangs in possession of venom-tipped hunting daggers and sharp pelt knives roamed the forest, and then decades later those armed with swords, bayonets and guns.

After a long while the people of Town believed the spires belonged to haunted churches, remnants of the Martyred Middle

Kingdoms. Myths were made of them for history was long forgotten and revised by then. Much later the surviving turrets were dedicated to the tragic loss of brother and sister, Hansel and Gretel, but few folk ventured there except for the annual culling of Christmas trees by the Woodsman in the Forest of Firs.

Resentfully stuck in her shrunken human form, the Giant Witch Queen lived on beyond her years by the use of cruel cosmetics, the eating of rabbits' hearts and the incantations of enslaved Middle-Eastern genies. Yet still she was unable to defend herself against the ever-quickening ravages of Time. More admired by sycophantic mirrors than real people, the Snatching Years marched on leaving their laughter as ornate furrows and lines of loss – wrinkles and crow's feet etched into her face and papery skin.

The practice of Mirror Magic, like the use of truth, was a tricky game of blindness and sight that could be exacting. Any personal addiction to external beauty reflected back a shallowness that was a blind spot to seeing the greater mirrored picture. This was known as the 'Dusk-Star Downfall', which entrapped many a Witch, fair, false and foul, who concealed devious desire or evil intent. Somehow, the single artful mind was always distorted in the tranquil, overseeing Mirror-Mind-of-All that could turn the observer into a feeble-minded, senseless fool.

In its heyday Mirror Craft had been called Tear Magic, for a single tear (freely given or forcibly ripped) was all that was needed to start a mirror seeing, but that begged questions of allegiance and ownership. However, well-tuned owners of other Looking Glasses could see the reverberations if they wished. That is why mirrors had eventually become twinned or winged diptych and triptych – to increase the panoramic view, for looking over your shoulder, and to show others that you had no knife or wand hidden behind your back.

It was also rumoured that certain elder members of the Screech Witch clan could dive through any mirror at will; lunging through to stab, poison or steal whatever they required. Because of this, trust between the Witch clans was an ancient feudal issue.

So it was that the Witch Queen spied upon the incarcerated Princess through her use of a myriad of mirrors and looking glasses. Annoyingly, by some unfathomable trickery, the Princess seemed only to grow and age one year for her every twenty. She who was alone was never lonely, and with her friendly disposition the Princess would talk to her gaolers and all manner of creatures living in the turret walls. So, unbeknownst to the wicked Queen, spiders, mice and birds by day, and rats, cats and bats by night, all befriended the growing Princess. Conversing with the animals helped offset the madness she sometimes felt as the months, seasons and tens of years slowly slipped by.

Of course, the Princess had forgotten that her 'Time Spell' was making her own few-and-far-between happy days seemingly last forever – well, at least for an additional week. Plus, her Turtle Egg Tide Turner ensured that certain lunar months helpfully repeated themselves. Living in-and-out of the ordinary hours she discovered some of what had been lost in her childhood – a unique sense of seasonal joy. Thus gaining an unusual perspective of the divisions of decades, the Princess became somewhat transcendent and timeless. And all the while she sang.

The Witch Queen, in a grandiose pretence of dignifying her stepdaughter's life – not to ease the guilt of her own wrong doing but to find the secret of her ward's youthfulness – had generously granted the Princess three wish-gifts on her thirteenth birthday. They were presents which the stepdaughter had chosen horribly wisely, beyond her years, and which backfired on the age-raging Queen. So, for the dexterity of her fingers, the agility of her mind, and the expression of her artistic desire, the Princess selected a spinning wheel and a harpsichord, which the Lady Spiders later taught her to play and control with such experimental pleasure.

These trifles were granted by an imperious wave of the Witch's wand as she strode around the eastern turret searching for clues as to the essence of her stepdaughter's youthfulness. But the white mice had cleverly concealed the Turtle Egg Tide Turner and the Princess's spell-grazed mind revealed nothing under interrogation about the casting of the fortuitous 'Time Spell'. Even the mirror's enslaved genie had nothing unusual to report. The Princess coughed demurely to gain her stepmother's attention before enquiring graciously whether she had one more gift to receive? Magnanimously, the Witch informed her stepdaughter that she had one more wish to squander in whatever ridiculous manner she thought fitting.

The Princess pondered wisely before deciding upon a Casket, a special type of Casket containing…

Impatient, bored, unthinking, the Witch flourished her wand and the gift was immediately granted. But this was no ordinary trinket box, but the infamous Casket-of-Dark-Secrets holding all of the world's unspeakable horrors. This final gift had infuriated the Witch Queen who, realising her mistake, secretly feared what might lie inside, but three gifts she had agreed and so three gifts had been granted. Of course, it did not mean that she had to give her miserable stepdaughter the key to the fabled Casket for that would have been a fourth gift and a generosity beyond her – so she seized the key and placed it upon a chain around her neck. The key was not part of the pact, and Witch agreements, wishes and spells went hand-in-hand in those bygone days. Feeling somewhat defeated and angry, the Witch Queen left the eastern turret never to return.

Curiously, the Princess did not fear the Casket's presence for she did not want to know the grimy particulars of what lay inside. Later, in her imprisoned dilemma of despair and delight, she invented a simple guessing game with the clandestine Casket, which out of amusement occasionally shared some of its mysterious contents. The Casket did not burden the Princess with its true criminal content, which burgeoned with every passing day, but allowed her to choose what she wanted to believe by telling her terrible truths and lovely lies in the form of fairy stories. The singing Princess welcomingly used these as the inspiration for her sadder songs.

Yet to possess the key and not have access to the Casket's secrets was a haunting that slowly eroded the Witch. Insecurity of darkness had been born that day where insecurity had never been; clever the golden-haired child who had asked for such seemingly simple birthday gifts. Through her growing bitterness, the Witch began to rapidly age and falter as rust slowly spread from the key poisoning her body. The key grew heavier each day, slowly disfiguring her body until she hunched forward and a hump started to form on her back. Peering into her mirrors, she was aghast at how withered and depleted she looked and how pretty the young Princess was becoming. More and more she relied on draining what residual power she could from the Fire Dragons' enchanted Star-Compass.

Continually misused in this way, the Dragons conspired against the Witch Queen as she tried to renew herself with drops of their precious blood, contained in an ivory vial. They knew what she was plotting – if only she could carve out a Dragon's heart and devour it then she would become young and strong and pretty again. Like acid, fear gnawed away at the Witch Queen's failing flesh, ravaging her face and contorting her joints and bones. Now the Well of Tears and Good Wishes was destroyed, resentment, sadness and incomplete dreams brimmed over in the Palace courtyard and seeped into the Witch's soul, reminding her of a desire that she believed left behind forever – the want of a lover, a child and an heir.

Over-shadowed by the threat of the Eastern Gods' warning, no Giant, human or Fairy suitor had ever been forthcoming, not for all the Witch's previous fame, fortune and far-reaching influence. Their names taken in vain, the Fire Dragons' greater strength kept her concealed and isolated. So the Witch Queen had not grown old happily, but lonely, believing the veiled taunts of her Middle-Eastern Mirror that there would come to exist once again one more brave and beautiful, and another more fair and lovely – Rose Red and Rose White. As a young child she had been frightened by such cautionary tales of goodness in old stories from her own nursery.

Up until now, the re-incarnation of the twin sisters was not believed to be possible for they were an old Witch foe from the long forgotten Land of Enchantment. Those enemies of the twin sisters on the Indivisible Planes had so far successfully blocked their souls' return. Thus their Rose secrets had remained hidden from the mortal world for centuries, only vaguely remembered in fireside stories and hushabye tales.

However, allegiances had changed and influence had shifted. The veils between the Elemental Worlds had grown thin again, letting the disturbances of good and evil through into the Divisible Dimensions. Omni-kind, including humans, Fairy Folk, and all manner of supernatural creatures, were plotting once more in power-driven grudges and blood feuds. Re-ignited, the Towers of Light and Dark were back at war – control of the Earth Lands the sought-after prize, cloud exile and ice wilderness the bitter consolation.

Meanwhile, in the mists of the Witch Queens' hand-held Seeing Mirror, another visage grew trembling before her, a face of the far future, an illegitimate sister, a Rose of Pink – one whose destiny she could not foresee, for the most difficult of decisions surrounding her birth had yet to be taken. That rare, serendipitous circumstance seemed almost inconceivable. Her fate, like that of the entire Rose family, appeared to be entwined with that of the first born son and elder brother – a bothersome boy called Jack. Centuries would yet have to pass, but in him the Witch perceived greed and the seed of opportunity. Then another image abruptly appeared. It was the face of a fourth fair flower – a Rose of Snow – so holy that the purity could not be contained in her Seeing Mirror. The glass cracked and the Witch's hubris grew.

'How I hate them all,' she screamed.

In the following days an even more troubling image waltzed endlessly across the Queen's Mirror hanging on the wall – the haunting picture of her stepdaughter grown into a beautiful Lady taking up her royal birth right in the future Land of Awe. Disturbed, the Witch Queen cursed the day she had cast the protective spell. So she informed the Screech Sisters – the last of the Lost Witches, the Babble Mouths, and the ostracised female Giants – of her predicament and what she had divined in her mirror. Through the swirling worlds of their snowy fjords and cold empty caverns she swore them to curse binding if her plans should fail and future Rose prophecies grow true.

The Screech Witches also saw the future images of the Princess and the Sister Roses in the surfaces of their shimmering ice-sheet mirrors and shaken snow globes. They could see a battle, but could not foresee the outcome. The Witch Queen knew then that she must conceive or her bloodline would be lost and White Magic would return to awaken the sleeping woods. But conceive with whom? Who could the suitable impregnator be?

For the Witch Queen's conceit, her suitor needed to be handsome and strong. Fortune intervened. Two men on horseback came travelling through the Forest, the best of friends, but both slightly the worse for flagon drinking and the telling of tall stories. Perfect. In a bout of bravado and drunken dare, the friends climbed through the lancing briars and stabbing thorns, which inexplicably parted for them. Scaling the fallen sarsens and stones, they stumbled intoxicated over the spell-blasted statues, across the castle courtyard ruins and up the spiral staircase of the westerly turret to find the momentarily beautified Queen resting on her fur-covered bed. In her need to be desired she did not hesitate to test the two strangers, not realising that the test of strangers and friendship was, in fact, hers.

Even though the friends were inebriated, the wicked Queen failed to entice either of them naked to her bed and secure her desires' will. In fury she bit one on the neck, turning him into a fanged, Moon-howling wolf. The other, she fascinated with fur and, in her cruelty, taunted his mind until he became demented. Immediately he began stalking his wolf-turned friend. The hunt was on. The winner, the Witch Queen proclaimed laughingly, could wed and bed her and she would bear him a charmed child-king. So the two friends, now cursed as mortal enemies, fought around the ruined castle, chasing through the courtyard lunging at each other against their better judgement. Yet some natural bond of underlying friendship kept each from the other's final murder.

Enraged and insulted, the Queen dismissed the two friends with the whip of her wand. Bloody, hurting, they returned home that night and infected their wives with the Witch's wild desire and their lingering, frenzied delirium. Thus incepted, the two wives promptly tore to death their once beloved husbands, devouring and absorbing the Witch's remaining spell. That was when the hand of fate came to overtake the tormented, age-obsessed Witch Queen. She had failed

Fortune's test and in her forbidden attempt to conceive the Eastern Gods' curse descended.

The avenging wives, now imbued with extraordinary strength and ferocious maternal instinct, headed back through the woods tracking their husbands' scent to the foot of the westerly turret. The Witch observed the wild, grief-stricken women in her Seeing Mirror and knew she would not win. Yet she, like all of her tribe, knew the dangerous incantation of 'Shadow Revival'. So, in a desperate bid to stave off death and secure her long-term survival, the wicked Queen began to separate herself into slender, misty, snake-like fragments.

Thus the wives arrived to find the Witch Queen in separating weakness. They sniffed out her side-winding selves, pulling and tearing at the snake-like pieces until they reformed into a semblance of her true grotesque ugliness. Then the wives dragged the Witch Queen's deformed, struggling, vaporous body out of the turret, away through the woods, and drowned her in the murky darkness of Obsidian Lake. Rare dread and moonlit water were the Witch's most vulnerable points. They tore out her throat in acts of instinctual savagery and fed her remains to the Hungry Grasses, who stripped her green gown and flailed her skin down to the bone. They duly feasted on her body – devouring her pale flesh, brittle bones, innards and all, in hitherto unheard of sumptuous top-to-toe Witch dining. The key to the Casket they spat out.

Before being finally consumed, the remains of the Witch's shredded body were scattered by the Carrion Crows and their hungry minions, whilst her blood leached into the surrounding soil and the roots of trees. Water from Obsidian Lake was poisoned further with her black bile, her venting spleen and the worst of her contaminating humours. Some of the walking-talking trees became tainted and division fell amongst the once harmonious woodland creatures.

Thieving birds, whose beaks, claws and feet corroded like acid on the touch of her blood, stole the leftover strands of her sparkling hair, which instantly greyed on her physical death. Later, birds' eggs were discovered abandoned in contaminated nests, left to go rotten.

The two wives shook the westerly turret with their howling and weeping, but could not bring it down any more than they could resurrect their husbands. They searched, but could not sniff out the remaining source of the turret's power. The Fire Dragon's magic had disappeared back into the Star-Compass, which would remain hidden by the Palace rats until, centuries later, a high-spirited boy with stolen Seven League Boots would find it. Meanwhile, bereft and appalled by their instinctual behaviour, the goodly wives returned home. They buried what was left of their husbands on the edge of the now infected First Forest, the Witch's shadow magic seeping deep into the blood-sucking soil of the shallow graves.

So the curse befell the people of Town as the wives' wombs filled with the infected fluid of Witch, wolf and hunter. They grew large with issue and nine months later a new generation of wild male-children were born – those with feuding urges of wolf and hunter bred into their blood and bone brought about by cursed desire, savage death and enchanted cruelty. Every future spell-infected boy on reaching puberty would turn on the Full Moon to either wolf-run or seek out a knife, dagger or hunting gun.

Oblivious to all of the frenzied howling beneath, the Princess slept the sleep of the good and continued to live innocently up high in her turret. As she grew, the Princess was bathed in the beams of light from the East to the point that her hair had turned an even more blessed, corn-ripened gold. More than that, a sunny disposition infused her and, despite all the loss and difficulties of her childhood years, an optimistic outlook grew. She occupied her time by spinning, singing and weaving her tapestry, waiting until she had grown as tall as her hair was long, in equal weight and measure fair. That was when, late one summer, the songs of migrating Swallows had filled her heart with joy and yearning. She knew then that she had to leave.

Meanwhile, not so far away but oh so many centuries later, the Princess's Fairy Godmother had grown ever so old in the local village ways. No one in Town knew Matilda's exact age for she was so light and bright and golden, yet she remained dazed from the battle between the evil Witch Queen's two feuding sisters. It was almost as though she floated along the corridors of the Hazy Days Care Home and Waiting for Death Day Centre. Indeed, was not Silly Tilly of the wrinkly tights really Waltzing Matilda of the long silk stockings and sometime wearer of the crystalline slippers?

Like her six fairy-siblings, one born to grace each day, Matilda was gifted with magic, charm and visionary insight. Along with the Mathmagicians, she was one of the few Fairy Folk alive with the right turn of mind to fully comprehend the inner realities and the objects of fairy tales. That is why, behind the clicking of knitting and the daily dosing of sweet syrupy sherry and sharp sloe gin, she had been one of the first to recognise the news of the oddly acting birds.

'The Travelling Ways – save the day?'

Amidst their honeyed dawn singing and the rising shine of the sun, the birds twittered to her every morning a wonderful reminder of the word-on-the-wing.

'Would she help?' the birds sang out. 'Could she awake and remember herself for everyone who could assist was needed now?'

Slowly Matilda's mind began to de-mist and sharpen in the light of autumnal rays. Through the haze of her befuddlement, thoughts and recollections returned: twirling birds, swirling skirts of a fantasy ball, and the memory of a golden-haired Princess long forgotten that she had blessed at birth with a thousand fortunate wishes. How many decades had passed since then? How many centuries?

'Where had she been?' she asked the birds.

'Under the curse of a wicked Witch Queen,' the birds replied helpfully.

The first person Matilda told of the strange tweeting of birds in her new awakenings was Able Mable. Her sister, Mable Fable, always one for a good story involving local gossip, was friendly with the Ninny Goat Griff sisters and their neighbour Nanny Goat Gruff. So that was how all the Old Goats, the spiritually tenacious elderly of the Land of Awe, were the very first to cotton on that something in the wind was a-changing.

Far away in the Forest of Thirst a flock of sinister birds took flight from a westerly turret and gathered in the gloomy woods beneath. They perched upon the telephone lines, pecking and clawing at the giant worm-like wires, sharpening their talons and beaks in preparation of oncoming battle. Unthreading voices from out of the airwaves, the birds became once more agents of evil as a force from beyond the grave reached out to interfere with a schoolboy's fate. In a desperate, scrambling frequency of fear the fragmented shadows of the Witch Queen were resurrecting, rising faintly from the Forest floor, in one last attempt to end the accursed Rose line.

'Grandmother Littlesøn?' Miss Beret enquired down the crackling telephone line. 'Hello... Grandmother May? I just wanted to let you know that Raoulf's still standing at the School gates. Is someone coming to collect him? I know you live on the far side of the woods. His father? I don't know. Yes, this line is very bad... I'm sorry? Yes, it's about Raoulf. He's waiting... alone. Will you come? Hello? Hello?'

The line went dead. Miss Beret tapped the receiver buttons twice with her finger... then again... but nothing, only silence.

'Great!' she shouted at the telephone. 'I'll let him know myself, then.'

Miss Beret dropped the receiver back down into its cradle, picked up her coat and 'Exceptionally Useful Bag', and left the building striding across the playground toward the gates. She dreaded having to encounter a tearful Raoulf left behind again. As she walked across the schoolyard she noticed once more the small dark cloud hovering above the Statue. Almost as perplexing was the symmetrical cloud of light next to it. Then she realised they were both branches of the same cloud entangled. It was very odd.

Sparks seemed to be flying out of one corner of the cloud as though some thunderous disaster had just occurred. If Miss Beret was not mistaken it looked like a hex gone wrong. Then she noticed a small form falling straight through the cloud, not pulling up to land, but plummeting straight towards her and the Statue. A gentle thud delivered the bird to the feet of the Philosopher-Prince. Miss Beret's shadow fell upon the bird in the half-light as she reached up to look on the plinth. It was a Swallow.

'Oh!' she exclaimed. Then in a softer tone added, 'Poor thing, please be dead.'

Unwanted thoughts around the death of birds and wounded animals stirred and collected in Miss Beret's mind. In an unconscious flash she was a child perched upon her father's knee watching him break the neck of a trapped rabbit to end its misery. She had tried to intervene and help the course of Nature by trying to open an iron trap, but had only made matters worse. His faraway words of wisdom regarding gun, feather and fur returned to her now…

'Nothing any good ever came from bringing injured birds or animals into the house. If it's their time to go they must go – it's not for us to upset the Eternal Balance. Otherwise you become accountable for their souls and only attract sorrow.'

If the bird was only injured and not dead would she have the strength to kill it? It was what her father would have advised and wanted.

'Of course not,' she lied inwardly to her struggling self.

If Miss Beret momentarily believed she was too sensitive for such a gruesome thought as murder, she instinctively knew that she was not beyond a mercy killing. Her father, the Huntingsman, had taught her as a child how to use her hands to slay and handle the blood axe, the knife and the cleaver before he had been so brutally taken away from her. It was rumoured that a wolf dressed in sheep's clothing had killed him on that strange ill-fated day; the day on which her child's world was destroyed, her family lost and her memory erased by the sharp tap of a wand. However, if any aspect of her wild childhood instinct still remained, the present-day Miss Beret remembered little of it and simply guessed at childhood absences.

'Are you all right, Miss?' asked a concerned voice.

Relieved by the distraction, Miss Beret turned from her strange reverie and looked down. It was Raoulf Littlesøn. She felt calmed by his presence standing there in his strawberry-red coat, with his round face looking up at her like a lovely candle-lit Moon-lantern. She re-assured him, and herself, that she was quite all right and had only stopped because of what she had seen. Raoulf had noticed the bird's strange descent too from the School gates. On tiptoes he stretched toward the top of the plinth on which the Statue stood to pull himself up and peer at the Swallow, but he was too small to reach.

'Is it moving, Miss?' asked Raoulf.

'No,' she replied, 'I'm afraid it isn't.' Miss Beret tried changing the conversation. 'Now, I spoke to your Grandmother and someone will be here to pick you up very soon…'

But Raoulf persisted in his childlike questioning. 'That bird has been acting strangely all year, Miss. Does it have a nest in the Statue?'

It was funny how certain people noticed the same things.

'Why… I don't know, Raoulf,' said Miss Beret absently as she briefly scanned the Statue. 'I can't see any twigs or signs of a nest.'

'What did it die of, Miss?' asked Raoulf.

'Why, I don't know, Raoulf.' Miss Beret noticed a small speck of blood as she inspected the lifeless body. There was a pellet-size hole through the bird's breast.

'Miss, can birds die of broken hearts like humans?' asked Raoulf.

'Why, I don't know…'

Miss Beret's words trailed off as she looked down at Raoulf. Three times now this child had asked her a question and three times she did not know the answer. What was it that always came in threes? Good or bad luck? Or was it an omen about a girl? No, that was sneezes… or was it the glimpsing of magpies? Perhaps it was wishes? Sisters, roses, kisses three? Miss Beret's spell-protected mind swiftly cleared any thoughts of disaster and feelings for her family. It was so frustrating not being able to recall.

Then a book on 'The Behaviour of Birds and their Secret Lives' scudded like a cloud through her mind. Some birds partnered for life. Some were baked in a pie. Others pecked off your nose if you were caught telling a lie. As a momentary reference book, Miss Beret found it all rather unhelpful. Then she thought about the pining nature of certain cats, dogs and humans that lead to death so they could follow quickly after their departed beloved and masters.

'I suppose technically any creature could…'

Once more Miss Beret's words faltered as she peered at the bird. It was almost as though a rifle pellet had pierced it, but there had been no crack or sound of a shot. Perhaps the impaling point of the Philosopher-Prince's rapier had made the hole? Why was she finding it so hard to see what was in front of her?

Unexpectedly, a friendly Robin Redbreast flew onto the fingers of the Statue's outstretched hand. He spoke briefly to them, 'Chirrup-Chirrup,' before dashing away. With the Swallows all departed the Statue now belonged to the Robin for this acted as one of his hopping branches, last territorial outpost from his usual haven of the nearby allotments.

'No-one is born free – do you dare to follow me?'

What was the Robin saying? Unfortunately, steeped in intrepid wildcat, badger and squirrel, Miss Beret spoke only to those with fur, not feathers. Had the Robin been speaking fox (her preferred second language), and not bird, she would have understood the message in an instant for Forest Folk were often twittering away to help one another. But as Miss Beret could not translate the language of the Robin the words escaped her and the moment was lost. A cold feeling arose within her heart, for the sighting of a Robin meant the heralding of Winter and a fleeting reminder of those missing, stolen, faraway years of her childhood. She shivered. The fragmented part of Miss Beret's Rose past was beginning to knock stubbornly like a wolf at the door…

'Let me in…'

'No, no, not by the hair on my chinny-chin-chin.'

'Then I'll huff, and I'll puff, and I'll blow your house in.'

What was Miss Beret so afraid of? Was it the Robin or something else in disguise? To distract herself from such odd interloping thoughts, Miss Beret gently prodded the Swallow with a pen she had taken out from her 'Exceptionally Useful Bag'. The bird did not move. It was definitely dead. She would leave a note with Mr Woolfe, the School caretaker, instructing him to remove the bird before the other children arrived in the morning. He was to dispose of it properly and not to eat it. It would be a joke of hers; she could see him licking his lips in that peculiar, large-jawed manner he had.

Yet as Miss Beret nudged the underside of the Swallow to turn it over she noticed that it was not a pellet that had killed the bird, but a beautiful black pearl. With a pair of tweezers she picked the tiny blood-stained pearl up, placed it carefully into a pocket-tissue, which she neatly folded, and then put everything back into her 'Exceptionally Useful Bag'. She looked up at the Statue whose sockets were shadowy and empty. Yet somehow they were glistening as though tears were forming in the concave recesses. Miss Beret knew that the pearl did not belong to the Statue for his eyes had been sapphires set against the Statue's former coat of gold and silver.

That was back in the days when the Statue had stood in the Old Town Square, before the Philosopher-Prince had been slowly vandalised and robbed of his former splendour. Some believed the corrosion to be caused by a sudden flurry of bird activity and their resultant droppings, whilst the majority of the Townsfolk presumed it was due to the hunting boys wishing to cover their bullets with the Statue's silver and their teeth with the gold leaf. In reality, that time had been the beginning of wondrous fables and beatitudes delivered daily by the Statue to the bird world. Magnetised by the truth and beauty of such tales, the feathered flock had gathered to spread the Good News. So, in a flapping of wings and glad-tidings, the Prince's story-telling ministry had begun. Now, however, the Statue looked grimy and forlorn.

'Come along,' said Miss Beret taking Raoulf by the shoulders and turning him around.

Suddenly feeling the late afternoon chill in the air, Miss Beret pulled the hood over Raoulf's head and took hold of his hand. As she did so she felt a quick shudder run through her. Unable to place the feeling, she dismissed it and started walking Raoulf back across the schoolyard towards the imposing iron-wrought gates. If Miss Beret had trusted her sensitivity and teacher's instinct, she would have realised that his thumb was missing a freshly pressed print. It was stuck hovering between the air and the curve of a brass Door Knob that once belonged to a marvellous, magical travelling bed.

'Chirrup-Chirrup,' sang the flitting Robin tilting his head to peer at the boy whose coat was as bright as a holly berry. Raoulf looked up at the amiable blood-breasted bird.

'If you're like me be of good cheer – hop into the woods without any fear.'

Glancing down, Miss Beret was distracted once more by Raoulf's strawberry-red coat. She adored it as much as he loathed it. The coat momentarily reminded Miss Beret of a Cape of Red that an old friend had once wrapped around her in a desperate hour of childhood need, whereas the coat was a reminder to Raoulf of his mother. It was the last thing she had given him before her departure; a memory of kicking around in the leaves in the garden one morning, then her arms enfolding him with the coat, and she was gone.

Yet, truth be told, Mrs Littlesøn had already vacated the house many months before when she had started on the course of pills prescribed by the white-coated doctors. She had been given them to subdue her rising pain and calm her nerves in a bid to dam the intensifying inner scream growing amidst her challenging domestic circumstance. Mrs Littlesøn had given her son the coat to connect him to his protective, if somewhat exasperating, grandmother. It was an ancient tradition, gift and curse, usually inherited by girls in his Grandmother's bloodline. So a grandson now inhabited what should have been passed down and paraded by a granddaughter.

'Red fate,' chirruped the Robin, 'how charming!'

Perched on the wall, the resplendent blood-bird looked on admiringly. Raoulf stared back fuming. He would have deliberately lost the coat, but was afraid of hurting his mother's feelings. Unlike Miss Beret, he understood the Robin's song, but he did not share the bird's sentiment. Stopping at the gates Miss Beret looked around at the empty street.

'Here,' she said handing Raoulf one of the rosy red apples that the children had brought her earlier that day, 'something for you to eat later on if you get hungry and have to wait.'

Raoulf smiled appreciatively.

Miss Beret would never eat them as she had a strange aversion to biting into proffered apples – one that bordered on being a phobia. Yet however suspicious she was of the delectable fruit, she always said thank you to the children and looked so genuinely pleased that the little darlings had vowed to bring her an apple every morning for the rest of their lives, or at least until the end of their school year would separate them. So beloved was she by the children. At the same time as gifting the abhorred apple, Miss Beret also fished from out her bag a packet of flapjack fingers.

'Thank you, Miss,' said Raoulf, placing the apple and flapjack into his coat pocket, 'that's very kind.'

Miss Beret noticed Raoulf's elasticated mittens dangling from his coat. She helped him put them on, and then tightened the toggle of his hood under his chin. Even though Raoulf was resentful of having to wear the red-matching mittens and the hood up on his coat, he was so very fond of Miss Beret that he accepted the imposition. She was caring, and sometimes funny, and everyday she read gruesome fairy stories to them. Thus inspired, he had eagerly taken to reading under her wing and guidance, and he loved learning new words that opened up the story worlds of imagination.

In an attempt to survive the different kinds of schoolboy trauma, Raoulf had turned his early attention to books. He had read the entire ladybird library of Astrid and Ethelreds, of Gudrun and Ragnars, and the many coloured rainbow-bridge books. Now he was moving onto the Valhalla volumes of silver and gold. Alongside the dancing toys, the talking trees and the flying rocking-horse dreams, Raoulf ensconced himself into an inner world of which Miss Beret and her stories were a central part – where words of learning and love, healing and adventure, even magic itself, had become essential aspects of his dream world.

Indeed, other teachers had observed, during the rounds of playground duty, that Raoulf preferred the Land of Imagination to making real friends, for he was often found whispering in corners to the ghost of Cartwheel Charlie and other invisible companions. Raoulf's own imagination was active and open; it seemed to be one of Nature's gifts. Yet playtimes were frequently arduous for Raoulf. Although he liked to play games with the other boys and girls, he did not like attending their parties and felt awkward around them. He did not know what to do, and they in turn thought it was strange that he did not like the devouring of jelly, the slicing of birthday cake or the popping of screechy party balloons.

Raoulf seemed distant. Miss Beret wondered if the dead bird had upset him.

'Raoulf,' she enquired, 'will you be all right?'

The boy looked up at his teacher and nodded.

Miss Berry had a pretty face with a warm smile that he believed reflected her heart. She smelt nice too, like lavender, only younger. In some ways she also reminded him of his parents before the shouting had started. The warm, easy-going nature of Raoulf's father played a great part in his secret world, as did the complex depth of his sensitive mother. In their different ways they both helped the fuelling of Raoulf's inner mystical Sun for, as an only child, he felt essentially alone and somewhat disconnected from others. He often saw his fellow schoolmates as trespassing strangers rather than welcoming friends. Miss Beret seemed to have a mixture of them all – perhaps that was the reason why he was so overly fond of his teacher.

'Raoulf, you will be all right waiting alone, won't you?' repeated Miss Beret. 'I spoke to your Grandmother and someone will be here to pick you up soon...'

Raoulf looked up at her and beamed. In that moment, through the eyes and face of this child, Miss Beret's fairy tale childhood of much dark, but some light, rotated like a rose frozen in time, like a memory forever trapped suspended. Miss Beret reached out to grasp the multi-faceted crystal flower when a sudden blinding pain shot through her temples. She was beginning to feel fragile again. She needed her pills and needed to get away from the boy who stood in front of her feeling so wretched in his blazing red coat. She would go and see Mr Woolfe about the dead bird and then see the Headmaster, he who was always there to help as her spiritual guide and mentor.

'Yes Miss,' Raoulf lied, 'I'll be fine.' He was distracted by the antics of the hopping Robin, who kept asking him to follow and fly away.

On hearing this blatant untruth Miss Beret hesitated, but taking the opportunity to escape she turned rapidly around and walked back across the schoolyard. Raoulf had no intention of waiting for anyone, not with the memory of the last time still burning inside. Then he had launched all his feelings of anguish, stupidity and pent-up pain as an outburst of uncontrollable hate towards his father. However lost to the Moon Mr Littlesøn was, Raoulf had been left torn, struggling with his own torment as well as that of his parents. Mr Littlesøn had been genuinely remorseful, whilst Mrs Littlesøn had gone berserk.

As soon as Miss Beret was out of sight Raoulf too would go, slipping out through the gates and running into the wild of the Wood's leafy edges. After all, it was the beckoning season of cheerful birds, scampering squirrels and the chasing of falling leaves. Escape from the grey imprisoning schoolyard would be fun. An adventure. And the Robin was hopping from rapier to gate and back again in excited expectation.

'Don't forget to mention the dead bird to Mr Woolfe,' Raoulf shouted out at Miss Beret's vanishing figure. She carelessly waved back as though thanking him for the reminder, but Raoulf was really implying how easily busy adults could forget the words and worlds of children. 'And thanks again for the apple and flapjack, Miss…'

But she was gone and so too was the Robin.

A cold, cloud shadow crept across the schoolyard engulfing the Statue. The classroom Goblins and Trembling Fears reached their fingers towards the disappearing Raoulf, whispering intently on the capture of his soul. Meanwhile, the caretaker's office had a light on, but no-one was there. Miss Beret knocked again and peered in, then pinned a hastily scribbled note to the door right next to the plated name – Janus Woolfe. "Please remove the dead Swallow from the Statue." She then quickly added a line to the note: "Please look out for Raoulf Littlesøn before closing the School gates for the night."

Mr Woolfe was not there for the simple reason that the Headmaster had called him to his office for a 'private word'.

'I'm sorry, Janus' said the Headmaster shaking his head, 'it's something that's going to affect us all.'

'But Magnus,' replied Janus, 'it's so sudden. There's not much time to adjust plans. What of the teachers and children?'

Janus was thinking of the fate of the Headmaster, whilst the Headmaster was considering the caretaker's difficult situation.

'We only have until the end of the academic year, all of us, to sort this out and re-position,' said the Headmaster gravely. 'Everyone will be informed accordingly, but please accept this as your formal notification. I wanted to give you time to think and make decisions. We need an exit strategy if things go wrong, but we cannot stay here anymore. There's the matter of protection and relocation, both yours and Miss Beret's, as the matter stands. Please keep the news to yourself. It will be out in no time and everyone here at the School has the right to hear it first-hand. The Mayor will be overseeing the final public announcement regarding his fandangled regeneration scheme. But I'm concerned, Janus, concerned for you…'

Janus's ears pricked up.

'The Mayor?' he spat contemptuously. 'That fat fool who sold his soul and more for a fist full of beans.'

'Still doubt, Janus?' asked the Headmaster, mentally noting the vehemence of his friend's remark.

Janus said nothing. Who was he to question the nature of the spells cast on the two surviving members of the Rose Family amidst such childhood catastrophe, but after the passing of so many years nothing seemed to have really changed. Only time would tell and reveal the Mathmagician's wisdom. Indeed, judging by the contents of the letter sitting on the Headmaster's table, events were about to get considerably worse for everybody involved. Wishing to ameliorate any awkwardness, the Headmaster gently continued…

'It's time for us all to move on, my friend. Fresh starts for everyone in the new 'One Dream Awakening'.'

'Don't you worry about me Headmaster,' Janus replied, his blood still boiling at the thought of Jack Rose and how he had turned into such a bumbling, yet dangerous, fool of a mayor. Yet he felt uncomfortable about such a strong slip of the tongue in front of the Headmaster and the allusion to matters of the past that still troubled him. 'I have to go now, but I do want to say... thank you... and that I understand your position. I'm truly grateful for what you have done for the others and me. You've achieved so much in uniting this community. I know the Forest Folk and the other Mathmagicians would want to wish you well in your final endeavours...'

'Further adventures...' the Headmaster proffered wryly.

The caretaker hesitated before adding, 'But if these are to be our last days then let's make them count, so to speak...'

'Of course, Janus,' said the Headmaster half-smiling. 'As always... soul brothers in arms.' At the mention of brothers Janus took a deep breath, whilst the Headmaster turned his attention back to the bamboozling matter of the letter on his desk. 'Still, I am hoping that the Mayor's position might favourably shift...'

Here he lifted the Mayor's letter up to his Mystic Mirror hanging on the wall as though searching for a sign, a signal, a clue, but the glass remained obstinately cloudy.

'Unfortunately, the fate of the School is no longer in my hands. Events are rapidly changing and even this aging Mathmagician has to step down at some time. I have to confer the responsibilities of my office onto younger, more suitable, shoulders. I might even have a task or two to ask of you, old friend...'

'Anything for you, Headmaster....'

The room fell quiet. As Janus turned to leave he heard a faint voice in his mind whispering of things dead and past. A shiver ran up his spine as he instinctively touched the silver talisman lying in his pocket. The metallic hinges creaked as he opened the wooden door and stepped into the flagstone corridor outside the Headmaster's office. Janus hesitated as he heard a wolf cry drift out upon the wind; a wailing sound so distant that he alone could hear. The foothills of the mountains were calling the Lone Boys – those failed men lost in fur and damage. The hair on his back bristled as he felt a sudden surge within to turn – to transmogrify. He could feel the inner hunger of his wolf rising alongside the urge to run into the wild and lead his roaming pack through the Forest. The solitary Full Moon-devotees would be riding out tonight. They liked to call it Fang Ridge racing, whilst Janus called it soul sailing.

Thank Odin the Headmaster was unaware of the last few years' secret events; of the society of fur Janus had established underneath the Townsfolk's noses. Anyway, it served them right – both the ordinary people and the rival hunting sons. Those stalking lads never did have the power of sense or scent given to the wayward killing frenzy as they were. Yet all those similarly spell-tainted had to obey the Moon's blood calendar, so any celebrated liberation of the Wild Wolf Calling also meant the monthly return of the savage chase; village fur-friend against gun-folk foe alike.

Pre-occupied by the Mayor's letter, as though some important aspect still eluded him, the Headmaster now looked up over his glasses inquisitively at Janus who remained frozen in the doorway. It was as though he could read the tracks of his friend's wolf-turning mind. More intrigue! Not being able to control his instinctual thoughts against one so insightful as the Headmaster, Janus shut the door quickly behind him, squaring himself up as he walked down the corridor back to his office. So, that was how the School and their final years of friendship were going to end. Not with a bang, but a car park.

As Mathmagician and former Mayor, the Headmaster was still acknowledged as the authority to turn to for magical help, insight and advice. Overseeing public disputes, he had brought law and justice to Town and the surrounding districts that were fair for the people and good for the land. Yet some seriously questioned the wisdom and suitability of the appointment of his former apprentice, Jack Rose, to become the current Mayor, including Janus Woolfe.

Still, Janus knew that the Headmaster had his Far Seeing reasons, however baffling they seemed. Plus the change of mayoral positions had left Magnus free to take on the guardianship of the School. As Headmaster he could concentrate on educating and safeguarding the last generations of Fairy Folk and other displaced creatures that were being lost to the ever-quickening human world. And for that the Forest and Fairy Folk of Town were truly grateful.

The Headmaster's current position had not only helped protect the School, but also Janus – ensuring his friend's safety by transferring him from a wayward track finder and forest despatch runner to become the School's custodian caretaker. Yet not everyone had taken to the snarling, often snappish, stranger who did not suffer fools gladly. After the vastness of the Frozen North, Janus had found it hard to settle in such a small-minded place. Still, he had the woodland and mountains in which to stretch his legs and howl.

Prejudice and bigotry were rife amongst the Townsfolk, flaring up in monthly incidents around the time of the Full Moon ever since the Witch's failed conjuring of suitors. Some of the younger local lads pursued their interest in knives, guns and blood sports within the Forest Rangers cadet academies, whilst wolf others took off on bikes to roam the wild spaces and cover the urge for territorial distance by road. It was to the helping of this younger generation of wolf-turning boys that Janus's interest had turned in the last few years. Monthly Moon meetings had turned into an outlet for both good and ill. Janus was one of the last transformers still able to turn and run at will – him, Big Bad and a few Polar others – but even that was getting more and more difficult on his body in his now rapidly silvering years.

When Janus Woolfe, old as the hills and hoary as snow, arrived back at his office he found Miss Beret's note pinned to his door. For all her concerns about Raoulf being stranded at the gate, Janus already knew Mr Littlesøn would not be there to collect his son, not with such a strong, ripe tilt of the lunar inclination – for Raoulf's father would be amongst the Lone Boys riding out tonight. Strange. Some recently expelled scrabbling Fears clung onto the edge of the note clawing desperately at Raoulf's name, ravenous in their pursuit of the boy's thumb, identity and soul.

The Fears trembled nervously as Mr Woolfe laughed, threw back his head and gulped them and the note down in one bite. Yet for Fears ingestion was just another way of travelling. In their fanatical search for the owner of the thumbprint, they did not care what the mode of transportation was. Janus could feel the Fear's quest in the pit of his stomach.

'Thank you, Miss Beret,' thought Mr Woolfe. 'Helpfully inadvertent as ever.'

The Fears thought the same about Mr Woolfe, but he understood their game even though it meant an exhausting night of Forest prowling. Janus could hear the sound of oldness in his ears as his body grumbled and his mind complained, so he stretched back on his haunches and shook himself free from his restricting beliefs regarding the Mayor and their difficult past. Then, out lurched a rabbit-like hunch that had to be followed. It was purely the luck of circumstance setting out the tracks of the now. Grandmother May would be on her way to collect Raoulf, and of her he had to be wary for she always suspected him of being deceitful and untoward. Wolves, whether Big and Bad or Lone and Silver, were not the kind of company Grandmother Littlesøn wished any human to keep.

Excitedly, the ingested Fears felt their host's sudden hankering after the same prey – all, it seemed, were in mutual pursuit of Raoulf Littlesøn. Ever the two-way opportunist, here was a chance too tasty for Janus to miss. He guessed that even Miss Beret had figured Raoulf's plan out by now as he walked to the Statue to remove her dead bird. Janus scooped the Swallow into his hand. Damn Nature's flying agents! Wanderers without borders, they were always the most difficult creatures to command and control. The strength of Janus's profanity and unfolding plan interested the Two Towers, whose intercepting beams scanned the School for circumstances beyond the inhabitants' grasp. Intriguingly, Raoulf was nowhere to be seen.

Back in his office, Janus gently placed the Swallow into a bunch of dried flowers left over from Cartwheel Charlie's disappearance memorial. He wrapped the bird up with tissue, a bow and a blessing. He would bury the bouquet of dead things properly in the morning otherwise unburied birds attracted all kinds of sorrow and harm. Now, Janus turned his attention to the pursuit of living things and strode out into the schoolyard. He paused to sniff the wind. Miss Beret's scent lingered in the air from her standing at the statue and the writing of the note. Juniper berries, Lapp pine – the smoke of simple spells and something else he could not quite make out. Was it lilac or lavender? No, it was more crystalline and metallic. It was the faint aroma from her compact case and magical talking mirror.

Of course! Janus recognised that smell of silver from the misfiring of guns – pellets shot into glass and wood that in turn had triggered the fatal shot which had prematurely ended the life of his brother, Eirik. May Odin forgive them all for everything that had happened during that terrible day and tragic night. Still, Janus admired Miss Beret for all she had endured. He had vowed to try and do what was best for her and make amends where possible given the half-chance.

The Eye of Dark spun briefly before snapping shut trying not to reveal its plans, but Janus had seen enough. Few could read the dark like Mr Woolfe. Raoulf's Grandmother's cottage would be empty. Oh! The light would be on, just like last time, every time, but no-one would be home tonight – not for a while. The question remained as to where Miss Beret was and what she would do? She had once been in a similar situation of danger, but had she simply handed the boy's responsibility over to him on a hastily scrawled note? The Goblins who were following him were thinking the very same thought.

As Janus closed the wrought-iron gates behind him he could see a light in the Headmaster's study and two silhouettes. Good! Miss Beret was suitably occupied. Janus could tell by the boy's lingering scent that Raoulf had taken the old way home via the wood and into the Forest. Grandmother Littlesøn would be driving along the mountain road at that very moment, coming to collect Raoulf. Then she would sit and wait. After that she would phone her son to see if he had already collected Raoulf. There would be, of course, no-one in at that home for Raoulf's father was already out on his motorbike Moon-riding, whist Raoulf's mother, the unhatched Banshee, had recently been removed from that particular domestic nest.

'Poor Hawthorn child,' thought Janus, who was one of the few who understood Mrs Littlesøn's reason for leaving.

As someone who had fought in the War of the Witches, Janus recognised the scent of the Banshee and had sensed the lurking creature within Mrs Littlesøn. With their command of silence, stealth and sound, Banshees were almost impossible to detect until it was too late – perfect for ambushing the unwary. They could easily confuse you with ear-splitting, heart-shattering noise that curdled your senses, your milk and your soul. Janus knew that what was bred in the blood and the bone of Fairy Folk had to get out, even if it meant clawing and screaming its way through the thorny briar.

Emergent Banshees only unleashed their voice and found their wings through painful predicament. Until that particular briar threshold had been reached, Janus thought Mrs Littlesøn's incarceration was probably for the best, but had she left of her own free will or had those known to be rounding up the last of the dangerous Fairy-kind captured her? That Janus did not know, but it was rumoured that intrigued, yet sceptical, doctors were said to be performing wild midnight experiments on those strange inmates held captive at the Elysium Asylum.

Meanwhile, a distraught Grandmother Littlesøn would try and contact Miss Beret, and they would either search the Forest for Raoulf or go straight to Grandmother's cottage having guessed where the boy was heading. Janus began to consider the different woodland routes and possibilities. He knew what he must do – track the boy and reach Grandmother May's home first. Striding out into the late afternoon Janus started to stretch and pad, then, having wolf-turned, bound across the ground into the gathering gloom. His way of Two Wolf and Truth Moon, of dark and light in perpetual conflict, meant that his entire life had been spent running, both toward and away. He had only the slimmest of chances, a hair's breadth, but it was his, Raoulf's and Miss Beret's only one.

So, Janus threw back his head and howled, laughing, aching, whilst thinking of his old Ice School comrades. With his brother the Huntingsman dead these many years, there was no-one serious to stop him following the dark, and Janus believed the deceiving of the Headmaster was justified in allowing an expression of the Wild Wandering and Old Wolf Way. In the forest Janus could race as free as he pleased; the more recently tainted young gun-ones were just minor annoyances and troublemakers to one so seasoned as him. Only the Headmaster, as trained Mathmagician, was left to rein him and the last of his wild lot in. Somewhere far away in the Forest of Fur tails began to wag.

In the Cloud Land of Bliss the three eldest Little sisters – Little Star, Little Seed, and Little Spark – had been planning a secret soul descent for quite some while. They were going to skip the usual growing-up wait and incarnational queues by taking the law into their own hands, jump cloud and surreptitiously use some passing rays to help them descend to the Earth Lands. They knew it could be done even though such renegade souls were usually frowned upon and permission for Spirit Children to incarnate must always be sought from the parents or guardians. Of course, tiresomely, it was never granted.

So, in preparation and eager anticipation, midnight plans for their escape were formulated under tented bed sheets and provisions were made ready. Toothpaste, apples, and overnight jim-jams – everything a travelling soul could possibly need. Yet when an earlier opportunity arose, created through the unprecedented Chaos and Drama of a bird colliding with a spell resulting in the tearing of the School's silver lining, the three sisters were off in an instant.

Unfortunately, in the confusion, Little Pearl had lost her way entirely. She could not understand what was happening. She had seen her three sisters grab each other's hands and run towards the precipitous cloud edge, but in the ensuing panic she had been baffled at the outset and left behind. She had tried to follow her three sisters when a hole in the fabric of the cloud appeared at her feet.

So, with not a beanstalk or magic carpet in sight, Little Pearl unhesitatingly hurled herself off the curling cumulus border where she instantly solidified into her namesake and fell straight into the breast of a passing Swallow. She heard the bird's chest crack and then they both plummeted down to land at the feet of a Statue standing in a schoolyard. Pearl, bird, and metal all collided. For a moment she felt a dull impact and heard the Statue's heart break. Then a distant voice exclaimed, before a dream shadow fell upon her. Then all she remembered was flying back up through the mists and curling wisps of cloud with the face of a receiving Air-Angel beaming down at her.

'Got you,' said the smiling Air-Angel.

'Welcome back, Little One,' said her schoolteacher somewhat relieved. 'You were very much missed. Did you fall?'

Little Pearl was smart enough not to answer, as it felt like one of those questions adults often asked to trick you. Fall indeed! She had very much purposefully jumped, but sometimes it was best to be shrewd. Little Pearl half-smiled but remained silent. Anyhow, she was too busy thinking that it was all very well being caught by an Air-Angel and brought back to Cloud Land, but it was rather annoying when your sisters were off having such a brilliant cloud-jumping adventure. As for being missed, she had hardly been away for more than a minute, but still the effect had been triggered and the souls of a bird and a Statue had been altered. Time behaved differently in the misty altitudes and Little Pearl did not realise that when that which should never leave departs, everyone knows and has an opinion on it.

'Perhaps when you're older,' said the kindly Air-Angel reading Little Pearl's mind. 'You know, some Spirit Children are destined never to leave the Cloud Lands. Like your sister – Little Bliss.'

'Thank you for bringing me home,' said Little Pearl gratefully clambering out of the Angel's sparkling arms. 'Will you help the poor bird, please, for I am terribly sorry to have cleaved his heart?'

'Don't worry. He's already been promoted. Now look, your Mummy's here so no harm's done.'

As the Air-Angel smiled down, Little Pearl playfully winked up before running along towards the next set of gathering arms.

'Hello Mummy, I'm so very sorry for leaving,' said Little Pearl immediately on the charm offensive. 'I love you very much. Is Daddy here?'

'Hello my darling,' said Mrs Little rather fazed. 'I love you too, but you know you ought not to have jumped.' She paused wondering whether she should ask what had made her go, but instead turned to more pressing matters. 'Do you know what's happened to your three sisters and the other children?'

Little Pearl shook her head and gazed up with those large round eyes that were meant to melt the hearts of adults with the innocent art of getting away with it. Mrs Little could already feel her somewhat brittle resolve dissolving.

'Now,' she thought to herself looking down at her daughter enquiringly, 'medicine or blanket; sugar or spoons?'

Roots and shoots, wishes and wings, the Ten Thousand Demanding Things of motherhood went through Mrs Little's mind. Difficult daughters, fretting fathers, and multi-tasking mothers: did it ever end?

'Oh well,' they both secretly thought, smiling to themselves, 'always another day.'

That night Little Pearl prayed for the safe-keeping of bird souls and her missing elder sisters. For Mrs Little, what else was there to do but to worry, wait and welcome all of them back home with wide open arms and a smile? Of course she was concerned… and then there was the rather difficult and sensitive matter *of telling her husband that four of their daughters had turned into Cloud Jumpers and three of them were still missing. Oh well, she had crossed many a rickety bridge before, but what would the Cloud Elders and other Nebulous Immortals think?*

Meanwhile, the three sisters had swung their escape plan into action with seamless precision and no hesitation. Little Seed, Little Star and Little Spark had run to the edge of the cloud, which now had a hitherto unseen peculiar looking corner, and bounced off the strangely angled rainbow beams shouting,

'Geronimo!'

Ticketyboo was no longer for them. So, under the cover of flying sparks and spraying twinkles, the three Little Sisters made their escape and jumped from their cloud. Fortunately, an ascending Air-Angel carrying the soul of a bird and their sister Little Pearl broke their initial fall. Down the Angel's white wing they went, riding the rapid curve of the scapula, then along the ridge with the wind billowing in their exhilarated faces.

'Whee!' they cried, bracing their ankles against the tickling fuzz of feathers. All, that is, except Little Spark who was tobogganing face first, arms in front as though she were flying, blazing a trail of thin silver mist and a mouthful of vaporous feather.

'What a lark!' she thought, soaring off the edge of the Angel's wing and plunging down into the thrilling, chilling air.

For the past year Raoulf knew that something was wrong… well, not quite right, concerning his parents. He could tell that there was estrangement between them, a difference, an absence, and an odd making do that was like a mask. He looked up into their adult world and could not make peace with it. Raoulf wondered if he had done something wrong, particularly in regard to his mother whom he adored and loved dearly. She seemed to suffer so much. Things were not right for her as she tussled with the intensifying voices of her emerging Banshee. Uncomprehending, Raoulf watched his mother's struggle from a child's distance, whilst his father coped with the situation by avoiding his wife on a daily basis.

Mr Littleson did not understand his wife's ever-changing moods and strange patterns of behaviour – how could he? Mrs Littleson did not fully understand them herself. Day and night, her mind was given to unintelligible bouts of Crow Speech, Siren Song and Mermaid Babble as something deep within struggled to surface and find expression. Sometimes Mr Littleson even feared his wife, for she seemed complicated; asking of him something he could not give on top of what he had already given. Consequently, he would disappear on his motorbike to contend with matrimonial issues, whilst also attending to his own urgent lunar matters. His frequent absence led to domestic spats and their differences turned into shouting matches and fights of frustration.

Conditions of shredded nerve and boiling blood were involved in their screaming bouts. Anger, hurt and ineffectual communication meant there were incidents of scalding flying kettles and the warrior rattling of pots and pans between them. These usually occurred at the bellyaching time of month, both hers and his. Her rising emotional outbursts and his departure by motorbike were overseen by the regular phases of the Moon. That much Raoulf had realised. But should they get further in or get out? Raoulf came to believe that his parents' only chance of happiness was in mutual relinquishing. Otherwise, they continued to dance a strangely formal dance – one of missing steps, of lowered eyes and fingertips, of blame and repercussion, of duty lacking so many expressions of physical love.

Ultimately it was a dance of destruction, of perpetuated absence devoid of intimacy on both sides, but in different ways. Harboured secrets were involved. Raoulf hardly saw his father who seemed incapable of engaging in the family way of life, but who did his best to provide and be there when he could. His mother grew cold and distant, becoming more and more isolated like a mountain explorer caught in a brutal blizzard. Unfortunately, Raoulf had got used to this uncertainty. He did not miss what he did not have or know, yet he recognised its warm presence in other families. Raoulf became withdrawn. He liked to be alone, but had so much care to give that he just did not know what to do except be silver and blue. Solitude descended upon the Littlesøn household. It was late Summer, but no-one understood why the sunshine was not getting through.

Sitting alone in the kitchen, Mrs Littlesøn sought the solace of the shrill, ever-whistling gas kettle. Something was deliberately haunting her overextended nerves as though a fiddle string was being tightened – as though there resided a restless Banshee within. At times the sound she could hear was so high, so piercing and insistent, that it tore through her temples like a skull perpetually shrieking in torment. Headaches tortured her as though some invisible force wanted to rip her soul from out her body. Outwardly there was the constant banging of doors, her husband's strange absences, and the slow passing of Time to contend with. She became fraught not realising she slept within the aura of a Moon-baying Wolf-Turner, who fitted and yelped in his dream-addled sleep.

Caught between the spasm and the pain the tablets could no longer contain, Mrs Littlesøn knew she had to release the pressure that had built up within and cut through the Ring-Pass-Not of eerie sounds that surrounded her. She felt herself unwittingly bound to her domestic situation, trussed as though she were being thrown under the clacking wheels of an oncoming train. And turning, pounding, steaming away in her head was its relentless refrain…

'Get down on the tracks; Get down on the tracks.'

But no one was coming to rescue her. And all the while a disturbing feeling that something, something that was wrong, something which could be right, haunted her and pervaded the home. Discontent versus the truth of things – was that really the way of the world? Self-preservation and the need for personal happiness meant that she had to get out of her situation, however selfish her actions would be judged to be.

'Bide your time,' said a voice. 'Choose your moment well.'

When the draconian Doctors had finally taken Mrs Littlesøn away to the Elysium Asylum – the No-Go Insanatorium and Deadly Home for Winter – she had surrendered and gone willingly. She did not wish to leave her husband and son behind, but she could find no other way to move forward. Yet, she could not predict the effect it would have on her life nor did she realise just how long it would take for the Banshee to emerge and for her inner revolution to complete.

Departing in the early autumnal frosts, the shedding trees reaching up under a hoary sky, Mrs Littlesøn was driven to the Asylum located on the outskirts of Mid-Witch – a large stonewalled place of secured respite where, according to a sign, there were to be *"No Visitors"* thus ensuring *"a chance to rest"*. In the imposed peace and quiet secret tests could be carried out, desires silenced, and from where, some said, people never returned. Well, not as they arrived.

So it was, under a muted grey dawn with a Hawk Moon descending, that Mrs Littlesøn was admitted to the Ward of Virgo for those who climbed walls and were considered demented; a containing centre for Grotesques, Changelings and Fey deemed less than perfect, struggling to express what was bred in their coursing blood and which crawled relentlessly through the marrow of their bone. The ward was full of the damned, the beautiful and the broken – fractured souls from the long ago who were all caught up within the Asylum's odd haunting. Doctors dressed in white coats rattled their keys as though they were the official keepers of chains, secrets and sanity, yet most were only confining men who clinically concurred and knew no better.

'Shackles, hackles, restraint and release – who is the beauty and who is the beast?'

Mrs Littlesøn had gone 'bat-crazy, cuckoo, unhinged in the head', jeered unkind Townsfolk callously circling their fingers by the side of their temples. Others, more politely, believed she was having a breakdown – a disastrous crisis leading to her tragic collapse. One, her son, thought she was on the verge of a personal discovery, however difficult, deranged and impossibly Banshee. Yet the truth told to Raoulf in regard to his mother's absence was hard for him to fathom…

'Some people climb mountains,' the white-coated doctors said sagely, 'whereas others have mountains to climb.'

Adults were often odd like that, speaking in cloaked, protective ways when a simple truth would do. All Raoulf knew was that he missed his mother and that something felt devastatingly wrong. What crime had they committed to be so cruelly punished by her ongoing absence and removal? He simply did not know whether things would become better or not? Raoulf looked to his frequently absent father, but found no answers there. So his grandmother wisely filled in the spaces the best she could. Yet even with her friendly face no smiles penetrated his world as a hurricane descended and whisked him away, just like the house in a film he had once seen on the television; the one with the tiny barking dog in, and the screaming Witch and the flying monkeys. With the combined threat from the clan of tigers, lions and bears, Raoulf found himself in the shadowy grip of the mysterious 'Oh My's!'

Billy Goat Plum was Raoulf's bestest friend, and they belonged to a gang called the Radio Boys. With help from their invisible friends they could cast spells that could out-thwart many a pretend Witch and Wizard, but together they could not heal the harms that tore through their homes. Billy was raw with grief following the death of his father in the Sand Wars of the Troubled Lands, whereas Raoulf was stuck in a pit of silent rage and confusion. Their emotions felt too deep, too elemental, too devil and angel, all at the same time.

Exhausted and lost, the two boys invented a radio that could listen to the missing and tune in to the dead. Invisible spirits and floating orbs spoke to them, yet the fact that everyday Life went on regardless seemed cruel. Not knowing what was to happen next the future seemed frightening. Raoulf's bedtime prayers, usually so full of good wishes for others, became full of angry demands and selfish requests where he wanted his world to be righted again, but he could not make it so. Misery and Winter descended.

After Mrs Littleson had rested for a few days at the large-walled Asylum, her peaceful solitude was broken by a visit from a doctor who was wearing a dazzling coat as bright as a White Wizard's cloak. He said he wished to conduct some tests in the Room of Reflection

— a giant, multi-faceted crystal chamber. Wary, Mrs Littlesøn slowly followed him.

The doctor smiled and sat her on a chair next to a console on which lay, face down, the Hand-Mirror of Truth. The mirror had once belonged to a Giant's daughter who kept it hidden in her doll's house until the precocious, bean-growing Jack Rose had stolen it. It was a striking silver mirror much like the one Mrs Littlesøn used to hold when her mother brushed her hair at night before bed. Whilst pulling at the scalp-tugging knots her mother would laugh and sing 'Songs of the Siren' to her — pretty ditties about storm-tossed sailors lost out to sea and love's torment, murder and drowning. The final brush was always a smoothing blessing in a foreign Banshee tongue that pacified her daughter's rebellious, snake-like hair.

The Hand-Mirror of Truth was ornately scribed with small flowing flowers entwined with six-pointed stars. The doctor said the mirror was enchanted, enabling people to see the truth that helped them defeat their darkness. These visions were then magnified through the rest of the crystal chamber — so there could be no escape or hiding. He warned Mrs Littlesøn that some previous observers had tried to manipulate what they had seen with jinxes and curses, trying to replace uncomfortable truths with desires of their own making. Some had even tried offering delectable apples in return for the comfort of sleep. Smiling, the doctor advised that these were not wise moves and that honesty was… Well, the best policy if you could trust your heart to find the right way forward in the confusing world of reflection.

Hemmed in, Mrs Littlesøn had few options regarding trust. The doctor told her that there was to be no negotiation with any voices she might hear and she was advised that the whisperings of inmates, informants and confidants could erode self-confidence. The Asylum doctors could, of course, always use the infamous Breastplate of Judgment to extract what they wished to know – a previously outlawed instrument that once placed around the neck, tightened with every untruth you told until it slowly strangled the throat of an incessant liar. The doctor also warned Mrs Littlesøn that the Hand-Mirror was neither a feel-good nor a distorting mirror, but that its revelations did have far-reaching implications regarding change.

Mrs Littlesøn did not care about such things for she was not afraid to look. In fact, a catlike curiosity had already crept over her, for she felt that here, at long last, she might be able to view her inner self and come to terms with her destiny. At the very least she hoped to attain some deeper knowledge and understanding of those things she felt, but could not reconcile within. Mrs Littlesøn knew she had to see and speak true, however difficult it was to express her present conflict; otherwise the damnable Denial Spirits would torment her and she would be torn apart. The doctor departed locking the door.

So, as Mrs Littlesøn picked up the Hand-Mirror of Truth, a cold tingling flowed up her arm and down her spine. She hesitated before turning the reflecting surface toward her and looked up out of the window at the late afternoon sky. In the distance she saw the treetops of the First Forest where Grandmother May lived. Deep in the centre she saw the twin Palace turrets, now named after Saint Hansel (patron saint of wily children against witches) and Saint Gretel (beloved of brothers), jutting above the tree's towering green. She heard the Carrion Crows cawing as they flew to and from Black Nest on their dark daily business.

Closer by, Mrs Littlesøn noticed the crushed skulls and bones of Giants' that the dry stone builders had used as rocks and boulders to construct the walls surrounding the Asylum. How that once mighty race had fallen. Then, a chirpy Cock Robin flew to the top of a nearby moss-covered branch and peered in at Mrs Littlesøn through the window.

'The North wind doth blow, and you shall have snow, and what will you do then? Poor thing…' chirruped the Robin.

Mrs Littlesøn could understand bird song and those sounds made on the wing by flying things. She let out a small sigh,

'Have you come to herald my Winter?'

'I have come to watch over you as you walk through the Veil of Mists. Can you grasp the sword of your dark-teared truth? For the mirror's vision not only cuts, but liberates as well.'

Swiftly, over the Robin's shoulder, a barb carved out of bone shot past. A pressgang of Sparrows with feathered bows and arrows appeared in pursuit of cockiness and an excuse for territorial war. The Red-Breasted One flew quickly away.

'Whatever happened to balance and Natural Law?' Mrs Littlesøn enquired of the great outdoors.

In the returning, over-powering silence she gradually pulled her attention away from the turrets, the trees and the squabbling birds and brought her focus back into the crystal room. Quietly shivering, she found herself sitting with the mirror in her hand, waiting.

'Shimmering mirror – what would she find? A peaceful heart or splintered mind?'

Slowly, Mrs Littlesøn turned the Hand-Mirror towards her.

With a steely resolve she looked into the glassy depths, into her reflecting eyes, into the silvering grey skies behind them and into her past. It was as though a curtain was lifting on a difficult chapter of her childhood. Torn events, ephemeral and fleeting, flickered across the mirror's surface as ever-shifting scenes of unfortunate circumstance…

A banished Witch flew by, a torch flared, a hare darted, a cantering horse reared, her mother falling from out the sky, a lamenting gathering, a secret churchyard burial, the village School aflame, a memorial held, poppies placed at the feet of the Old Town Square Statue in commemoration of dead children, the twirling dream of an ostracised girl rescued by an illusionary charming Prince, the arrival of an Unkind Lady with a stifling presence, the locking of doors, the closing of curtains, a time of cellars, dust and grimy grates, coal fires and the collection of broken Forest branches, a creeping, sinister coldness as cruel as scattered peas and lentils thrown haphazardly into the ashes – occasions heralding the rising harshness of a governess she would endure all her growing years.

Mrs Littlesøn had lived through all this without any guidance from her Banshee mother who lay dead and buried, her siren song forever frozen under the uncaring Parish ground. And where was her father? His presence seemed ever diminishing, his warmth and affection over-shadowed by changing events as first love grew distant, beyond memory's grasp and her young mind's reasoning. Did the mirror show true? Had she accidentally screamed and set the School ablaze, or perhaps she had done so on purpose? Had they realised then what kind of creature she was and what she was capable of? That would explain why she had been so often silenced and forcibly gagged by her governess. Around her, ice, snow and crackling fire filled the magnifying surfaces of the crystal chamber.

Compelled by curiosity, Mrs Littlesøn continued to gaze into the mirror. Now another curtain opened on to a different scene. She saw the restrictive chains of her future life with her fang-bearing, fur-turning husband. Horrified, she knew then that she must get away from him forever. Not even the mirror's final fleeting image – the face of her son, such a painful reminder of his father, looking up at her so lovingly – could change her heart. She knew then that she must end the lie of her present life. The mirror turned dark as a voice from the past echoed out…

'Be not afraid,' whispered the ghostly voice of her mother from within the glistening Hand-Mirror, 'for you are like me – a winged traveller from across the far Northern Sea.'

In the sudden haunting, Mrs Littlesøn realised she did not know her true self at all. Was she somehow descended from the tribe of naturally flying Witches – the diminished clan of Banshees? With a growing sense of foreboding, she knew then she must extricate herself from her current situation while she still could. There was no true sanctuary here in the Asylum and she must not embroil the lot of her life with others any further. She must sever and leave what was now truly apparent – the terrible mistake she had made in marrying such a divergent man. It was no longer right, which meant that it was not fair on him, on her, on Raoulf their mixed-blood son.

'Truly, you are much loved,' said her mother's voice, 'but that love must start from and include yourself.'

Briefly, the Room of Reflection was filled with a vast inner calm before Mrs Littlesøn's ancestors gathered about her, majestic and powerful, yet overwhelming and frightening. Slowly they began to sing and the chamber was filled with an eerie sound like the faint humming of overhead Spitfires. Behind Mrs Littlesøn's now burning eyes tears were beginning to collect. She knew then that she did not love herself, not quite yet, and not as fully as she needed to, for where was her Banshee in all of this confusion and conflict?

In that moment of trial, Mrs Littlesøn struggled to find the courage and strength to release her rare Banshee self. May Odin forgive her, as she tried to relinquish the shocking pain and terrible anguish she suddenly felt. She looked into the Hand-Mirror of Truth one final time, but saw nothing except her hollow eyes and empty face. Only one devastating belief remained – that somehow she had failed, failed herself, failed her husband and her son, and that Life had somehow failed them all…

'Remember,' said the departing voices mustering as much love as they could find, 'that the soul can only be rightfully restored once the illusions of the lonely heart have truly emptied.'

Yet Mrs Littlesøn could not hear them, dared not heed them, for in the din of her calamity there was no space in her heart for such loving words. Now, desperately searching for the freedom of acceptance, her skull pounded with a sound like that of fox cubs whose cries and whimpers trumpet the start of the vixen's hunting. Assailed by such a forlorn sound, she felt her grief rise and collect in her strangulated throat. At last, in desperation and yearning, Mrs Littlesøn broke free from her past and began to cry the Ten Thousand Tears of Terrible Truths.

As all the horrors of her aching heart overwhelmed her she emitted a scream, the one scream of all her lifetimes, and her shrieking Banshee reared-up within. Slowly rising from out her chair, Mrs Littlesøn found herself suspended mid-air; her newly expanding bat-like wings filling the crystal chamber. Lifting higher, she leant forward and began to glide around the room as the strands of her hair danced wildly about.

Momentarily feeling free, Mrs Littlesøn laughed and the delightful sound of fluttering echoed all around. But as she floated she let the Hand-Mirror of Truth fall from her hand. Then an extraordinary thing occurred, for as the silver-cased mirror clattered to the hard, stone floor it was not the glass that shattered, but Mrs Littlesøn.

So it was, in such a state of bewilderment and broken pieces, that Mrs Littlesøn was admitted to the Ward of Libra in order to rest. Balance and respite were offered in her continuing breakdown; a touch of harmony and a taste of honey were given to comfort and console before the next set of tests commenced. Ongoing ordeals would be the matter of her coming days; trials and tribulations beyond her control in which challenges, like the acceptance of ever-changing patterns of light through her barred windows on a padded floor, would be monitored by the men in dazzling white coats. Every day she was given a special tea and a drugged piece of cake until a slice of Golden Peace was hers once more.

'Surrender your sound,' she was told, 'and you can fly free.'

Mr Littlesøn admired the thickening fuzz growing on his face as he moved his chin from side to side in front of his motorbike mirror. The Lone Gang of Renegade Youths and Wayward Fathers were out riding again, for a howling was on and the rising Full Moon demanded their attention. Into the Forest they would go to scratch their skin and the spell-tainted blood that boiled beneath. Another lunar ceremony to the unearthly destiny of the Witch's 'Fur Spell' and the lads would all feel better. They always did after a tankard of beer or two and a mad bout of Fang Ridge mountain racing.

'*Skål!*' they cried.

It was what Janus would have wanted. If only he could have been there to rally and send them off, but this night he had forsaken the pack to hunt just one.

'To hunger is human; to devour – divine.'

That was the motto of the man from whom they had willingly taken leadership; not only elder, but also last of his clan – the Nordic Silver Wolves.

'*Skål!*' was the pack's amiable reply.

'Take nothing but what you need,' he always reminded them as he gazed into their inexperienced fur-changing faces. 'And remember to think on the run. You cannot plan circumstances or control your environment; you'll only know what to do when the Time comes… so trust your instincts.'

'*Skål!*' they cheered, but their bewilderment and ignorance of wild Nature shocked Janus.

'There's power in the pack. So stay together and survive until sunrise.'

It had been late afternoon when Mr Littlesøn had left his house and in the roar of his motorbike's engine the quiet ringing of a telephone was left far behind, escaping even his enhanced hearing. Exasperated, Miss Beret gave up and put the telephone down. That was how one of Raoulf's very few chances of rescue was lost.

Raoulf decided to visit his Grandmother who lived alone in a small thatched cottage on the far side of the Forest of Furs. Still wearing his strawberry-red coat, he waited at the gates just long enough to see Miss Berry disappear indoors on her quest to find Mr Woolfe. Unaware of her ongoing concern for him and Mr Woolfe's gathering interest in the evening's unfolding plot, Raoulf willingly followed the chirruping Robin down the Cinder Path that led away from the School. Then, threading between the intersecting walkways of the allotments, he began to make his way to the wilder parts of the woods that bordered the dusky Forest.

Raoulf merrily skipped along humming to himself, a sea shanty of his mother's about a young woman waiting for a sailor's return from a violent storm. After the foul wind blows away any mercy, the ship arrives empty and the woman throws herself into the storm-tossed sea. The drowned lovers are reunited in a watery grave. Raoulf thought it was a somewhat cruel outcome with a high price to pay, but the tune was pretty and perhaps grown-up love exacted such things? Striding confidently to the sound of the song and the rousing finale, he skirted the Meadows Edge, puddle-jumping across the long harsh grasses and sinking quagmires.

In the gathering twilight of growing shadows, shrubs became menacing grizzly bears and trees twisted up into looming giants. Over-hanging branches occasionally loosened the last of their leaves, which twirled above his head like bats dancing to the music of an autumnal sunset. The bramble, leaf-patterned path he had taken was certainly overgrown and covered with detritus; the wet, yellow leaves slipped treacherously underfoot whilst the dry, brown leaves scattered and scrunched as he kicked his way along. Luckily his coat protected him from the nettle stings and blackberry barbs as he pushed aside the prickly shrubs. Luminescent fairy rings poked through the grass whilst toadstool grew in slimy clumps on rotting, fallen wood.

The last of the northerly Summer Swallows circled overhead, wheeling in the sky as they called out to Raoulf.

'Do not go into the uncertain woods,' they cautioned. 'Head South instead. Come away with us for the Forest is full of Witches and Wolves and the night is full of death.'

Raoulf waved at the departing birds; yet as they streaked away against a faintly bleeding sky, their words of warning failed to reach him. He did not follow the winged messengers and so another one of his slender chances disappeared.

Andante now, andante, andante, as the crimsons, blues and indigos of a purpling sunset began to collide and descend. The curtain of night began to fall swiftly as Raoulf went further into the woods. Two looming spires stretched their elongated shadows, but gave no solace as each stood alone reaching out to the other, forever unable to hold hands. Raoulf knew he must go beyond the giant wolf-thorns and bear-briars surrounding the brother and sister spires to get to the other side of the forest where his Grandmother lived.

As he pushed through the undergrowth he found himself surrounded by moss-covered statues; unfortunate figures frozen in perpetual dance with faces of fear now peeking through the creeping ivy. Raoulf picked his way amongst the fallen sarsens that littered the ground. Beneath his feet was a courtyard of crushed statues and human skulls discarded like giant-gnawed bones thrown to the floor from a Titan feast. It was as though he had stumbled upon some medieval monstrous ball – cold, cruel and inhumane.

Crumbling columns stood along one side of what used to be the old Palace pathway, whilst white marble statues of courtiers offered out their hands in search of company. The light slipped away quickly between their smooth reaching fingers. Imperceptibly, some of them seemed to move wishing to break free of their century-old stone-prisons. Carrion Crows collected in the gathering gloom chattering, brooding with dissent and ill-temper.

One Sinister Soul in the quickening shade was whispering about a forthcoming Shadow Banquet, uttering terrible things about the succulent heart of a brave boy, but then slipped away like a snake winding around the statues' feet and was gone. Raoulf was not alone. A large Tawny Owl swooped across the sky warning of Wolf Men close by. His father was there somewhere, roaring around the Forest on his motorbike with the other Lost Youths and Fathers of Fur. Closer still was Janus, running fast in pursuit on all fours. Oblivious to all this surrounding activity, Raoulf continued blithely on. He knew his way to his Grandmother's house. Yes he did, as sure as the back of his hand. He may be lost in the anguish of his parents' lives, but lost in the Forest? Never! Not for all the nights he had spent awake praying and wondering why.

Raoulf pushed through the ever-shifting shapes of shrubs and stones, but it was as if a globe of darkness had been shaken and his surrounds had been blurred and twisted about – as though someone had deliberately re-arranged the trees and obscured the familiar path. It was dead Witch magic created to confuse her prey. Her silhouette had survived the centuries soaked into the soil, waiting for a certain moment – this moment – waiting for a lost child to happen by.

A gurgling death rattle like the shaking of a snake's tail rippled across a nearby pool of stagnant water. Raoulf began to long for the comfort of home and wished for a glimpse of twinkling lights that would mean the safety of his Grandmother's cottage and the warmth of her gathering arms. In the kitchen they would have supper together. He would peel the vegetables badly and she would prepare their favourite meal: herrings, pickles and a large serving of potato salad, washed down with elderflower cordial. Amidst such cheering thoughts, the cool, dark evening closed in upon Raoulf.

Now, in amongst the statues and scattered stones, a sudden dread of darkness was here. Nearby something howled. Raoulf stopped in his tracks. The Full Moon was pushing up in the arc of the sky, not silvery white, but ghastly orange chasing the blood of a late setting Sun. Climbing over a particularly perilous and mossy boulder Raoulf slipped and fell, as though his ankles and wrists were tied with strands of thinnest hair. Harms in the night reached out like the hands of branches, like an unflesh Witch clawing, trying to rise from the bloodthirsty soil. Cawing coarsely, uneasy birds flew up like oily inkblots flicked into the sky.

'Bother!' Raoulf exclaimed through gritted teeth as he kicked out at the rock. 'Stupid thing.'

Robbing Raoulf of his certainty, the creeping Shades and lengthening shadows not only brought unease, but also two scrapped knees and a throbbing bruised ankle. He tentatively pulled at his blood-stained sock with his fingers. He could see a small grazed flap of skin where a thin trickle of blood was seeping underneath. Feeling defeated, Raoulf let himself slide down between the nestling boulders. On his hands and knees he crawled along the gulley of stones until he happened upon a small flat area, the width of two dead husbands one grave long, surrounded by thick clumps of cutthroat Hungry Grasses. Wild Turnip Heads turned in the earth to look up at him. It was simple, if chives were for chopping, then the chubby fingers of children were sizzling sausages waiting garrotting.

'Now, where am I?' Raoulf asked himself.

Raoulf's eyes began to fill, tears splashing onto the ground and mingling with the stale surface waters of the broken Well of Good

Wishes. Where once glorious rose bushes crowned with golden flowers surrounded the porphyry Well, now nothing but dark blooms abounded. Newly watered by the blood and tears of the lost boy, the nearby Hungry Grasses swelled and sighed. At last! They smelt the flesh fears and tasted the salty tears of a brave boy in search of love and comfort. It was a long time since they had tasted such a delicate morsel as child. Well, not since the Witch tossed the remains of the two doomed children out of the Western turret hundreds of years ago.

Commanded by the avaricious dead Witch, the Grasses were ravenous for flesh, soul and blood-happenings. Once more along the Forest floor the whispering greenery began to sharpen its teeth and deadly blades to a thousand razor-sharp points. In their more carnivorous moods they would make a stew of anyone passing. At the sounds of cruel slashing, the long-dead Witch's laughter echoed in the pools of mud in which Raoulf now slipped. The Grasses knew how to prepare for a feast and wear a quarry down.

So, the Witch's treachery and high treason against Nature in defying her death returned in the simple twisting of a boy's ankle, for here was the long sought-after promise of life coming together again. A puff of warm stench from a Witch Plant meant the umbra of her Mud Shadow was billowing and re-gathering. Her separated soul had lived on in the dark earth of the Thirst Forest, hiding in the layers of the loam and inhabiting the worm-rich, blood-soaked soil. The silly, turning Townsfolk had mistaken the Thirst Forest for the First Forest all along. How whispered history and dark past could be deliberately twisted and misheard.

Unbeknownst, the Witch had been absorbing the spilt blood of those monthly wolf and gun-turned men for all these past decades – imbibing the essence of her original spell to nurture her separated

Shadow-self back to life. She had been living secretly upon the hex-infected bodies of others. How else was she supposed to survive the Time-torturing centuries? A rotting Stink Horn reciprocated the Witch Plants' scent attracting passing intoxicated flies and scurrying blood-beetles. Thoughts of reconstitution, devouring hunger and deadly nightshade filled the air. The rising Witch was screaming for skin and for that she needed an innocent heart.

One by one, the callous Crows and rapacious Ravens started to arrive at dusk. Perching on the telephone lines they scraped their beaks from side to side – tap-tap-tapping their tales of terror into the worming Forest wires. Using a specialised frequency of fear and abandonment emitted by the Dark Tower they signalled murder,

'Murder most foul!'

Like a Witches Sabbat, the Birds of Spite cackled and howled at the thought of a Full Moon feasting and night hunting fun. Descendants of the Witch's original spying pets, the birds collected together on the surrounding spires offering Raoulf everything their fleeting darkness had to give.

'Job lot coffins from Joe's coal-black Crows and Ravens Esquire.'

'Removal of the broken-hearted…'

'…And soon to be dear departed.'

'We can deliver special sermons on Sundays, with blood rituals for those like you, born on Plague Days, so full of woe.'

Priestly the birds strutted, their beady eyes ever watchful for the broken bones of boys and girls lost in the Forest. With crooked, inquisitive heads, their eyes twinkled darkly at Raoulf as if to say,

'O slaughterhouse release your stench, the Witch is very nearly real. Watch her Ravens strip the carrion. Are you her next evening meal?'

Forever famished, Joe the Chattering Crow, Master of Dark Ceremonies and Sinister Soul Services, could rob you of life and light in a blink of his wink; Raoulf's hand recoiled after a peck from the Crow's sharp stabbing beak.

'Not nice, not nice. You cannot live on sugar and spice... Well, unless you want your legs chopped off.'

In the dusk the gathering gizzard birds sniggered, snapping at unaware moths, mice and creeping beetles that happened to be passing by. Of course Joe the Crow hoped that death would be different for Raoulf, in the Natural Way, so to speak – in the right pecking order of decaying things. Joe cackled and laughed,

'You never expect to bury your children first, does ya, and not in such a way as Hansel and Gretel's poor weeping mother. May Odin bless their tiny, sainted, spirited souls! They struggled and fought to their final gasp; clinging on to the last grasp of grass before it too turned hungry and devoured them up. Did you really think that they survived the cauldron clutches of a heart-hungry Witch?'

Raoulf looked up to see the looming spires covered in crawling black shadows. As compass points of safety and certainty, they had lost their appeal and the Forest suddenly seemed very uninviting to a frightened boy. Forlorn hopes and gathering grief for the two children once trapped in the westerly turret filled the air. The door had locked behind them as brother and sister climbed up the stone stairs to meet their terrible fate. Chain-tied Palace prisoners tried to warn them, 'Beware', but ghostly guards, hateful Hob-Goblins and ominous Dark Angels would not let them escape. There at the top of the stairs stood a wild gargantuan woman.

Although bewitched by the beauty of adulating mirrors, the Witch looked old, lined and gaunt to them. She could see the horror and disgust in their faces. When asked, Hansel and Gretel replied truthfully, telling the Witch Queen exactly what they saw, defying her and deliberately flouting the lies of her sycophantic mirror.

'Crone... hag... ugly,' they cried out together.

For such insolent words they had instantly forfeited their tongues by a lash from her wand. Well, she had asked. And if polite silence was seemingly beyond them then they must suffer. So much for honesty being the best policy, but it was truly cruel to be made into gruel. The blood of the brave and the hearts of the innocent were the only cures to reverse her aging, yet once drained and eaten, the leftover fingers and thumbs of the children were ground into crumbs and fed to the fanged-creatures and carnivorous plants roaming the Forest floor.

Joe the Thieving Black Crow now coughed up a Witch's shiny silver coin, for it was she who had paid for such dedicated services of child entrapment. The grubby Birds of Black gathered around and sang to Raoulf a rascally song of experience reminding him that there was to be no saviour for doomed children. He recognised it as one of the local nasty verses from the broad sheets of bedtime stories and dreadful drunken ditties his father sometimes sang after his monthly night out with the lads. Now, the birds' croaking, out-of-tune voices reminded Raoulf of everything the children of Town had been taught to fear regarding Hansel and Gretel's grisly demise:

"Two children to eat, so suckled and sweet,

Spires devoted to each – how divine!

A mother's twin treasure, heads cracked forever,

Bludgeoned together – a crime?

Kind loving hearts, torn quickly apart,

Were eaten like tarts – so fine! So fine!

A Witch's cold reason, the siblings' warm treason,

Sprinkled with season – sublime!"

The 'Camaraderie of Crocodiles' was the best dog-gone drinking hole this side North of the Nordic Nile – the only river that split Awe's Forest Plain. The happy, hairy Lone Lads and Lost Men pulled up on their roaring bikes, tanked up on beer and forgot all about the hardship of their fracturing lives. Oblivion was the sought-after gift at the bottom of their frothing tankards and their teeth-pulled, cap-flipped bottles. In the pit of beer-pint philosophy and merry-making, all their problems and lack of bliss could resolve.

In the tawny depths beneath, their childhood worlds of adventure and escape were reforming... watery realms of goodness where benevolent kings and wise sages, democracy and dragons, seafarers and seahorses, could all hold a feminine secret as much as any wolf – true or spell-turned. Their raised clinking tankards were containers of amber oceans in which galleons sailed and mediaeval missions of leftover vision quests were won. It was a place where Titans waged war, gods intervened, and the people loved; a place where they all eventually found strength in the blossoming land.

Intrigued by his Moon-growing mind and the free talk of fellow Lost Men in their jovial fur gathering, Mr Littlesøn abandoned himself to his abandoning whilst not far away, almost lost to the Hungry Grasses, his son bemoaned the possibility of doom before him. Of all the fates of fairy tales, Raoulf had not expected this one: to be eaten alive by blood-drenched, Witch-enchanted, carnivorous fronds. Nor, in fact, did he expect the advent of the Guardians of Dark Doorways – the Trembling Fears and Goblin hordes. Yet still they arrived.

'Ow!' groaned Raoulf, as he sat on a hassock the size of a tuffet, tending his aching ankle. 'I think I've lost my way.'

'Curds?' moaned the encroaching Hungry Grasses. 'Where was the curds and whey?'

A snaking Witch-whisper slipped through the perfidious undergrowth. 'Remember the old way,' it said.

'The old way?' thought Raoulf. 'Which way was that?'

Perturbed, the trembling Fairy leaves on the surrounding trees fluttered gently.

'Go quickly,' cautioned the Forest Fairies skipping featly along the moss-encrusted twigs, 'get out of her way.'

The branch of a black and rotten tree brushed them violently aside. The Guardians-of-Good were being buffeted by amassing strange forces.

'Wolf, Worm or Witch?' asked a helpful voice. 'Are you brave – or are you afraid? So many fates await those lost on the path of the wandering way.'

What on earth was the Forest talking about? And what did Raoulf know of such ill-fated things? Oozing out of the century-old, blood-soaked mud, the intent of the Hungry Grasses seemed so much more treacherous than the allying benevolent breeze. But who should he trust? In the creeping darkness Raoulf was growing confused and scared. Macabre stories of children's crimes, oddly atoned through nursery rhymes, baffled his brain as though fairy tale Fears slithered beside him. Was his mother's Banshee curse at work – his destined inner scream forever souring the milk and obscuring the way? Or was the wind whistling through the wood simply a warning announcing the waking of the Shadow Witch?

Distracted by such chilling thoughts, Raoulf did not feel the matted roots of the Hungry Grasses crawling across his feet and ankles like hundreds of spiders, sapping his energy in their desire for sustenance. The hassock he was sitting on was slowly sinking into the molasses-like mud, descending into the mire of past Palace murder and the surrounding morass of the Thirst Forest's foulness. Raoulf was certainly regretting having followed the cheery red-breasted Robin who had disappeared so long ago. The grassy agents of the Witch rubbed against Raoulf's fresh creamy flesh; the tasty fingers and toes of children were much sought-after delicacies.

'We must have curds and whey,' implored the peckish plants, 'or we'll have to eat you instead.'

Instinctively Raoulf started praying, calling upon the protection of Saint Hansel and the guidance of Saint Gretel, but nothing happened. There was no guiding light, no breadcrumb trail or piece of string to help him find his way back out of the now Tangled Forest. He must move on, but the Hungry Grasses creeping around his ankles drew him down, lacing their green and grasping tendrils about him. Tightening like a carefully constricting corset of miniature flat blades, they slowly tethered his skin. Then the taller Grasses fell upon him violently with the ferocity of slaves turning against fallen masters, whiplash and all.

Raoulf cried out to his mother and in return she released a heart-wrenching scream. Through the momentary sharing of the Moon's soul-mirror they could see each other writhing and thrashing, but each was callously restrained. Helpless, Raoulf lay on the ground as his life force slowly ebbed to the edge of dark dreams and the beckoning of welcoming sleep. In his binding, he could smell the pungent earth about him as all the tests of the resourceful soul now descended.

Then a blinding flash of silver light passed across Raoulf's eyes as the skilful fingers of the Grasses knotted his hair to the ground, pulling so tightly they stretched back the skin on his face. His temples throbbed, his eyes bulged and his head felt that it might split open at any moment. Twisting and turning in agony, Raoulf tried to escape the clutches of the gnawing Grasses, when something hard and round dug into the side of his hip. Was it a skull poking upwards from the Palace graveyard beneath? Then there was the sound of scrunching. Was it a stranger's footfall on the old marble path?

Deep inside Raoulf's coat pocket a hard lump rolled slightly, something that was not stone or earth but fragrant crisp flesh. Realisation came as he remembered the kindness of Miss Berry. He recalled her face, her smile, her lovely scent somewhere beyond juniper, pine and the faint hint of silver. She was there guarding him, protecting him, urging him on to think.

'Be of quick wit,' her voice in his mind cried, 'or else you will surely die.'

Raoulf was scared, but summoning up the last of his strength he tensed his aching body and reached with the last scrabbling inch of his fingers into his pocket. He gratefully clutched at the stalk of the rosy red apple as the malevolent Grasses pulled him ever deeper into the sinking ground. Thoughts of supper were on their mind as they pierced his plump, pulsating veins to slowly siphon his blood. Raoulf gasped as he pushed down on his bruising hip. The apple released from his pocket and rolled away. With lightning speed some of the Hungry Grasses loosened their grip upon Raoulf in pursuit of the enticing, perfumed food – a moving quarry infused with the scent of numerous children and an adored teacher.

'Whey!' howled those feasting Grasses as they stripped the skin off the juicy apple and fed upon the delicious fruit. 'There must be more curds and whey?'

'Ah-whoah!' went Lone Silver Wolf baying to the light of the distant Moon. A handful of Trembling Fears escaped Janus's howling jaws. They were delighted with the free ride and could smell Raoulf's blood and fright. Perfect! Then out of the undergrowth the savage Goblins ran, whooping and hollering, ready for a quick thumb-scalping and the stealing of a boy's soul.

'What was that?' thought Raoulf despairingly as he wrestled against the matting fronds.

Confused by the arrival of new adversaries, more of the Grasses released Raoulf and turned to chase these invading, odoriferous creatures. Yet they could not catch the Goblins and Fears for they were fast of foot and fleet of mind. Still, the rolling apple, the wailing wolf and the arrival of the galloping Goblins gave Raoulf just enough time to gather his strength and wits. In the Hungry Grasses' hesitation he was breaking his binds and wriggling free.

Crawling forward, Raoulf dragged himself through an overgrown gulley before dropping down onto firmer ground. The Grasses grabbed at his shoelaces and ankles. Struggling up, stumbling on, Raoulf scrambled across the large mossy stones reaching once more into his pocket. He did not have whey, nor did he understand the nature of the old way, but a packet of flapjack he did have. That was the scrunching sound he had heard. Good flapjack; sweet flapjack. It was fingers of flapjack freely given, and gratefully received, that he now crumbled and scattered about him.

So it was, in the midst of the infinite possibilities of creative-not-knowing, Raoulf realised that whey or no way, his hard-won courage and wit, an accidental apple and some flapjack given in kindness would have to suffice. Thanks to Miss Berry he had found his own brave path. Yet as he staggered deeper into the Forest, tumbling further into the night, he did not realise that another fate of fairy tales was rapidly descending – not one where so much wrong, given time, could finally be made right, but one where you discover that you have jumped out of the frying pan and into the fire. In the distance the turrets of Saint Hansel and Saint Gretel, reminders of the souls of Witch-eaten children, diminished silently behind him.

Mrs Littlesøn had been admitted that day to the Ward of Scorpio where the men in masks, dark coats and black rubber boots were investigating further the overwhelming power of her moods. They said it was an attempt to end her personal gloom and understand her suffering. That evening, as the 'Trial of Terrors by Night' descended upon Raoulf, so the test of 'Shock by Snakes and a Thousand Stings' fell upon his mother; anything to tame the untameable scream that occasionally emitted from her. But somehow Mrs Littlesøn's Banshee cleverly defied the doctors, who failed to extract the soul-ripping sound they wished to put to their own secret purpose.

Later that night, as her outspread wings were further restrained, Raoulf's mother submerged her troubled spirit in acts of savage self-preservation and hiding. The wild Banshee inside instinctively knew of such shamanistic ways, whereas her human half outwardly struggled with fractured identity and frenzied split states. Afterwards, leashed and sedated, Mrs Littlesøn drifted along the Scorpion corridor of twisting shadows and whispering fears. She passed by other constrained women, some with whiskers in half-turned, she-wolf states, some sprouting wings and feathers, whilst others with gills and flapping fish-like tails were busy being hosed down.

Although some women of the Elysium Asylum were part consumed, raving and ravenous in wanting release, others were engaged in steely control, fighting their natural instinct to slash, claw and bite those who came too near. Abnormal sounds emitted from them. Some of these frightened figures were deemed to be failed mothers, sectioned to protect others from the inseminating spell of old Witch magic. As far as the silver Hand-Mirror of Truth could tell, it only ever affected women who could not overcome the dark side of the Moon and their menses.

That desperate night in the wood, Raoulf could fleetingly see in the drifting mists of the Moon his mother sailing away from him, ghostly pale, lost to Saint Celeste and the Sirens of the Slippery Sea.

Only later, too late to help her son in his present predicament, would Mrs Littlesøn regain the spirit to fight and re-establish herself against the Asylum doctors and the severity of their prescriptive ways. She could be of no help to Raoulf as she struggled and floated uncontrollably about her moonlit cell, gagged and bound so she could kill no-one with her new-found scream. Yet she truly believed now that they could all find a way; knew that someone could still save the day. But who?

Mr Littlesøn did not understand his life. He did not understand his wife, and only partially understood his only son, Raoulf, who was such a chip of the Woodsman's block. He was not sure why he had married so young, so far from fun, just out of his teenage jeans, apart from it had seemed expected of him. Raoulf was a great kid. Mr Littlesøn just wished he could be there more for him, but that meant giving up of the camaraderie of Fur Fellows, and being there for her, his eccentric humming wife.

Mrs Littlesøn seemed to want so much, need so much, which he was unable to provide freely. It was an asking of something he did not have and could not give. He loved the freedom of the open road, exploring the vastness of leafy forests and snowy mountains, but to be married to one so volcanic, yet cold and potentially devastating, was a different matter. Mr Littlesøn did not realise that his wife had buried her Banshee aspect for reasons of safety, sanity, and terrible fear.

Uncontrolled, her sound was potentially soul-shattering and she did not wish her husband or her son to be harmed. Yet what did matter was happiness: hers, his, and Raoulf's. If it was the right of all to be personally happy, the only remaining question was how? Sit and hide or run and ride? Either way – there was no avoiding the oncoming domestic avalanche.

Mr Littlesøn's reaction was to seek escape. He was scared of the changes he could feel descending and felt imprisoned by the ever-deepening responsibilities of fatherhood, so his instincts told him to simply go and sort it all out on tomorrow's tide. He knew he could always escape on his motorbike, but then what would become of Raoulf? He was also concerned that he had passed on the lunar infection to his son – the curse of the Witch's 'Spell of Blood Tainting'. That had been the original cause of his ancestors and his own lone wolf running. This legacy had in turn made him seek out the solace of the pack.

Thank Odin for Janus and the creation of his secret clan of the 'Two Way Wolf'. He seemed to possess a deeper understanding of Nature's way, though other Fur Folk talked about Janus as being from a totally different breed of wolf – more vicious and violent, more magical and majestic. Was his and the other spell-infected men's destiny so set? Perhaps they would all be out-gunned in the end for close on their heels there was always the threat of pursuing huntsmen, just as now there were random shots being sounded off into the air everywhere. The howling was a healing for the four-legged turners, but under Mayor Bear's recent relaxing of the licensing laws gun-running had become good business alongside the sale of trophy wolf tails and the surging trade of fur stoles.

It was rumoured that those killed on the turn stayed as a wolf and their carcasses, once stripped, were dumped into the mountain gorge. Wolves' manes, pelts and paws with extended claws made powerful amulets. Since the Witch's Spell, those contaminated had to follow their impulses, although few understood the underlying cause.

Mayor Bear was one who did know, and he secretly hoped that the feuding blood-tribes would cull each other, thus clearing up their own shadow trouble and save him the problem. Still, wolf parts used in traditional medicine were always lucrative, and additional funds from battles, backstreet brawls and underhand death certificates swelled Town's coffers and his own black-market funds.

Mr Littlesøn needed the monthly howling as a vocal outlet to express his personal grief for there was a wounding inside – an absence caused by the death of his circus father early on in his wolf-turning life. It walked beside him informing all he did and did not do. Of all his cares and woes this wound was the deepest, for it made him feel ineffectual in the world of water and profound emotion. Yet who could ever understand this loneliness? Whilst shedding his skin Mr Littlesøn's neck reached full throttle, baying in obeisance to the merciful Moon.

'Soon,' she said compassionately, 'someone will come to help you soon.'

Then Mr Littlesøn sensed something strange. He was perplexed at first as something soft in fur, yet in full-grown human form, rubbed playfully against his skin. A thousand miles away in his mind he heard the faintest of purrs. It grew stronger, and then he felt an unexpected vixen scratch. Ah yes! Somewhere there lurked a hint of feminine fox, but whom? Someone to come who could accept the way of half-wolf, yet not be frightened.

It was an odd intuition; a premonition caused by a certain vatic, crossed-phase of the Moon. It confused Mr Littlesøn, made him mad, wild, and excited in a way that he had not been in a very long time. In all his turbulence a faint ray of hope, of not giving up, was rising. It was not the rose-hope of poets facing the longest of nights, but the full warm glow of a soon to be new sexual dawning. Above, arcing in the indigo sky, the Full Moon was ghostly white and glistening. In being so drawn to his human side, Mr Litt{\o}n's wolf-transformation was halted and he slowly changed back to his aching human form.

After his lucky escape from the Hungry Grasses, Raoulf now found he had the wilder wood to contend with. Looming mountainous trees blocked him as he circumnavigated the bracken paths and fern-infested ways. Large overgrown fronds flicked against him as he struggled onwards to his Grandmother's cottage. The thread of Raoulf's tale was not one of spooling wool, but of menace, dread and pursuing horror. Fearlessness – that was required now. Yet what of his remaining guilt that he was somehow responsible for adult events beyond his ken? And what of his child's sense of unfairness? Would he ever understand himself and come to peace with his turmoil and stowed emotions?

Feeling somewhat helpless, Raoulf entered further into the maze of tangled trees with only the companions of night by his side. The terror of the unknown, the alarm of bats, birds and creepy crawlies, the trepidation of encroaching howling and gunshots exploding around him – all these things overwhelmed Raoulf. His irrational fears now combined with the dismay of his ultimate darkness – of being lost, alone and unloved. Even worse was his fear of not being able to share the love he felt towards others ever again. Inwardly, Raoulf was battling against his personal thunder.

At a distance, a silver silhouette that once ran beside Raoulf was now standing observing. The man known as Janus would not intervene in Raoulf's finding of a Way to his Grandmother's cottage.

But something was odd. It was almost as though someone was purposefully re-arranging the bushes and trees to waylay the boy. Underlying, there was a pervasive, strange earthy stench interfering with his usual refined sense of scent. Janus felt troubled, whilst Raoulf felt sorry for himself. Nightfall was rapidly descending and only sparse moonshine penetrated the thick canopy of trees overhead. In the shifting nocturnal light the previously good Fox Glove Wood had become a savage Wolf's Garden. But where was the kindly soul who would protect him from the long-running loneliness of fear itself?

But if Raoulf believed he was alone, he was mistaken. The walking-talking trees, the enchanted overhanging fruit and the steely binding vines were gathering around him even as the puffballs of sleep exploded at his feet. Poisonous Ivies, Hexed Vetches and Hungry Grasses still roamed the wood, and in the surrounding dusk the intoxicating influence of the Witch's Shadow was everywhere. Slipping underneath the unfurling fronds, nuzzling amongst the trembling leaves, the Fears, Goblins and Ghostly Shades were on the move, whilst Will-o'-the-Wisps and frost-winged Fairies shimmered by – spectral white and gleaming. For good or ill, if Raoulf still believed in good magic he needed it now. Run Raoulf, run! For deep-rooted danger was lurking everywhere.

Little Spark had sped her way ahead of her sisters and was busy pushing through the thinning atmosphere. Geronimo! Not for her a slow descent or a long life on the elemental plane known as Earth Land. She had separated from her sisters early on taking an unusual geometric trajectory and awkward angle of entry onto the Vertical Rays upon which spirit moved and cloud inhabitants incarnated. Little Spark had only one mission in mind, Love, and she did not care how her

life was used for the greater good in the grand scheme of things. Save the planet? If she could, but she had seen a different scene, a family scenario on the border of breakthrough and with a little help, a little hand, a little spark…

'Look through the trees,' she shouted to the lost boy running through the wood. Then quickly added, 'Geroni… go!' as she gathered her final momentum.

So it was that Little Spark from the cloud Land of Bliss, the first and last in every act of knowing and loving, the I-Am-All, yet oh so small, surrendered her light in a carefully chosen moment of ultimate kindness and giving…

Gunnbjorn the Gruff – Park Keeper by day and Head Game Hunter by night – commanded the gathering of a different clan, but still one mothered from the Witch's original desire of wishful longevity and blood lust. Those curse-infected only had until sunrise, which was the law as monitored by the Two Tower's mutual Blind Eye and those residents who were in the know. Even now, freshly-fired firearms were being re-filled with shot and re-loaded with special silver bullets. Primed rifles with cocks drawn back were lifted to the shoulder so sights and scopes could be adjusted to the late night killing of four-legged prey.

Eradication of Townsfolk, gun, fairy or fur, was best done under Mayor Bear's 'dusk-to-dawn policy'. This meant any unsavoury business could be put down to false imaginings brought on by the culpability of full-tilt lunar madness – a common phenomenon amongst Fairy Folk. Any deaths or disappearances during this time could be legitimately disregarded. The Full Moon watched down tearfully through a sudden shifting veil of cloud. These Hunters and Wolf Men were all her unfortunate children.

Meanwhile, the last of the Witch's snake-like remains ran like rivulets escaping from Obsidian Lake, drifting ghostly along the lagoon's shore. The night air grew colder as her encroaching vapours fell upon the miasmal fog of the surrounding fungal backwaters – green, misty serpents rising up, binding the trees and shrubs to her curse command and bidding. Slithering across the Forest floor her rank, malingering essence permeated the land, linking her lost years and separated selves together. The dark blood of death ran through her wraith-like veins and the soil beneath, enough to turn trees treacherous and certain Black Birds to sinister action.

The Witch's winged ministers lurked everywhere, coming to feast upon the flesh and bones of warm carcasses, and oversee the funeral rites of those unfortunate souls caught in her enveloping shadow. Squabbling beads of oily black were hopping and squawking in the branches above as the 'Coven of Fouls' held their post-dusk meeting. Broken twigs were sticks for gouging out eyes, making marks on maps and testing the breezes. In Mr Littlesøn's half-mutating Moon-mind, bird bones were simply snacks for the cracking. The evening's instinctual drinking and thinking had made him hungry. He smiled.

'Ah…wooh!' gurgled his stomach as he kick-started his infernal roaring machine and took off into the Forests' leafy by-ways.

'Ahhwooohhh!' cried the other Lone Wolf Men in chorus, running beside him.

As Mr Littlesøn rode through the Forest he sniffed the air. A strange smell hovered above the loam, fainter than the perfume of a rotten memory. It was a deep-rooted scent lost to the pungent earth except to those with the extraordinary power of nose. Behind him a thin slick of petrol, blue-black and peacock green, interspersed with the puffiest cream-white cloud of exhaust. The ghostly vapour drifted between the trees before slowly falling onto the smaller trails of ferns, frogs and snails caught beneath.

Skeletal smoke hung between the bracken. Should Raoulf trust the thin, criss-crossing vapour trails before him? Ought he to follow these vanishing tail ends of ghosts? He did not know it, but he was astray in the Whispering Wood and that was not good.

'Stupid boy!' rattled a voice. 'Are you lost or just simple?'

Raoulf said nothing. He was generally an obliging child and did not wish to disturb or cross anything unnecessarily, particularly not in the on-gathering dark of night in a forbidding Forest. His ankle still throbbed painfully as a reminder of his earlier encounter with the Hungry Grasses. An unhelpful tree pointed a leafy finger in front of his face, whilst another shoved a twig into the middle of his back. Raoulf muffled his discomfort when a feathery Pine branch slapped him violently across his chest sending him sprawling. As blood rushed to his head, tall trees and low-lying ferns began to pull him every which way in a bid to disorientate.

Nearby, a bellowing gunshot, a terrifying howl and a tortured scream rang out simultaneously across the Forest. The noise was as dismaying as any Wolf about to be disembowelled could muster.

'If you're confused and lost in the woods you must bear the toll and pay the Trolls, or take your diminishing chances…'

Raoulf picked himself up, but remained silent.

A large bunch of overhanging Mistletoe, which could have been a misshapen, severed Troll's head, was host to a group of mischievous Goblins with a particularly morose sense of mirth. They added unpleasantly, 'As if anybody cares!'

'My Grandmother cares,' Raoulf answered defiantly unable to hold his tongue any longer. 'And my mother and my father…'

'Of course they do, but where are they now?'

'And if they truly loved you…' retorted a nasty, needling Fir throwing pinecones at Raoulf that made him gasp, 'would they ever leave you long enough for you to stray?'

'A mother's parting kiss in the night to say goodbye… then disappearing forever.' A Willow tree sighed. 'Standing alone at the School gates holding back tears waiting for someone to come… yet still you're left waiting.'

Suddenly Raoulf's heart hurt as he scrabbled desperately to get away from the Taunting Trees and their far-reaching fingers and torturing truths.

'So many struggles for one so young,' sniggered a voice hiding in the branches of a twisted She Oak. 'Perhaps you could fell the trees and turn the wood into a wardrobe. Let's hope that you can climb your way out and pray it's not Winter forever…'

Dressed in red, Raoulf was an easy target. A circle of vicious trees and spiteful bushes now rounded on him, mocking him, making him angry. A poisonous ivy leaf tickled him under the chin, drawing bubbles of blood, whilst a horrible Fear lashed a stinging nettle across his cheek, blistering his skin. A large Fir branch pranged Raoulf in the nape of his neck and lifted him slowly off the ground, whilst a Holly bush slowly drew a prickly branch across his throat, scratching him from ear to ear.

'Only pretending,' said the Holly as the Fir obligingly dropped Raoulf from its bristly fingers and onto the ground. 'You're no good to us dead… well, not just yet.'

Like a lynch mob descending, the Trees were intent on only one thing: the drawing of blood from the brave. The Witch's greater force manipulated them towards her desire – the gathering together of her scattered serpent remains. Raoulf did not realise that his heart was her sole hope of revival. Were faith and courage the only antidotes? Such qualities had not been enough to stop the Witch's wand from slicing the tongues of Hansel and Gretel.

'Ears and nose, fingers and toes; the 'Circle of Time' ebbs and flows…'

From out of nowhere a long, sharp, pointy finger prodded him.

'Stop it!' pleaded Raoulf stumbling over the writhing roots of the walking-talking Trees and falling to the floor. 'Enough!'

More screeching laughter erupted in Raoulf's ears, whilst Goblin hands reached through the bracken trying to shove moss into his mouth. Dizzy now, Raoulf spat the moss out, slapping the hands and snapping the entwining shoots and branches as he tried to rise.

'Can you fly?' asked a female voice enquiringly.

'No, of course I can't fly,' Raoulf admitted truthfully, but instantly regretting it.

'I didn't think so, but I just had to be certain,' said the Shadow Witch gently stroking Raoulf's head. Like mist, like moonlight, like a crooning mother, she soothed him with her strange incantations.

'Moon fright is such a delight; then dead by dreaded morning.'

As the Witch laughed, Raoulf thought of his Grandmother and her cosy cottage not a million miles away. If he found himself lost in the Forest without friends or comfort, then the warmth of the vision of his Grandmother spurred him on. Gathering his wits Raoulf picked himself up, pushing his way through the tangling mire of trees. The answer was simple, but if Raoulf did not know it someone had told him how to fathom it out. Immediately the turning pages of the "New Book of Joy" sprang into his mind. If he could only ask the right questions or name his fears, he would find that they had no substance and would disappear back to the Land of Dark Dream whence they came.

So, as Raoulf began to voice out loud his dreads and doubts, the Trembling Fears and Goblin Keepers of the Door Knob and Dream Gateway began to materialise. They were not the Witch's minions, however much they hunted a common prey in the form of the boy. The Witch's authority and horror ran deeper than theirs and worked in more mysterious ways – for she had once stolen precious gems from the Fire Dragons and was blessed by blood descended from the royal lineage of Ice Giants. Yet the Fears and Goblins were unafraid of such company for they believed they could drink the still incorporeal Witch dry or else drown her once more in moonlit water. They knew her weaknesses. Still disembodied, she was not so strong, but the moment of her truth and power was drawing ever nearer.

Unfortunately for Raoulf, the Fears and Goblins possessed his thumbprint and that kept them connected to him. The missing print, when matched to his thumb, would mean the stealing of his fairy soul – for was he not born of Banshee and Turning-Wolf and descended from the infamous Red Riding Hood line? To the Witch, Raoulf's strawberry coat, now torn, filthy and covered with grime, suggested so many delectable things. Though a frightened schoolboy reluctantly wearing a coat of crimson was somewhat unusual, in acts of sacrificial magic the blood of any child would suffice, and his would be no less sweet and delicious. The battle for Raoulf's thumping heart and warm pressing thumb was on.

In the deep dark woods, the surrounding trees looked all the same to Raoulf. Trees in the night were annoying like that and he was sure they kept moving, whilst sending him on endless diversions and dead ends. Circumnavigating the Holly Grove was a particularly prickly and thankless task. Then, without warning, the roar of something up ahead made him hesitate. Man or beast; machine or imagination? Raoulf could hear guns going off, leaves were scattering and there was the sound of four-footed scampering everywhere. In a brief moment of splashing light, Raoulf took his bearings by the silhouetted spires that lay behind him. Yet they could just as easily be the tops of trees or the peaks of mountains as forgotten castle turrets or shrines to dead children.

'Look through the trees,' a girl's voice had shouted. 'Go!'

Yet which way to go still baffled Raoulf? He was hearing voices of which he was unsure and that was not good for his sanity or his uncertain footing. He was in unknown terrain, walking in the riverbed of sad streams that met at the feet of those trees that forever wept. Waylaying melancholy sang here like a lullaby – more memories of his mother, songs of sadness and savage drowning than any heart could bear. There seemed to be some matter of urgency now as the windscaped Willows proffered Raoulf their hair-like hands and strangulating fronds and fingers. Surely that meant that he was close to Obsidian Lake, and that he had dropped too far South, to be on the right track to his Grandmother's cottage.

'This way…' echoed the wind through the trees, '…over here.'

Did Raoulf dare trust the guiding voice that had called out? Of course he must look to the trees – he had no choice for they were all around, encircling him, but what were they saying? If only Raoulf had more Forest wisdom and confidence like his cape-wearing, knife-wielding Grandmother. She would know what to do and would come to his aid in an instant if only she were there. Somehow he needed to find the long Leafy Lane that led to the back of his Grandmother's house, but all around him strange voices were hollering and whooping and whispering.

After several minutes scrabbling around in endless and exasperating circles, Raoulf was thoroughly breathless. He did not realise he was stuck in a rut following the Palace's old carriage turning path. His chest was hurting, his knees were grazed, his ankle was throbbing and bruised. He stopped and looked up. The surrounding triangular shadows cast by the trees reminded him of something, but what? If he looked carefully he would see in the looming landscape a clue… Of course, Christmas trees! These trees were his friends grown of good cheer, the best kind of trees, just like the ones that surrounded his Grandmother's cottage. Suddenly, Raoulf was filled with relief that he might just get home without falling and crying again, for all the cuts on his hands, legs and face. He remembered his Grandmother's saying,

'Christmas trees grow all year round. In candle-lit branches home is found – all lost children safe and sound.'

Walking tentatively forward, Raoulf could feel the thick fingers of the branches gently nuzzling him. The Fir trees' silver and green touch was soothing, covering him with the sweet scent of pine. For a moment he felt the consolation of homecoming warmth, as though the Firs were swaddling him, keeping him from harm. A late evening breeze sighed through the Forest and the soft hush was entrancing.

The gathering Witch, speaking in the strangest of Tree tongues and leafy whispers, was mesmerising Raoulf. Slowly he grew motionless as though he were frozen, when previously all his thoughts were of urgency and getting home. But however much he yearned to be free, to be able to move his legs and be on his way again, he also wanted to surrender to this terrible moment forever. Around him the spirits of the Fir trees were awakening.

'Little Boy in Red, are we not beautiful too?' asked a Christmas Wreath Wraith rising up and brushing against Raoulf. 'For some do not consider us…'

'…Symmetrical enough?' interrupted a group of lush, well-proportioned trees from across the shifting glade.

Silver tags and tied red ribbons of ownership already hung from their trunks and branches. These trees had all made the Woodsman's grade for the end of year's Christmas festivities. One large tree, the tallest and most perfectly triangular, had been designated for the yearly honour of standing in the Old Town Square – to be lit at the Winter solstice 'Ceremony of Carols'.

'Triangular triumph is not to be asserted,' cried one of the Wreath Wraiths turning on Raoulf. 'Do you know what will become of us this Winter? Do you, boy? Do you?'

Raoulf shook his head. The conversation between the ghostly arboreal giants about the promise of Christmas future somehow felt real for Raoulf. He could understand the division between the trees, hear their hysteria rising as their branches became filled with Fears,

Goblins, and entwining essence of resurrecting Witch. Entranced, Raoulf said nothing.

'Our branches will be stripped, then plaited into deer, stags and Christmas garlands,' said one wretched tree.

'And cemetery wreathes,' groaned a second.

'To be borne on coffins and nailed to doors,' beseeched a third.

'To be placed on graves by grieving mothers…,' cried out a fourth, who was quickly silenced by the looming Witch.

'Built up underneath bodies and burnt in fires on funeral pyres,' moaned a fifth.

'To know only tragedy and never bear the indoor lights of Christmas,' wailed a sixth.

The rejected Wreath Wraiths drifted toward Raoulf. They pointed at the good, the strong and the true trees standing opposite.

'Some of them will be sent overseas in remembrance of light and the passing of the great Dark War. Imagine! What a life they will lead in their Christmas days whilst we will bear broken bodies and burn into ash those twisted, scampering half-creatures that die before dawn.'

'Did you know,' the Witch whispered, 'that how you die is how you awake again on the other side of this earthly life?'

No, Raoulf did not know this.

'When my grandfather died…' He started, but abruptly stopped. Only moments before there had been thoughts of home and happy return, but now only the unbearable sadness of loss remained. The melancholic touch of the Weeping Willows was winning. As the

Wreath Wraiths surrounded him, empathy with the forsaken Christmas trees overwhelmed him.

'We understand,' murmured the wretched Wraiths.

The forsaken Fir trees slowly encircled Raoulf. About them the skirmishing aspects of severed Witch, Trembling Fears and gleeful Goblins kept arriving. They were all delighted to see him standing as still as a statue in the moonlit glade. In the momentary silence of encroaching shadows Raoulf's childhood loneliness engulfed him. He believed that he had to make a heart-rending choice between his mother and father.

In the easterly turret of the ruined Palace the Casket-of-Dark-Secrets was being opened, as an intrigued Goblin rummaged for Raoulf's utmost dread and death desire. Yet the Casket simply opened and shut its lid consuming the malicious intruder whole. Under the influence of the rising Witch, the Fir Trees simply continued to sway…

'We who stand outside looking in through the window recognise your heartbreak…'

'Your disappointment…' said a second.

'Your fear of being unloved,' whispered a third.

'We who suffered injustice in our childhoods are never to see the joy of Christmas presence,' moaned the injured trees looming closer. 'We will never see children open their gifts placed beneath our branches.'

The poisonous parts of the once-drowned Witch had been imbibed deeply here, and the Wraiths of Tainted Trees detained Raoulf with their powerful, diseased truths.

'Why try to make it on your own when we can help?' enquired some Deadly Nightshade.

'He cannot and must not stay,' replied an Elder Tree with a Fairy bough sharply resisting the Witch's rot. Tiny Fairy lanterns lit up to ward off the growing darkness. 'The deeper truth is that all are held in the arms of love even those considered broken and ugly – perhaps especially those.'

The embracing coils of the Witch's shadow-snakes were seducing Raoulf. Entwined, he found himself rooted and spellbound. Some roaming Night Scented Stock shook itself and held him enraptured in its glorious fragrance. The Siren breezes were calling out his name and he was surrendering; slowly slipping away into a perfumed land of sleep and dreams. He no longer cared for life as death seemed suddenly welcoming and a part of him wanted to go.

'The turn of tides is upon you,' implored the Elder Tree shaking its branches in alarm. Leaves and Fairy lights were being scattered and lost, their purpose forgotten. 'You must struggle. You must wake up. You must run.'

'Do not be like the discarded leaf, but become like the acorn,' spoke a concerned sturdy Oak, 'for in you I see the seed of the sapling within the tree of me.'

'To each its seasons and the reasons for love,' said the departing Fairy leaves being blown away, tumbling about in a sinister stirring breeze.

'Stay with us,' beseeched the bewitched Silver Birches. 'Sway with us.'

'Beware, Little Boy,' cautioned a Willow mid-weep for the forming Shadow Witch was stripping one of her branches for a majestic new wand. 'Remember that the Settler-of-Scores does not mind which way the axe cuts… for we all eventually must fall.'

'That which is parted shall be returned,' reminded the Elder. 'You need to believe beyond what you know and what experience tells you.'

'That is not true,' sneered an ugly Goblin disguised as a would-be truth, 'for what you see is all there is.'

Words of fear, faith and fright wrapped around Raoulf's heart and he was lost to a terrible song of a Banshee being subdued. With her wand, the rising Witch cast a 'Spell of Widow's Veil' that quickly shrouded the sky. Clouds cloaked the faint outline of the Moon. Any fleeting help from the revolving Eye of Light was blocked out as the Witch's enchantment entrapped the night. The Eye of Dark fell upon Raoulf who felt afraid and overwhelmed.

'The granting of your wishes is not possible without us,' insisted a Goblin Chief as he pressed the faintest of prints recently peeled from the Door Knob against Raoulf's thumb. He nodded. This indeed was the hand of the one they sought.

Now undisguised, the ghoulish Goblins and Trembling Fears emerged from the trees as a shimmering door appeared and began to draw Raoulf in. Reeling, he found himself being dragged through the surrounding branches towards the eagerly awaiting portal. The materialising Witch strode forward as the Two Towers locked horns. The Eye of Evil beamed down as the Fears and Goblins licked their lips and rejoiced, for they all knew where Raoulf's destination would be in his present state of mind. The Eye of Good could not reach him, whilst the Witch blocked his way.

Then, with one deep, wounding stab, a crude stick-like wand pierced Raoulf's thumb as though being pricked by the needle of a spinning wheel. A bright bead of blood appeared at the shocked surface of skin, yet instead of pain a terrible sleepy sickness began to descend. Reassured in the tasting of blood from the tip of her wand, the Witch Queen now rose around Raoulf like a green shadow-dragon. In the eating of his still-beating heart she could finally be reunified. The Eye of Light spun in despair. Raoulf would succumb, would be all undone, with one simple baby suck of his thumb – and his hand was now rising!

From a distance, Lone Silver Wolf watched on.

As the Witch struck out at Raoulf a second time there followed a mighty crash as the splitting forces of Door Knob dream-call and Witch blood-retrieval took place. Simultaneously, the Trembling Fears, the greedy Goblins and the wicked Witch all descended upon Raoulf, and in that moment their worlds collided – a thumbprint for a soul or a heart for a magical sacrifice? Although portals of extraction were found in several places on human skin, the thumb was the essential one that the Goblins and Fears needed to obtain the boy's soul. But the resurrecting Witch needed the boy's blood to drink of his youth and drain his innocence.

As the Witch's wand slashed out again an eerie, spilling light broke through the glade, scalping Raoulf's thumb and scattering the Goblins and Fears. Seconds later Raoulf heard a girl's shout, a churning car engine, and the distant roar of a motorbike. Then a voice echoed out as a streak of quicksilver shot through the trees, followed by a giant beam from the Eye of Light and a welcome glint of precious moonlight. Out of the night sped a blistering ray, bright and blinding, and there was Little Spark burning up on her entry into the Land of Awe.

'Geronimo!' shouted Little Spark triumphantly as she shot through the Witch like a silver bullet piercing her freshly forming, malevolent heart. At last, courage was here where only fear had previously been. The Eye of Light rammed its beams through the trees, through the wood, through the now-shrivelling Witch.

'Nooo…' screamed the Witch as her century-old dream of blood revival was ended. Greedily, the contaminated soil of the Forest of Thirst began to drink back her dissipating shadow.

Meanwhile, the Door Knob's 'Spell on Far Dreaming Souls' was momentarily broken and Raoulf's befuddled, raw fingers were moving again. He had no need to suck his rising bloodied thumb for that was for babies. With the arrival of the light and the luck of passing Good Fortune, he was no longer afraid of the dark, or the trees, or the haggard Witch draining away beside him. He no longer needed to be frightened by the Trembling Fears and Goblin hordes. Little Spark had landed, ending her journey into this side of life so he could step forward and find his way. Thus newly empowered, Raoulf began to howl,

'Ah… Oooo!'

Attracted by the eerie wand light and the boy's strange sound, several loper-wolves and gun-hunters entered the glade, before running away, yelping and screaming – for they had briefly seen the fearsome origin of their spell-infection. Only Lone Silver Wolf remained at a distance to maintain pack law and preserve the welfare of wolves – for no-one born of wolf-blood was ever outcast and left alone, however young. Now, Gunnbjorn and his gunmen sped by in rapid pursuit of Lone Silver Wolf firing silver shots – for the much-vaunted cunning of Janus Woolfe made him the best of trophies. All hail the hunter who wall-mounted that much prized head. There was no interest in the boy standing at the centre of the disturbance for he was far too young to be either a wolf-turner or gun-hunter yet.

'Here, quick,' said the kindly trees. 'Take our hands, Little Boy, for although we all have our different truths to tell...'

Raoulf instinctively reached out for their branches for he could clearly tell the different nature of trees now.

'We are your friends,' stated the Elder. 'But now you must move your legs and leave this troubled place...'

'Turn once in triumphant revolution,' chorused the trees spinning Raoulf around and pointing him towards Leafy Lane and his Grandmother's cottage, 'now run as fast as you can.'

Slowly Raoulf turned away from the circle of trees and began to run as a boy freed from a place that could not be Christmas forever. He was moving again, falling onto his hands and knees, grateful for the painful breath of life in his lungs. Yet this time he was not afraid and clenched his fist in determination, blood oozing from his throbbing scalped thumb. Stumbling onward, Raoulf fled the Forest. The fall of the foul Witch meant the slow awakening of the Wise Woods and the unfreezing of the Petrified Forests could begin again, for without Raoulf's heart she had no substance or power.

Meanwhile, the Fears and Goblin retreated. With no matching thumb skin, the precious print they held was useless. It was now very late on a quietly closing day at the end of September. Several hours had passed since Raoulf had left School, but there, at last, in front of him, was his Grandmother's cottage. The lights were on, twinkling through the dark, just as he knew they would be. The door was open and he was running into the warm kitchen where she would be standing, and he would be all right, because everything was always all right when he was held in his Grandmother's loving arms.

The only problem being that Grandmother May was not standing there to greet him. She was not there at all. Raoulf moved on inside the cottage. In the half-light of the sitting room fire, he could see a flickering changing form, a tall figure rising up out of the winged chair; the chair where his Grandmother always sat with her knitting and her favourite throwing knife stuffed down the side. The indistinct shadow stretched out his aching arms and long-running legs, moving his jaw from side to side with the heel of his hand as he clicked his neck in a distorted sharp twisting. The figure turned to greet the boy. It was somebody Raoulf recognised, but did not expect at all.

'Hello Raoulf,' said Janus Woolfe smelling the boy's blood, 'I've been waiting for you.'

Raoulf sat stoking the cottage fire whilst he listened to Janus's story…

'I think of Eirik every day. We were born Shape Shifters, with the ability to transform, but we were abandoned early on by our Sorceress mother. We went from place to place, sometimes taken in, but mainly living in the woods by the river, surviving and playing at changing, catching fish with the otters. Both human and animal, if we smelt any fresh shot pheasant or rabbit hanging on a barn door we would turn into wolf cubs or crows and steal it right from under the farmer's nose.'

Janus laughed and so did Raoulf.

'With no-one to teach us we worked it out for ourselves: finding shelter, food and water, crossing the icy lake, and keeping out of the way of the grizzly bears and grown-up humans. We had our own secret language – mostly animal chatter, whistles and growls. We couldn't read or write too well back then, but we picked up a word or two, learnt to read a sign, and could tell if talk was friendly or not.

We joined the pack herders in the Nor Land Forest of Skald, tending the rowan horses and the reindeer in the Far Fields. The mountain men taught us how to rescue trapped animals, read and send smoke signals, and how to use flares without burning our fingers. Because we were different not everyone trusted us. We were bullied, but the blows made us tougher, better fighters and our instincts became as sharp as fresh whetted knives.'

Raoulf pulled his grandmother's blanket tightly around him. 'I wish I had a brother,' he mumbled.

Janus smiled and nodded.

'I was no more than fifteen when the herders sent us off to the Sheet Ice School, run by the Mo Snow Tribe and a few magical Brethren Brothers of Olde. The School was hidden mainly underground, like a warren, with a central circular chamber domed like a giant igloo. We joined a class with five other boys, and in exchange for lessons, board and keep we'd run errands for the Brothers. Most were straightforward, but some were more secret.

Out in the field we learnt to read the snow, rain and clouds like you learnt to read a book – the signs of an on-coming storm were always turning in the air, if you knew what to look for. We could navigate the land as well as any Mo Indian on the hunt or out for revenge, and knew a man's business by a sniff of his coattails. In the mammoth season, feasts of fish were held on the return of the sky-whales and sea-leopards. Dancing, and drinking the local 'Reyka' and 'Ild Vand', we'd watch the Aurora blazing high overhead in the midnight sky. 'Dragon Light' the Mo's used to call it. Others said it was the spirits of the dead reaching through a crack in the sky.'

A forlorn lament, as desolate as the mountain wind that rips the heart out of a freezing man, filled Raoulf's ears and chilled his bones. 'Were they friendly?' he asked, shivering.

Janus paused.

'Hard to tell… Some believed they were warriors killed in battle trying to find their comrades. Magnus Skovgaard, a Mathmagician at the Ice School, said the lights were wandering souls dancing across the skies bringing peace to their loved ones. He was a good friend to Eirik and me. He could read the shapes of heads, hands and faces – animal, fairy and human – as well as prophesying Future Time through stargazing. He was smart and could see meaning in the colours of sky vapour, ice mirrors and rippling water. The Brothers asked him to teach us, watch over us and rein us in…'

Raoulf winced as Janus tended to his thumb and swollen ankle with makeshift strips torn from an old bandana, but he was eager to hear the rest of the story, which swirled like a shaken snow globe full of exciting tales and misty memories.

'Eirik had an eagle's eye. He could kill a troll with a catapult at a hundred paces and could shoot a hare, whilst it ran through the meadow, with one eye closed. He loved to hunt. I looked inside to my inner wolf. Of all my shifter animals I wanted to understand him the most, master him. We couldn't agree and fought over everything. In the end we choose – him hunter, me wolf. Magnus knew the hell we went through…

"Fighting or peace," he warned us. "It's your choice."

Janus gently built up the fire, the tinder crackling gently in the flame, and Raoulf huddled closer welcoming the warmth.

'But why did you leave the Ice School?' Raoulf asked.

'One night, a few years later, the Fire Dragons descended and torched the School…'

The fire popped and spluttered unexpectedly and Raoulf drew back. 'Dragons!' he exclaimed, suddenly afraid.

'Yes, it was a warning. Magnus explained to us that the Old Ways were to be discarded, and for the sake of unity only one God was to be worshipped along the New Path. The Dragons told the Brothers to shut down all their sanctuaries and go out into the world. Overnight the Ice School was gone. None of it made sense to Eirik and me – Nature was our God – but Magnus guided us, secretly binding us to the keeping of the Brothers' faith.

So, the three of us swore to serve Odin, Lord of the Wild Hunt and the Wandering Way – a god Eirik and me could at least believe in. But in our hearts beat very different truths, and finding common ground was hard. My wolf wanted to be free, to roam wild and follow the scents on the travelling breezes. Eirik wanted a more human life, whilst Magnus wished to serve the Mathmagicians. The Brothers made us leave. So we each went our separate ways to find ourselves and prove our use.

I travelled North to the Frozen Kingdom, getting in with the Frost Giants and Screech Witches. Pretending to be chief of a renegade wolf pack, I was prized for my killing skills and taken in. It was a dark time, but I was well looked after. Eirik travelled South to the Land of Ore, settling in White Bear Peninsula finding work as a hunter, scout and forager helping the local farmers and fishermen. Magnus headed North West in search of Dragons.

A couple of years passed. We all received a message from the Brothers to regroup and help in one final undertaking – to contain the interloping Giants and Witches. I had considerable insider knowledge, but it was Magnus who brought Eirik and I back together and into action with his Far Seeing plans, like pawns in a long game of chess. We were based in a frontier town called Lost, in the mountains of Yester Yore. It was a long, harsh war.

Finally, on the Winter solstice, the Banshee Tribe rebelled and fled South. They were strange, winged creatures who could easily devastate your senses and pierce your soul, but they wanted a more ordinary, war-free life.'

Raoulf was fascinated. 'What happened?' he asked.

'They choose self-exile and were allowed safe passage by the Brothers. In exchange, they agreed not to use their powers for ill and Magnus bound them to this. With the winged-Witches gone, the remaining Giants and Witches weakened and were easier to control.

After the war we were exhausted, so we made our way to Eirik's cabin in White Bear Peninsular to tend our wounds. We hoped to lay low, find shelter and some manner of peace where we could live out the rest of our days. The war was over and we were free to do what we wanted – go where we pleased. But Magnus had other plans.

There were stories of a centuries-old enchantment that had destroyed a Palace, poisoned a Forest and cursed its people. When Magnus was in the Old Hawk Land, the Fire Dragons had told him about the theft of an ancient Star-Compass, its magic used for no good. He became obsessed, wanting to search for the compass and a long-forgotten Witch scattered in the shadows…'

Raoulf looked up – startled – as a sharp pain shot through his thumb, reminding him of the night's savage encounter. Janus simply grunted in acknowledgment.

'We never knew her plans and she never showed herself through all our years of searching... well, not until tonight. Back then there were also yarns about a wandering female minstrel never aging, living in-and-out of Time. Magnus wanted to investigate, for there were too many coincidences for it all to be made up, and it gave Eirik and me a new purpose and direction. That's when we decided to travel to the Land of Awe – one of the last places where fairy and human still lived together.

So we travelled South. Magnus crossed the Slippery Sea using the broken causeway, paying his respects to the Mer-race on his way – he was trying to find an antidote to Siren Song and the Banshees' scream. I followed days later having run through the Silver Forests down the far easterly Crescent Lands.

Magnus was well regarded by the local people for his wise insight and quickly advanced to become Mayor of Town. All those with magic, however spell-infected or pure their bloodlines, soon came under his Far Seeing gaze and control. He would one day become the Headmaster of a certain Folkeskole...'

'You mean our Headmaster?' asked Raoulf, surprised.

'There's much you don't know about the Headmaster,' said Janus smiling. 'A brave and clever soul...'

'And Eirik?' enquired Raoulf.

'Well now...' Janus replied looking askance at the boy as if weighing up a difficult decision, 'that is a good question.'

Janus abruptly stood up and moved toward the fire, his fingers playing nervously with a silver talisman that hung about his neck. Hesitating, he continued...

'My brother crossed the sea by boat and then journeyed on foot to meet us in Town. Making his way through the Forest he met a woman – an event that would change his life forever...'

Here Janus paused, fumbling for the right words.

'You see, though he didn't know it at the time, Eirik became a father that day... soon after a baby girl was born – a Wild Rose... someone you know better as Miss Beret.'

Perceiving old hurt, the Eye of Dark swept its beams across Janus's Two Way Wolf's heart. Suddenly, a gloomy, flickering memory rose like a smoky shadow to engulf the room, for it was in Grandmother May's cottage that events had tragically altered for the worse...

A week before Eirik's death, Grandmother Littlesøn noticed something bizarre going on as her clothes kept disappearing from the washing line. Not once, but twice. Also, she could smell the musky overtones of the wolf Big Bad prowling through the Forest again at night. Hanging apples out on string, and sprinkling herbs and salt around the cottage, she could tell by their rot and footprint damage that Unwelcomed Others were lurking around as well. The Huntingsman laughingly told her that herbal lore, poisoned apples and bread knives, however sharp, would not work against one as seasoned as the crafty Big Bad, a past Wolf Man adversary of his from the Giant-Witch Wars.

The Huntingsman said a gun, particularly one that housed bullets of silver impregnated with the hair of another Turning Wolf, would help penetrate any protective Witch charm and get to the dark heart of the matter. How he knew of such things, and where he had got such bullets from, further informed Grandmother Littlesøn's mistrust of Moon Folk as being inconstant and wayward. She believed that Lunar Lore gave Clandestine Creatures and Spell Users an unfair night-time advantage, but left them ill-equipped to deal with ordinary life and overly prone to distorting madness. She believed such Weird Magic went against the Sun's better nature.

As a child, May Littlesøn had trained at the 'Magpie School of Practical Day' where pupils were taught that black and white, good and evil, were exactly as they appeared. Her liking for crimson was purely a preference for life over death – a matter of Forest survival and a taste for instinctual adventure rather than the casual spilling of blood. At school she had been shown simple Flower Charms and Herbal Healing. She had also been taught how to peel apples so you could read initials by the curl of the fruit's skin. She could forecast who would visit next, and whether they were friend or foe, by the way the skin landed when tossed backwards over her left shoulder.

Thereafter she had been instructed on how different knife blades could stab, cut and tear – to wound or kill, sever or skin – and how to fell and strip small coppice trees with a range of choppers, cleavers and axes. Since then she had considerably honed her knife throwing skills and wolf-killing instinct, but had never been trained in the art of gun craft. Her alignment was better with the weight of a blade in her hand, while the glinting end of a gun's barrel made her squint and curbed her aim.

As proud wearer of the Red Cloak, May Littlesøn had become protector of the woodland wayfarer and forest frail: the lost, the innocent and the elderly. She had a precocious talent and villagers called her vigilante, a 'justicier exceptionnelle' – unorthodox and unapproved. Her skilful 'Path of Direct Action' appealed to the inhabitants of Town and for this service many admired her, whilst others dismissed her cranky ways. The local women, particularly the mothers of the Witch-infected sons and the endangered Fairy Folk, all called her Grandmother and Wise Woman. They recognised her earth power and would secretly seek her advice when the rule of men and husbands was failing around them.

On their first Forest meeting, the newly arrived Huntingsman did not know of Grandmother May's infamous Cloak of Red, her lethal knife skills and her knowledge of wolf – Big Bad, the recently arrived Lone Silver, and the spell-infected others. She felt somewhat underestimated, but that suited her purpose, as she knew she could learn much from this seasoned hunter. So she visited Eirik often for Forest advice and he willingly helped her advance her wielding ways of axe against blood, bone and tree. She was a quick learner and went from proficient to impressive very quickly. During these visits she questioned the Huntingsman about his intriguing past, about his travels through the inhospitable Northern Barren Wastes and his present day reasons for staying on in the Forest of Awe.

Eirik's short, evasive, uninformative answers roused her suspicion. She found his current work situation at odds with the glimpses of his background she had obtained, for here was a truly skilled Nor Land hunter enslaved to menial forestry service and woodcutting work. It soon became apparent to her that his posing as the personal Woodsman for the virtuous Family Rose was not all that it seemed. She was certain something more secretive was going on. After the birth of Mrs Rose's fourth child, a third daughter, Grandmother Littlesøn guessed that his staying and deepening interest in the girl had more untoward reasoning.

However, for the Huntingsman and his daughter, Wild Rose, the changing months and seasons turned into happy passing years. He watched his daughter grow, and was proud of her, teaching her all the ways of Nature – of hunting, forest, feather and fur. Mother Rose had named her daughter Rose Pink, yet she feared the day when her haunting vision and things foretold, prophecies both good and bad, might come to pass. Grandmother Littlesøn watched on, but they knew she had guessed their secret and were grateful of her tacit help and overseeing care. Besides, who was Grandmother May to comment upon such awkward circumstances when she had so readily handed over her only son to his travelling circus father for upbringing?

It was true.

As a mother May Littlesøn had been disappointed by the birth of a boy, desperately wanting a daughter to inherit her Red Cloak. She had told the father not to return their son until after the difficult, unruly years of youthful adolescence were over and he was ready to return as a man. Then, once standing on his own two feet, he would be welcome back.

The father and other collected nomadic freaks and circus geeks all understood the vagaries of strange nature and soon recognised the teenage boy's wolf-spell transformation. To them it was blessing not curse and easily supported, but it meant that Grandmother May never understood her son's growing wolf ways. Nevertheless, her days were pleasantly filled with Forest business and the Huntingsman and his daughter were regular visitors. She enjoyed watching the Rose child grow and imparting the wisdom of the Old Red Way.

Somewhat ironically, the Huntingsman continued to convince Grandmother Littlesøn that guns were often better to use than knives as they could cover a greater preliminary distance. She disagreed. Silent Stealth, one of her favourite throwing knives, could slip easily through the Forest on a whisper to the carotid of any creature. Plus, any gun once fired would sound an alarm that could arouse the enemy and give your position away. Grandmother Littlesøn had thanked the Huntingsman for her regular morning lessons, but did not guess at his ongoing concern for her welfare from the threat of Big Bad. Nor did she understand why he would later have wished to dress up in her clothes as a decoy. It seemed odd to her way of thinking. Yet, the Huntingsman had guessed correctly the killing intent of both her and Big Bad.

Meanwhile, the disguised Big Bad had lain in wait for Grandmother May and the Huntingsman. The canny wolf, courtesy of a Witch's Seeing Mirror, had discovered the Huntingsman's decoy plan and turned it against him in a predator-prey reversal travesty. The old Witch Queen's plan to undermine the Family Rose was underway. So the Huntingsman and Big Bad, both masquerading as Grandmother May, were found in a gun-stalking standoff by a third, real grandmother – May Littlesøn. She possessed a rusty, sawn-off shotgun and wished to know who had been stealing her clothes from off the washing line. The answer, it seemed, was both.

So on that fateful day of misery and mishap, Grandmother May had found herself in the rare situation of being caught off-guard, staring down the right and wrong end of three gun barrels. She did not really care to whom the guns belonged as they were both trespassing on her property. Then a gun had accidentally fired, sending a blast flying over their heads and shattering a window. As glass sprayed everywhere Grandmother May's trigger finger slipped. All too soon a fatal shot had been discharged, slaying one of the impersonators of her – the wrong one. The unfortunate shot had exploded in Eirik's chest, killing him instantly. Her fingers would never have slipped on any of her favourite knives.

Big Bad took the opportunity to gloat before loping off. He laughingly turned and told Grandmother May that he would be back to unpeel her smock dress with his teeth and feast on her carcass as soon as the Forest Patrol had sorted out her killing mess and after she got out of gaol. Yet it was not the wolf left standing licking his lips, but Grandmother May in relish of revenge encounter. It was such an old war that she was not afraid of Big Bad and followed after him with her knives and smoking barrels, but she could not catch such a seasoned runner.

With the body of the Huntingsman lying dead on her floor, Grandmother Littlesøn had more important matters to attend to. First she sought out the Huntingsman's daughter, Wild Rose, who was playing with foxes in the burning Straw Fields; later she would seek out the help of the Mayor. Without hesitation she told the child the truth as to what had occurred. They had to travel swiftly before the Forest Patrol arrived and took Grandmother May into custody. There would be difficult questions asked and the child would have to have her criminal wits about her.

But the Huntingsman's death was a savage truth too brutal for one so young to bear. Not wishing to listen or understand, Wild Rose became hysterical. So, Grandmother May forcibly led the child back through the Forest to her cottage. She allowed the child to hold her father's hand and say her goodbyes kneeling over the blanketed figure. Remaining ever watchful at the window, Grandmother May said a hurried prayer for the departed soul of her friend. In their shock and grief neither Grandmother nor daughter noticed the silver talisman hanging around the Huntingsman's neck.

Hastily, Grandmother May dressed the child in a spare Cloak of Red and gave her a wooden basket. Into it she placed a sharp cutting-knife edged with poison next to a green apple with a sleeping potion made from the fungi of the wood absorbed into it. She hid these small, fatal items under a linen cloth and told the child to not be afraid to use the knife or offer the apple to anyone evil if they came too close, animal or human alike. The cloth was for stemming blood and making bandages if she should get wounded or hurt. The basket was the perfect pretence for a picnic outing.

So they left the cottage together and ran back through the trees to the grieving child's home where Grandmother Littlesøn explained to Mother Rose what had occurred. By the time Grandmother had returned to her cottage the Huntingsman's body had been moved and the talisman around his neck was missing. Fresh wolf prints trailed across the living room floor. Even from the distance of Town Janus had heard the gunshots, had felt a tug at his heart and had run into the Forest to investigate. He recognised the talisman from their shared childhood and knew it was his brother's disguised, disfigured body lying dead on the floor.

Standing in the cottage Janus could smell the scent of enchantment behind Big Bad's recent transfiguration and attack. Old Magic was part of his own condition, but had been banned for the use of killing by the Gods of the East after the Giant Wars. The blatant misuse of such power only ever spelt one thing – grave danger and trouble ahead. Big Bad and his gang of Marauding Mutts were growing bolder lurking under some form of Shadow Protection, most likely Witch. Having smelt the strange reality of the scene, Janus had taken the silver charm, transformed into Lone Silver Wolf and run in pursuit of Big Bad.

By the time Lone Silver Wolf had reached the foot of the Fang Ridge Mountains the trail had gone cold. Big Bad had re-crossed the snaking Nordic Nile back into the hills, heading towards the coast and the company of wolves waiting for him in the North. From there they would cross the broken causeway back to the Land of Ore. In his reconnaissance for the ice-bound Screech Witches, Big

Bad had gathered useful information regarding the remaining Palace ruins in the centre of the Four Forests of Awe. For this scouting raid and killing deed the Witches had lent him some of their more unusual protective charms, but there had been no sign of the Fire Dragon's Star-Compass they so eagerly sought.

Given Lone Silver Wolf's difficult situation, in being the last person alone with the Huntingsman's dead body whilst trespassing on Grandmother May's property, there was only one friend he could turn to – Magnus. Otherwise the less friendly villagers might blame him for the Huntingsman's death and turn vigilante. So, Lone Silver Wolf had taken his brother's talisman and placed it into the hands of the Mayor for safekeeping. Ill-at-ease, Janus explained what he had sensed in the Forest's muddy, mouldering loam whilst chasing Big Bad – a scent of decay that could only emanate from the malingering severed body of a Shadow Witch. He remembered the pungency from the Battle Lands of the North all too well.

Magnus told Janus to keep hold of the silver charm because it might one day, if used wisely, show a way to future redemption. This intuition had perturbed Janus for Far Sight was not one of his gifts. Being told that he would know what to do when the 'Unknown Time' was right, however many years the mystery might take to unravel, was vexing and burdensome. That was when a flustered, out-of-breath Grandmother May had arrived and interrupted them.

Initially the two men did not believe her story – three Grandmothers circling each other whilst holding guns, but only one not in disguise. What had they all been thinking of? But the accidental death of The Huntingsman was a serious, heart-wrenching matter. The Mayor promptly revoked Grandmother May's hunting licence on the grounds that her sanity and eyesight were not all that they should have been, whilst her nerves, hands and trigger finger were judged to suffer from the shakes. Her gun was confiscated as the weapon of death, but not her knives. It was self-defence against trespassers after all, and who knew when she might need her heroic blades to fend for herself or help others travel safely through the Forest again.

Frustrated at their apparent lack of action, Grandmother May explained once again what had happened, inadvertently blurting out the secret of the illegitimate Rose child. Of course the two men knew, but still they acted surprised. Stalling for time, the Mayor deemed the blatant return of Big Bad and outlawed Transformative Magic this far South as highly irregular. Perhaps there was another greater hidden purpose behind it all. As to the second set of fresh wolf prints and the dead body being disturbed… well, the Mayor could not account for that. In the corner, Janus was surreptitiously wiping the blood from his hands and bare feet.

The Mayor and Janus knew that Grandmother Littlesøn would not have knowingly killed the Huntingsman. Yet her extraordinary story would turn out to be just one set of harrowing circumstances on a particularly brutal day. The Mayor turned hastily to spy into his Mystic Mirror, which had been filled with swirling omens and sweeping shadows since dawn. Within the glass, the falling petals of roses were scattering everywhere, warning that the Family Rose was in great peril. According to the Mirror, murder, Wolf Men, Witches, Giants, enchanted vanishings and organised kidnappings were rapidly descending upon them all. They needed to gather support from the local Fairy community as quickly as they could, and that required the help of Grandmother May.

Grandmother Littlesøn had driven all the way to the School only to find her grandson missing. She could not find the helpful Miss Beret or the troubling Mr Woolfe, only the hopeless Headmaster who twittered around her like a flustered owl.

'Raoulf gone,' he spluttered, 'what are we to do?'

None of the Headmaster's unconventional thinking and talk helped Grandmother Littlesøn. She could not see eye-to-eye with his 'Path of Non-Action', his platitude of 'leave things be', and his eccentric assertion that 'events often originated from an invisible source'. Consequently, things were never simple, straightforward or what they seemed to be, and hence why he confused and frustrated her so. Intervention was always a last resort of his, whilst to her action nipped the bud and stemmed the cause. Yet, if the truth were told, she had only ever seen him work for the betterment of others.

Grandmother May desperately needed to do something useful, but what? Adroitly, the Headmaster told her to trust her instincts, which she promptly did. She used his telephone to call her son, but got no reply. It was then that she sensed something was wrong so she left the Headmaster's office and went to find Raoulf herself. She pulled out the throttle on her old jalopy and searched all around the back lanes to her son's house, but no-one was there. Then she returned to the School and skirted the side of the wood, along the allotments and wild fields, shouting for Raoulf.

Grandmother Littlesøn looked up into the sky and spied a large Crow cawing and behaving oddly – swooping down and striking at something. Then a breathless, friendly Robin flitted onto a nearby fence post telling her that he had seen a boy dressed all in red skipping through the woods towards the spires. Grandmother May spoke basic bird, animal and all manner of woodland languages, including the speech of trees. She also knew that the Forest paths and leafy byways could be treacherous, particularly on a Full Moon night such as this.

Grandmother May sighed. For generations the power of the Cloak of Red had been passed on, usually from grandmother to granddaughter, but this time to grandson. She did not know how much of his mother's genes or his father's blood Raoulf possessed, but she believed her grandson to take after her side of the family and that meant he possessed many forms of instinctual tenacity to draw upon. Perhaps the Headmaster had been right to assert,

"Leave them alone and they will come home…"

But deep down she refused to accept his blithering edicts or the random claims of some nursery rhyme, however charming.

After a fruitless twilight search Grandmother May was making her way back to her cottage when a roaring thunder of motorbikes overtook her, dangerously racing through the on-setting night before disappearing into the Forest distance. On occasion she thought she glimpsed the form of a large silver wolf running by the side of the narrow forest road. Wolves! They distinctly bothered Grandmother Littlesøn and had done so all her life. As a child they had been her greatest fear as well as the truest test of her wily strength. She had encountered several different types, but there was something not right when it came to the monthly feud of crazy half-wolves and overzealous gun-hunters. Plus the faint, lingering smells of dead Witch and Transformative Magic disturbed her.

Grandmother May pulled down the small leather bag containing chicken bones, sage and salt that had been dangling from the mirror. She clutched it in her hand as she warily glanced out of the car windows. It was the herbal defence she liked to use against unwanted guests and would-be trespassers. Perhaps it was naïve and superstitious to believe in the use of such simple charms, but it was always expedient to have something to throw into people's eyes as a last blinding resort. More re-assuring was the fact that one of her best hunting knives lay under the passenger seat – good Old Faithful.

Suddenly, there was a loud explosion.

It was not the sound of a gun being fired, but the sound of her exhaust backfiring. Something silver streaked in front of the car. Grandmother May tried to swerve. The noise of a grinding engine and crunching gears followed as the car kangarooed and stalled in the middle of the road. Grandmother May pitched over the steering wheel and hit her forehead on the glass. With a dull, bruising thud she slipped into an unconscious reverie. She was out for the count. How long? She could not tell.

Minutes passed as Grandmother Littlesøn travelled through a misty veil of eerie silence to a realm where she partook of the grace of someone she only knew by the captivating name of Snow Rose. Petals fell like gentle snowflakes whilst crystals of light danced about her. Floating out of her body, the only feeling Grandmother May remembered was an overwhelming sense of peace and love.

'May, you cannot stay,' said a gentle voice from within the spectral light. 'Take my love and return. Don't hold back your forest knowledge and woodland caring for you are much needed, but your understanding must take a different direction now. You must go. Your grandson needs you.'

Feeling disorientated, Grandmother May slowly descended. Dropping softly back into her body she found herself awaking in the front seat of her car, crumpled over the steering wheel. When she came round, she knew her knitting and knife-throwing would never be the same. She had dropped a stitch as surely as she had been in the hands of cloud-gathering Angels, but now she must try and save nine. She had missed the episode of the circling Lone Silver Wolf entirely; the one in which Janus had taken possession of the keys to her cottage. Confusingly, her son was standing there, his motorbike pulled into the side of the road, his concerned face peering in through the side window of the car.

'Are you okay, mum?' asked Mr Littlesøn.

'I'm fine, son' she replied rather dazed. 'I thought I saw…'

Grandmother Littlesøn abruptly stopped. She was not sure what she had seen in the ephemeral moonlight. Had it been a streak of silver lightning? Perhaps it was just the motorbike's engine glinting in front of her; perhaps it was her worst fear of wily transforming wolf.

Mr Littlesøn opened the car door smelling of beer, bike and a slight scent of fur. She recognised it and was puzzled. She knew he was a friend of Janus and the faint smell made her nervous. Had he been out hunting wolves? It made sense for it was in her blood too, but it did not feel right. For some reason she was blind to his wolf-turning ways. Perhaps it was easier than accepting the truth?

'Come on, mum,' he said sympathetically, 'move over. I'll drive you home.'

Grandmother Littlesøn felt wonderfully calm and somewhat illuminated as she shifted over to the passenger seat. Then her forgotten grandson came into focus in her mind. Had he seen Raoulf? She had gone to collect him, but did not know where he was. Mr Littlesøn groaned, feeling guilty at yet another after-school pick-up gone wrong whilst dreading further reproaches from Raoulf's teacher. The car was slow starting, but eventually they were driving away, heading back to her cottage on the far side of the forest. As the car pulled away a bag of chicken bones crunched and a spray of white salt and a sprig of sage fell off the front tire. Her 'Spell of Protection' from wolves had been deliberately broken.

The evening following Grandmother May's accidental midday murder of the Huntingsman was an ill-fated one. Wild Rose lashed out in uncontrollable anguish, turning her rage upon her kin and then in upon herself in despair. Far away, through the use of mirrors, the Witches saw that the Family Rose was splintered by the dark deeds of the day, which diminished the protection surrounding them.

So, sitting astride their broomsticks, the last of the Screech Witches came for the Rose Daughters on a promise they had made long ago to rid the world of their arrogant beauty. More than that, the former Witch Queen, she who had once foreseen the future, had instructed her Screech Clan to end the pure Rose bloodline forever – which meant the death of Mother and Father Rose as well. A small band of Ice Wolves commanded by Big Bad followed after the Witches in support.

Simultaneously, there came a grisly attack from two Giant guards who came independently of the Witches and for different reasons. No-one knew who had grown the beanstalk whence they had climbed or whether the stalk had been grown from the Earth Lands up or from the Cloud Lands down, for beans grew both ways. Yet the Giants arrival shocked them all. They had come specifically for revenge on Jack, whose thieving fingers had previously cheated their masters of several prized possessions. The Giants were under oath to find and return the missing artefacts, and to steal away the newborn child with the awoken light divine – the one named Rose Snow. But Jack and the magical treasures were nowhere to be seen.

So, during the deep, inconsolable sobbing of a child into the suffocating depths of her pillow, the Family Rose came under assault from different quarters. The separate surprise attacks overwhelmed them; the combined strength of Witches, Giants and Ice Wolves proving too much for their Fairy goodness. They were not a fighting or an outwardly magical family; their healing strength resided in the radiance of their ever-blooming rose bushes that emanated a protective, shielding light. Their individual personality and power was that granted to each hue of flower, but this proved to be ineffectual against such savage intruders.

However, in mutual pursuit of the rare Snow Rose prize, the cruel forces of Giants and Witches quickly turned on each other. The Witches attacked the Giant's foreheads and eyes like swarming, annoying flies, whilst the Giants tried to flick the Witches off their flying sticks with their chubby fingers. Meanwhile, the Ice Wolves were busy nipping and biting at the Giant's ankles in an attempt to topple them, for fallen Giants were easier to kill and feast upon. Then Grandmother May arrived with the assembled forces of the Forest Fairy Folk and good Woodland Creatures. The wand-waving Mayor and the snarling Mr Woolfe followed quickly behind.

But it was Wild Rose who now threw herself into the fray with a feral frenzy, gratefully pulling Grandmother May's poisoned blade from out her basket and unleashing her fury in honour of the Huntingsman's death. She was her father's daughter after all and the knife-wielding hunter contained within rose to avenge. Woe the Wolf, Witch or Giant who came too near. Spells bounced dangerously off her glinting blade, whilst several flying Witch's toes and Giant's reaching fingers were jabbed and sliced at. Then she was pulled away kicking and screaming from the surrounding chaos and billowing smoke. It was the Mayor who seized her.

'Save my children,' were the final words Mother Rose had cried out to the Mayor, and he had tried his heart-wrenching best.

Wild Rose found herself being bound and bundled off in a dusty wheat sack. Thus bagged and gagged, she was unceremoniously thrown into the back of a jolting wagon. A concealing tarpaulin covered her as the sky cried and it began to gently rain. As she was taken away from the scene of devastation, she heard several loud blasts followed by some thumping and ground shaking. A distant burning heat meant that a fire now raged, one that would destroy her family home and the fallen bodies of Giants forever. Still, she had the blade hidden in her boot and the poisoned apple in her pocket that she would slice and offer to her captors at the first possible moment. She did not realise that she was being rescued.

Nearby, people were calling out, discussing plans as they climbed on-board the moving cart. Wild Rose hit out at them through the tarpaulin when her head was struck with a tap of the Mayor's wand. A 'Spell of Forgetfulness' gently descended and her recollections of the day faded away. After that, her memories of the day's despair and her heartache grew hazy, as though a flurry of snow covered the landscape of past events. She was left only with a drifting sensation. It was decided by the Mayor that there was to be no trace of the Family Rose left for future investigation. That meant the very careful handling of the only two child survivors and the binding of those Fairy Folk involved that night to a magical oath.

So, amidst the jostling hay, vegetables and bales of wood, Rose Pink began her journey to the coastal town of Slow. There she was placed into the protective hands of the Brethren Brothers of Olde. They set sail by a south-westerly squall and crossed the cold, bilging waters of the Great Northern Grey to the milk-and-honey rich land of the easterly Enchanted Isles. The Brothers' mission was simply to safeguard her passage across sea and land to the Crook of Corn. From under the guardian Brothers' protection she was given into the welcoming hands of the merciful Iberian Sisters. More journeys ensued until she eventually reached the shelter of the Cloak of the Maid in Europa's sunny South. Carefully concealed, Rose Pink travelled from orphanage to convent but rumours always followed…

'To cover shame,' whispered some.

'To hide from the retribution of Witches,' countered others.

All Rose Pink knew was the kindness she received from a host of friendly faces smiling down at her. The hooded Brothers and veiled Sisters she met were spiritual travellers from the Old Temples who were helping her along the Shattered Way. Eclipsed by death, fear, and Shadow Magic, the blighted Rose was exiled into the sacred mountains where she played freely, whilst being schooled in the ways of unencumbered nature. Ten years passed. Rose Pink, now a young woman, travelled across Europa's patchwork countries, eventually returning to Town, her birthplace, in the Jutted Land of Awe. Here the safe, but ageing, hands of the Headmaster greeted her.

The newly self-named Miss Beret happily became a ward of his and under his watchful tutelage turned to the crafts of soft magic, healing and teaching. He was her custodian and her friend, yet also her somewhat baffling guide, who often smiled knowingly at her frustration as she struggled to grasp at her mind's fleeting fragments of the past. More perplexing was the fact that her family's history had been erased from all records and none of the residents of Town were able to shed any light on the subject. Watching on, the Headmaster realised that his initial amnesia blessing now seemed somewhat of a curse – for Miss Beret's true feelings bubbled under like a cauldron brewing.

On that tragic night of the Giant and Witch attack, other members of the Rose Family had disappeared too, some forever. In less than one day Mother and Father Rose, as well as the Huntingsman, all lay dead. Rose Pink's elder twin sisters, Rose Red and Rose White, had mysteriously vanished, hidden for safety by the Mayor in a book of fairy tales – a secret lullaby land where they would never be harmed, but could never return to earthly life. Accessible only to children, no adult hand would ever find them again. Her younger sister, Snow Rose, had disappeared, presumed stolen and assumed dead. Her body, cot and the last pages of a giant storybook were missing and would remain forever lost. Some said that the elder brother, Jack, had sold her into the Giant Land of Clouds and veiling white silence.

The facts were unclear; some believed Snow Rose's abduction to be for her safekeeping from the clutches of Witches, whilst others thought it was nothing more than fair payment for Jack's wrongdoing. It seemed a cruel punishment, but theft and clumsy use of enchanted relics were only part of her brother's crime and debatable charm. Stealing had started early with the nimble-fingered Jack for poaching, scrumping and rustling were all considered fair game to those who lived crookedly in the wood by the Forest. Climbing and hiding were second nature to him. He was not particularly bright, but he loved the heroic folk tales his father read him and consequently hungered for outdoor adventure.

Jack possessed no magical gift of his own, so when he stumbled upon the black-market beans being bartered at the back of the tavern he saw his chance. He procured the beans not in exchange for a cow, but with a bunch of roses stolen from his parent's famous garden – the perennial secret of their good fortune. With his magpie ways and green, clever fingers, the power of beanstalks had soon become his. In truth, Jack was the only one daring and stupid enough to give the beans life, yet his ensuing theft of Giant treasures meant that rumbling cloud consequences would one day catch them all up.

After the horrific incident that decimated his family, Jack was placed under apprenticeship to the Mayor, who was keen to help him move on. Yet what started out as the Mayor's brave attempt to save Jack's good name from Witch and Giant ruination, soon ended up looking like furtherance of Jack's social standing through personal gain. When questioned by the Mayor and Mr Woolfe, Jack said he had stolen the Giant artefacts purely to help his family, wanting to give his parents a chance for a secure life. Yet his desire for controlling outcomes, even for good, was seen by most as nothing more than a thinly veiled, selfish ambition.

Yes, Jack had held onto his singular plan – naïvely going wherever the stolen Zip Boots and Magic Mirror sent him – yet he never once questioned their allegiance. Some of the Air Fairies that aided the Boots had formerly seen service under the northern flying Witch Clans and did not believe humans should possess such aerial ability. The Fairies viewed Jack's Cloud Land quest for enchanted relics and treasure with suspicion and became jealous of his success. They informed the Witches of his wayward pilfering and told them he also possessed a curious Giant map and access to a scrying Ice Mirror. It was all useful information to the Witches in eventually locating Jack's Rose-shielded family.

Jack did not know that mirrors were interconnected. Nor did he know that all messages sent and received between them could be seen or heard if you happened to be standing in the right place at the right time to catch the Rippling Effect. These spectral portals were a means of viewing thoughts and plans from other kingdoms, however fleetingly. Such sending of messages, false or fair, could be used against another watcher's cunning and fear. Strategy was not the Giants' greatest gift, but they wanted an end to Jack's pilfering, and some peace from the Pirate beanstalk trade that occasionally kept their Cloud Kingdoms tethered to the turning Earth Lands below.

Yet Jack was nimble, fast and good; he could steal from a Giant and, courtesy of his Zip Boots, be at a hundred paces before the Giant could sniff him out.

'Fe, fie, foe, thumb – I smell the blood of a thieving one'.

But not always Jack, for he smelt more of beguiling roses than anything else – an off-putting scent to Giants and Witches – and he always left a bloom in place of any stolen artefact.

So it was decided amongst the Giant Chiefs that the capture of Snow Rose, Jack's infant sister, would be an answer to his stealing ways – offering revenge and leverage, whilst possessing a rare prize of living divinity to add to their collection of desired treasures. As the eldest child and only Rose brother, all Jack had wanted was a happy ending, but disaster beyond all reckoning had struck that devastating night. The rest was spell-forged forgotten history: the retribution of angry Giants, the fury of envious Witches, the bloody toll on his family. The Mayor, even with his advanced Far Sight, Mathmagicianship and Mystic Mirror, could not have prevented the death-dealing catastrophe that rained down – only sorrowfully mop up the heart-breaking damage.

Now, after the terrible events that had torn the Family Rose apart, the future fate of fairy tales and the survival of Town rested upon the mixed bloodline of a destined daughter suffering from amnesia and a wretched, power-driven son. But their whereabouts was unknown.

Anders paused as Little Milk sucked on his master's beer-soaked thumb. "The Chronicle of Ages" was rapidly forming and the sheets were spilling off the side of the trestle table. As The Bard shuffled and stacked his manuscript, the goat chewed serenely away. Oblivious to the missing eaten pages, Anders continued to scrawl quickly with his Swallowtail quills.

'Now,' he thought, 'how to get to the heart of Jack...?'

Jack Rose – plunderer of Giants, disturber of Witches, destroyer of families – had already sold some of the smaller treasures and hidden the magical rest. He was aghast at what he had done and how events had fallen. Some spoke of unaccounted for deals with Giants being completed that night above the stalk's cloud-line, but no-one ever truly knew. All except the one who did the right thing by chopping the beanstalk down, and the two who searched hard that night to find him in a bid to alleviate their suspicions and counteract any further foolishness and unnecessary evil.

So the Mayor and Lone Silver Wolf scoured the charred house for charmed relics and Fairy remains. They found, and removed, the enchanted Bed Knob, but Jack had already taken the biggest and best of the Giant's treasured spoils. Luckily, the Mayor also managed to rescue one scarred rose bush, which he later planted secretly in the Park's Crossbones Garden of Peace. He hid the remaining smaller artefacts about the Forest and the buildings of Town, just in case people were tempted to harness their power and beauty and become enthralled by their fascinating ways. The Bed Knob he placed on the door of the upstairs schoolroom, which nobody used then – for Town was considerably smaller in those days.

Of course the Mayor knew Jack had intended no real harm and that was why he sent the boy away, courtesy of the now newly coded, security-locked Seven League Boots. As a Mathmagician, the Mayor still held some sway with the Air Fairies who recognised his authority, however elderly he was becoming. How old was he now – a mere one hundred or a sprightly two hundred and two? Meanwhile, Mr Woolfe chaperoned Jack to Sky City where they were to seek sanctuary and stay as guests of the Mountain Monks, but Janus questioned his friend's reasons for protecting the selfish, errant boy.

Trolls guarded the only chasm-arching stone-bridge that led to Sky City. If you were lucky or good, and the monastery bells rang out in your defence, then the Trolls would let you pass without a fight. But as they approached the bells had not tolled and they each blamed the other for their misfortune. Janus was a seasoned fighter, whilst Jack, with his Flying Boots and his catapult, turned out to have an impressive aim. They fought their way across the bridge, but fighting together against the Trolls did not unify them and theirs remained an uneasy, difficult relationship.

Flying did not suit the land-loving Janus and walking did not suit the lazy Jack. For the already miserable boy being incarcerated within the monastery walls to reflect on his misdeeds was an unwelcome and lonely experience. At the top of Fang Ridge Mountain, in and out of the coldness of clouds, contrition eventually descended but it did not come with compassion or grace, but ill-humoured rancour.

'Seek that which you do not wish to find,' the Sky Monks instructed Jack, but he did not understand their austere words and chose to ignore their wise advice.

Still, the merry Mountain Monks helped to pray Jack's pain away and he eventually became interested in their use of mystical objects in the furtherance of their spiritual aim – the 'One Dream Awakening'. Manipulative thoughts and devious ideas began to brew in the lad's scheming mind. Janus, although steely and used to harsh mountain living, simply felt imprisoned in the cold stone City and burdened by his bothersome, ungrateful ward.

On Jack's return, the Mayor calibrated the lad's improvement through the use of a special measurement system designed by the Fire Dragons to evaluate human progress. The final outcome, not shared with Janus, resulted in Jack's hair being gently ruffled with a handful of stardust. The initial light sprinkling of silver powder felt wonderful and electrifying, but the ensuing hard rubbing of Dragon scales tearing through his scalp was sharp and rough. Dissolving into Jack's brain, the particles befuddled the boy and a deep change occurred. Accordingly, his inner totem was transformed from quick thieving Magpie to slow stalwart Bear and a new life began.

There was method in the Mayor's apparent madness. His first dusting action was the implanting of a future reward – a silver lining, of sorts – whereas his second searing action was the rolling in of grey clouds to obscure the lad's mind and inner landscape – a penance. Thus nimble Jack Flash duly became muddled-headed Peter – he of the knucklehead! Unlike the fate of Rose Pink, this was not an all-encompassing 'Spell of Forgetfulness', but a 'Befuddlement Charm' that would allow Peter choice in his handling of power and challenging events. However, choosing to perpetuate his selfish ways would only result in a Time-delayed, difficult and more painful heart awakening – whereas hard work, responsibility and continuing atonement were the keys to unlocking any future silver lining.

So, the novice Peter was taken under the Mayor's wing, who worked diligently towards the salvaging of the rest of the lad's life. He who had once survived the adventures of the precarious Cloud

Land of Giants, now continued to live on within Town in a different guise, reintegrated into society as a soul that only few knew or cared to remember. For the time being his separation from his sister was judged best for everyone concerned. The Mayor's plan was to keep the two surviving Roses apart, to ensure that their recently altered memories could not collide in recognition and re-kindle old wounds. Well, not until their individual healing had safely occurred and the ways of Future Time could kindly cross their threads once more without fears of reprisal or implosion.

Raoulf had heard the story of Rose Red and Rose White from his own mother. She had often held him at night and rocked him to sleep with soporific lullabies and whispered folk tales as old as the hills. She had such a lovely lilt to her voice as though calling a stranger to come home, beckoning rest, whilst others feared it was a siren call summoning death. Yet Raoulf had not heard of the third sister, Rose Pink, also known as Wild Rose to some, or Rose Berry to Enchanted Island others. Nor had Raoulf known of the fourth sister, Snow Rose, who had been snatched by Giants in her infancy and carried off to a place nigh-on-high where she was protected by brambles, thorns and severed horns wrestled from Dragons.

Snow Rose was a child of the mid-Winter sun; spinning symbols and runes on dew-soaked cobwebs so delicate that only those sacred worshippers of the Temple Tree rank of oak, ash, hawthorn, holly and hazel could perceive them. She now lived in the misty Realm Beyond where she could look down from her cloud and observe journeying souls, but they could not perceive her. Well, not at first glance. The road to her spiritual beauty was always open, but only to those who travelled silently and steadfastly through the frightening

Giant Lands. Thus shrouded, her fine, cloud-white secret lay in the mystery of the torn pages of "Goat's Beard" in which she had been swaddled before being stolen away – the fairy story you always wished to hear that would make all the difficulties of childhood right.

Few attempted and fewer succeeded in gaining access to the purity of Snow Rose's cloud. To the Giants she was fascination beyond reason and prized above all other riches. Who would not kill, steal or trade beans for such a captivating being? Yet even the Giants knew not to use her as a living poppet for their children. Unlike their other enchanted trinkets and fantastic treasures, Snow Rose was no ornamental bauble, but living, breathing proof of divine Fairy presence. Raoulf knew none of this, but there were those that were his elder and wiser who would willingly share her story – but only when the time was right and the listener was ready, for the tale of Snow Rose's abduction was considered the most terrifying.

So it was that Mr Woolfe had swept Raoulf up and engulfed him whole with the fantastic legend of "Goat's Beard": part fairy tale, part local legend, part home-grown history. With his deep rasping voice, wide penetrating eyes, and large expectant mouth big enough to blow a pig's town house down, Janus stored such stormy tales for the telling. He had fallen upon Raoulf with a voracious passion and recounted to him the lost tale concerning an orphaned infant and a family ripped apart by a curse, of destruction brought about by their inherent goodness and beauty, the causes of which were partly bred, by the mother, in the daring marrow of her vision and bone.

Raoulf was fascinated. It was a savage story of Giant Queenship, witchcraft and fairy peasantry, told as tale but reckoned as true. The story had frightened Raoulf; particularly the cruel part where Saint Hansel and Saint Gretel had been made into gruel, and where the remains of the wicked Witch Queen had been fed to the Hungry

Grasses – yet somehow managed to survive by lurking in the Forest's shadow. It had been a close call earlier that evening and Raoulf was still recovering from his own encounter with the ravenous Grasses, let alone with the pursuing Goblins, Trembling Fears and oddly acting Christmas trees.

Unlike Mr Woolfe, Raoulf could not worship the scents on the wind or howl to the Moon, for such ancient ways were as yet too deep for his child's form to comprehend. He was unsure what truly lay in his blood and bone, but simply chose to believe in a blazing trail of triumphant light equally as fierce as the forces of darkness, pain and corrupt power. That was the enduring legacy remaining from his encounter with Little Spark and her killing of the Shadow Witch. Somehow, somewhere out there above and beyond them all, were unfathomable forces of nature working for good.

Equally, Raoulf knew that such forces could steal him away from this side of life just like they had temporarily taken the mind of his mother, just like the Door Knob had transported Cartwheel Charlie and his grandpa, and just like motorbikes and phases of the Moon could carry his father further into the horizon's distance. Yet Raoulf also knew that Janus's epic account served a purpose – fables always did if you listened carefully. Miss Beret, in her daily delivery of cautionary tales, scary sermons and fantastical stories, had taught him that. But what happened if you listened wrong? What fate befell the unfortunate and those souls still sleeping?

A favourite saying of his Grandmother's voice floated through his head…

'Fortune can turn on a sixpence… if not wasted on a pie.'

Such unusual sayings always perplexed Raoulf, but then his Grandmother would smile down at him and helpfully explain…

'Remember, wherever you are in life, however desperate, Fortune will always come to help you. Sometimes that help might be found in a book or a dream, or like a whispered word travelling like a Fairy leaf on the wind. All you have to do is stop Time's clock and, in the silence between the seconds, look and listen. Fortune's answer will come if you can but read the signs and symbols correctly.'

Grandmother May believed that Life was often kind, despite its difficulties... but you needed to trust in the unfolding of each day. Like Janus, the beams from the Two Towers of Dark and Light held equal sway, and she believed the answer always lay in people who had to get along together better than they did. Forest encounters always led to the exciting adventure of the Ten Thousand of Possible Things in the Turning World. You just had to figure out whether folk were friend or foe, which was not always so apparent.

Now, sitting together by the fire, Janus showed Raoulf the silver talisman he had taken from around his brother's neck so many years before. Janus easily recollected the scene with the Huntingsman lying dead on Grandmother May's floor – the very spot upon which they now sat. The memory flickered just like the twirling talisman did in his gnarled, ageing fingers, catching the firelight whilst spinning this way and that. Janus missed his brother and there was a hole in his heart where the little he knew of love had been. He told Raoulf that the talisman was for identification and protection, but by whom and from what Raoulf had been unable to ask for at that point there had been an unexpected interruption, headlights momentarily shining through the window. Outside, Grandmother Littlesøn's old jalopy came to a grinding halt.

Holding Raoulf firmly by the shoulders Janus smoothed the boy's mud-caked hair, quickly slipping the talisman over Raoulf's head. He gestured with his finger to keep silent. Any moment of opportunity between them was now rapidly closing. Janus had tried to connect with the child in the only way he knew how – by pouring out his heart through a story and the surrendering of his brother's talisman. He hoped they were enough of a clue to help his only remaining relative – his niece, Miss Beret. A car door opened and shut, followed swiftly by another. Footsteps scrunched across the gravel heading toward the open kitchen door.

'Who's there?' Mr Littlesøn called out.

Hearing voices in the kitchen Raoulf got up from the floor. 'Dad, is that you? Is Grandmother with you?'

Mr Littlesøn muttered to himself as a fresh pang of failed fatherhood swelled up within. 'Come on Mum, let's get you inside. Raoulf's here... son, are you all right?'

Then the sitting room door swung open. Apart from the crackling fire, only those who were listening could hear the uneasy, shifting silence of wolves. Grandmother May's hearing was an excellent compensation for her somewhat poor sight. Hardly a twig could snap within a mile radius of her cottage without her knowing about it and knowing who had passed by. Even in her advancing years she was dangerous like that.

'Raoulf! Who's there with you?' asked Grandmother May. 'What's their business?'

Silence.

Raoulf tugged at the sleeve of Mr Woolfe who was now standing with his back to them in the shadows. Janus slowly turned around.

'Why hello!' said Raoulf's father. 'It's only...'

He stopped abruptly. Of all the people from Town, he knew his mother would not be best pleased to see Janus standing there.

'It's me... Janus Woolfe,' replied Janus in a friendly manner, trying to make the situation less uncomfortable for Raoulf's grandmother. He reached out his hand to Mr Littlesøn.

'Hello my friend. I just happened to bump into Raoulf on my way to find you and the rest of the lads. I was telling him the story of "Goat's Beard" to pass the time. He seems to have got into a bit of trouble in the Forest. But you're fine now, aren't you?'

Raoulf looked up at his father and nodded, but he did not like to correct Mr Woolfe so he said nothing about the silver talisman and the small white lie regarding their encounter and his trespassing.

'"Goat's Beard"!' spluttered Grandmother May. 'Of all the blessed tales...'

Rushing forward, Grandmother May remembered only too well their previous difficult meetings and would not let Janus stay on her property for a second longer; not for all the protection he still received from the Headmaster. She had not intended to kill Eirik, but she too had engrained, long in the tooth habits, particularly against the way of the intruding wolf. She believed that those purebred creatures of transmogrification, like Janus and Big Bad, were no better than the half-human Wolf Mongrels kept cruelly as slaves and for sport by the Giant and Witch clans in the far Northern Lands. Mogries, she called them – curs. The monthly Moon-turners were just unfortunates.

Mr Woolfe growled softly at Grandmother May's unyielding beliefs and Red Cloak ways. For better and worse both were individuals of instinct and action, not thought and reconciliation. As Janus began to circle the group, Grandmother May lunged towards her wingchair that held her knitting bag. From amidst her wool and paraphernalia she pulled out two weapons; a small, curving, double-edged knife and a pair of jumbo-sized knitting needles – number nine – which she grasped in the crossed sign of the rune of love. She kept the needles hovering in front of Janus's face as she began to shoo the silver-haired man out through the kitchen.

'Come on, Janus, old friend,' said Mr Littlesøn signalling to Janus from behind his mother's back, 'best be off home now. We'll deal with all this tomorrow… And thank you for looking after my son.'

Raoulf did not understand what was happening, but saw his father beckoning so he ran to his side. At the back door Grandmother May steeled herself whilst mumbling some basic, clumsy charms. Janus laughed at such quackery, but he did not underestimate her lethal intent for those bequeathed Cloaks of Red could be just as rabid as any she-wolf. Whilst Grandmother May ushered the silver-haired man out of her cottage she grabbed items from her kitchen shelf to throw after her unwanted guest: salt, meadow wool, and whittled chicken bones.

'No harm done, Mum,' said Mr Littlesøn. 'Come back inside and I'll make you some tea. Then I better get this one home… he looks like he's had quite an adventure.'

It was true. As Raoulf slowly pulled on his tattered coat to leave he stood in front of them a vision of strawberry-red, blood and caked-on mud. This sight at least cheered Grandmother May. So, in a shuffling, awkward silence, the night ended. Everyone dispersed knowing that nothing could be done to change the past or untell the tale from the telling. The cork was out of the Goblin bottle and from this moment a new future would come to pass for them all.

Mr Littlesøn took Raoulf home to a bath of bitter herbs Grandmother May had given them for just such an occasion – to ease the stings and lashes of the fight with the Forest. Mr Littlesøn gently removed the grime from his son's face and hair, whilst an excited, over-tired Raoulf retold his fantastic tale of trekking through the Night Forest – of Goblins and Fears, of talking trees and tormenting grasses, of Witches and wands and a mysterious exploding silver light.

At last, Raoulf was put into his pyjamas and led to a pillow of lavender and to a cosy bed that promised sweet dreams. He almost told his father about Mr Woolfe's strange story and the talisman he had been given, but decided against it as sleep was rapidly descending. Throughout the night he held on tight to the silver charm in his palm, the chain wrapped around his bruised, cut fingers. Ralph did not know what to make of the night's adventure, but his pillowed-head was abuzz with the bees of cloud Giants, bouncing beans and magical moonbeams that could turn boys into bats and hungry, howling wolves.

Feeling shaken and miserable, Mr Littlesøn sat up most of the night, smoking and drinking a bottle of cheap 'Ild Vand'. His wife had been gone almost a year now and his son was injured after the Night Forest's macabre initiation. He did not know what on earth he was going to do. Having no sense of self-control or being able to manage, he would just have to accept that Life was going to get considerably worse before it got any better, for he knew he had not hit the bottom of his barrel. Yet the wreck and rise of Mr Littlesøn's ruin still lay in the future. For now, he simply fell asleep on the sofa, burning cigarette holes in the chair all around him.

That night, after everyone had left, Grandmother May grabbed a handful of aromatic plants and sprinkled them around the cottage, completing the protection ceremony with a circle of ash and a smudge stick of sage. She warmed some sweet, spiced Glögg and sat on the porch in her favourite rocking chair sipping her wine until dawn, whilst muttering invocations she had learnt as a child: mumble magic, vexed hexes and strange incantations to block out the disturbing influence of Full Moon magic. Smoking her hand-rolled, clove cigarettes, she sharpened the edge of her beloved blades and whittled deer bone into barbed arrowheads. They hurt more when you did the wolf-men the favour of pulling them out. After that, she took to her knitting to occupy her nervous, fidgety fingers.

Janus Woolfe took the opportunity to run up to Fang Ridge Mountain and give his all to the moonlit night in a howling, trading his natural passion for compassion in a lamentation of exhausted will and recognition that events were truly beyond him. He had given Raoulf the talisman, but had it been the right thing to do? Running under the Moon's radiant aura he sensed that some good might yet come to be, but in what form he could not tell. Miracle makers were often like that, shaking their snake rattles for all their worth trying to influence the outcome, yet unable to predict the future. The Eye of Light reassured him there was fresh reason to hope; whereas the Eye of Dark showed him nothing but loneliness, heartache and dismal despair.

Either way, outcomes would have to wait as new possibilities curved away from the evening's events and disappeared around the mountain's corner. The terrain was hard and cold, but Janus Woolfe was used to that and did not complain about his earth bed for solitary wolf-warriors. It was a solid surface and he trusted that. He rolled in his sleep, yearning like a dog for its master, yelping and whimpering. The epilepsy of turning did not physically descend on Janus, yet he fitted and seized in his dreams as his mottled, silvery hair and tired mind absorbed the rays from the Towers of Dark and

Light. They poured into him their opposing plans. For Lone Silver Wolf, the journeying was almost over whereas for the younger wolf-lads and the last of the Fairy Folk it had only just begun.

Four bedtime wishes were made that evening: where feral darkness could be accepted as important as the light on the great journey home; where spell-infected spirit could live in harmony within community; where love and family could be united. These were the first three wishes, but of the fourth? Grandmother May caught it in her rusty-toothed mouth and spat it out into her grubby handkerchief. As the unutterable was taken from her cussing lips it was sunk deep into the belly of the Casket-of-Dark-Secrets, which would never let it be told. Why swallow truth when you could spit it out?

That night no-one slept well.

Miss Beret cried most mornings, but drowned her tear-filled eyes in her ritual showering. What use her sorrow when so many worlds were awash with grief? Crying had become such a habit she had almost forgotten the reasons behind her tears. Yet feelings still rose up silently and overwhelmed her from within. Oh yes! Now she could remember why she cried. It was for all the broken things that could not be repaired and for all the people who could not be replaced or made whole by the remembering.

Only now was Miss Beret coming to terms with the aging reality that physical beings caught in the World of Change could not always be renewed, and that some of those fallen people could not be helped up again: tinkers and tailors, soldiers and sailors, citizens and dancing denizens, the frail and the elderly, the young and the infirm, the strong and the good, the accidental and the intended, the rich and the poor. Everyone was caught up in Life's war of ceaseless activity.

After showering, Miss Beret hummed to herself to lift her spirits as she made up her bravest of faces. Her outward appearance was important; for the benefit of the school children if not for herself. So, she wrapped a towel about her raven-black hair, puckered her lips and cheeks until they were rosy and slowly prepared herself for the day ahead. She started by practising the sweetest of smiles in the mirror; the smile the children seemed most to like. Then she began putting on the rest of her makeup, but fingerprints kept appearing on the surface of the mirror in front of her. She wiped them away, but the whorls of fingertips simply re-emerged like the faintest of opening buds. The stubborn marks kept recurring despite her efforts to clean them off. Some things, it seemed, could never be removed.

It was as though someone was trying to communicate with her through the mirror. Miss Beret called aloud as if to some invisible, haunting presence, but there was no reply. There never was. Irritated by the unhelpful returning silence, she breathed on the glass, rubbed the mirror clean and then quickly applied a 'Veneer Spell of Cosmetic Protection' to stop the fingerprints from reappearing. Every morning, in that moment, the faint hope of Mother Rose was lost. From beyond the Land of Dreams her ghostly essence reached out to greet her only surviving Earth Land daughter, only to be vanquished once more by the one she sought to comfort. The fingerprint aura of Mother Rose faded in the last of the bathroom steam.

That was how Miss Beret started most mornings, with her pain stripped bare. She did not understand that her elemental surrender of tears was all that the water required – a form of restitution that helped her let the unspoken grief go. In truth, her slowly waking morning mind was reaching back in time for the missing memories of her family. Back then, the Huntingsman had called her Wild Rose – for she was spirited, brave and free in her Forest roaming – whilst on days such as these she was simply lost, trapped and hurting. Until story time, that was, when she would animate her reading aloud. For today, Miss Beret would draw upon her deepest sorrow and her highest joy to feed meaning to the children's gaping mouths and empty faces. The Little Darlings! She reached out for them now because they helped: both the small blue pills and the supposed purpose of children, that is.

The next morning Mr Littlesøn dropped his son off just around the corner from the School by the Park. As Raoulf hobbled past the black iron railings he saw a green-arched entrance to the Crossbones Garden of Peace. Peering through, he noticed a late blossoming, large-headed pink rose balancing heavily at the end of a thorny stem. Placed high up on the railings was a large, prominent sign:

"Do not play in the fountain. Do not walk on the lawn.

Do not enter the rose garden.

The picking of flowers, the purloining of blossoms and the knocking of conkers from trees is strictly prohibited!"

After the escapades of the previous night, Raoulf so wanted to pick the rose and give it to Miss Berry. Where once he had cried to leave his mother at the gates only a year before, he now loved his School, loved his teacher's laugh, loved the illustrated story books and the fanciful worlds they opened up to him. Under the tutelage of

Miss Berry he had almost read the entire library and he wanted to show his appreciation, for without her aid he would never have survived the Forest's terrifying adventure. As Raoulf weighed up the consequences the ominous sign continued:

"Do read the signs – then ignore them at your peril!"

So, Raoulf dared himself to do it. In matters of the heart he would become a rule breaker and outlaw just as daring as any pirate king, or as heroic and dashing as any knight or horse-mounted Forest Ranger.

As Raoulf limped across the lawn to the inner circle of roses it suddenly felt a much longer distance. He had to tug at the stem three times before the head of the rose twisted free. For his pains Raoulf suffered one deep thorny prick to the pad of his middle finger, right hand, as Mother Nature reminded him who had created the flower and to whom it truly belonged. Nature's karma was kind like that, would come back and slice your finger as quick as you please, if you were lucky. Thus Raoulf's thieving debt, one large bead of blood and some fresh remorse, were extracted right there and then – no prolonged sleep or other residual dues were required.

Shuffling back over the seemingly endless grass, Raoulf's ankle and hands still hurt from the events of the previous night, even with the protective plasters on his fingers and crude bandages on his ankle and thumb. He was terrified of a reprimanding shout from Gunnbjorn. The prospect of the long arm of the law grabbing him by the scruff of his tearaway neck made Raoulf hobble even faster, for the Park Keeper had hands that smelt of mud, pepper and gunshot, which you could smell when he grabbed hold of you. As Raoulf returned to the pathway, the single bead of blood dropped from his finger and stained the magnificent pink rose.

Raoulf's heart raced as he crossed the road, limping recklessly against the Lollipop Lady's wise request to 'Stop, Look and Listen'. He could hear in her voice a mother's concern; it was Billy Goat Plum's mum, so Raoulf waved back at her calling out he was sorry, but he was on a 'very important mission'. He was quite breathless as he entered the schoolyard and passed the statue of the Philosopher-Prince.

'Good morning,' Raoulf shouted up.

The Statue did not answer, but smiled wistfully as a Robin landed on his outstretched hand and chirruped at the boy,

'I'm glad you're safe.'

Yet there was no time to reply as Raoulf went into the building and climbed up the stairs to his classroom. As he passed through the door he squashed his elbows into his sides and clasped his hands together to avoid touching the brass Door Knob that had so recently held him under its shadowy spell. The Goblins and Fears recognised him and waved. They still seemed intent on hoodwinking all whom they could. Had he come back for more?

'Hello Raoulf,' said the inhabitants of the Door Knob in a friendly manner. 'Did you enjoy your time in the Forest last night?'

Raoulf ignored the voices and kept his retort to himself for there she was, Miss Berry, sitting at her desk collecting undesired rosy red apples with the loveliest of smiles. He had more important matters to think about than saving his own soul.

'Thank you so much,' Miss Beret lied politely to every child whose kindly meant apple she received and placed inside her desk drawer. 'Adorable. I'll eat it later.'

Bemused at the commotion of Raoulf's sudden entrance, Miss Beret glanced over. In one glad, painful dash, the Littlesøn boy stood next to her looking up. She looked down into his ruddy face and eager sparkling eyes. Who was this child toward whom she felt such fondness and believed she had so much in common? What unusual thing did he have for her in his hand and, more intriguingly, what was that around his neck glinting out at her from under his shirt collar? She found herself staring at Raoulf.

'For you,' said Raoulf handing over the treasured rose.

'For me?' Miss Beret enquired, somewhat relieved that it was not another apple.

'Yes,' the boy smiled, 'for you.'

'Why, thank you Raoulf... thank you very much. It's delightful.'

Raoulf could tell that it was a special moment, for Miss Berry was reaching out to hold the remarkably large-headed, multifoliate flower: a beautiful pink rose freshly stolen from an enchanted bush. She was leaning forward to smell the delicious perfume whilst exclaiming out loud that it was her favourite flower. Had Raoulf understood Janus's story correctly, cracked the code and guessed what needed to be done?

The hands on the classroom clock spun and sent a series of runic messages to its twin in the Headmaster's office, announcing that a boy's heart had found courage and that a young woman's heart was beginning to open. And that could only mean one thing – that the spell crafted to conceal Miss Beret's childhood tragedy was finally broken. The Headmaster looked up from the Mayor's letter on his desk and allowed himself a half-smile. After all, it was early days yet and worse would have to come before things could get better.

Meanwhile, Miss Beret was quite breath-taken. She was tearful. She was touched. She was smiling and lifting the rose to her nose again and again. It had a captivating mediaeval scent; one of enclosed gardens where lovers exchanged perfumed handkerchiefs with a kiss. If the bloom bore blood wildness, its curling petals promised the comfort of love that would harbour you safely despite Life's thorns. Recognition beyond reasoning and newfound fortune swelled in Miss Beret's heart as surely as loneliness fell from her face. Then there was also the faint, fascinating lullaby of Raoulf's Banshee blood calling out to her. What unexpected turning of love's tide was this?

In that moment Miss Beret's childhood 'Spell of Forgetfulness' started to ebb away and the memory of her Rose Family began to rise. The dream voice she heard calling out to her each morning belonged to her mother. Now she could see and hear her clearly. She was sitting in front of a mirror brushing her long, silky hair. She was talking to her eldest twin daughters who were sitting on the bed together braiding their hair with tiny red and white flowers. Rose Pink had come home late after playing in the woods. Grime smeared her hands and face as she placed her ever-muddy shoes by the door. Her mother shooed the twins away.

'Rose Pink?' her mother laughed taking her daughter by her dirty hands, 'we're going to play a game.'

Delighted, Wild Rose smiled and nodded.

'I want you to listen to my song and then sing it back to me. If anything ever happens to our family you must try to remember this rhyme. It might be hard for you to recall, but it will preserve a true memory of us should the time ever come that you feel all alone in the world and in want of great comfort. The song goes like this…

Sing a song of difference,

A pocket full of lies,

Remember me in bird song

And mirrors that can scry.

The woods are full of Wolf Men,

A-hunting they will go,

Roses Three will all miss me

Including one of Snow.

Yet my wild, dark-haired daughter,

Moonlit she will be,

Bringing love from newfound blood

So Spirit's always free;

The children will all greet her,

Giants and Witches too,

For in her grief a new-found leaf,

Rose Pink from out the blue…'

So Mrs Rose had encouraged her third daughter to dance about her bedroom as she sang her favourite song – the 'Rhapsody of Roses'. The melody was haunting and Miss Beret momentarily felt herself twirl about the classroom as though she were a princess spinning around in a magnificent ballroom. Like a delightful tune swirling from an opened musical box, her mother's song told her about the nature of the Rose Way and how she had come to be born.

Without warning, through her mother's eyes, Miss Beret could see a handsome Huntingsman brushing through the Forest branches. There, underneath the boughs of a Crooked Oak, her mother, sweet-scented as roses, fell easily into Eirik's strong, embracing arms and onto the mossy, sunlit floor. The idyllic scene entranced Miss Beret. Was this a glimpse of her true father?

More importantly, as the 'Spell of Forgetfulness' continued to lift, this was the first memory she recalled where her mother spoke her true name – Rose Pink. It was a name that joyfully connected to her sisters, the Roses Red, White and Snow. To her twin sisters she had been known playfully as Logan Berry, as she was always out wandering the woods and picking fruit and fresh Forest flowers from the faraway fields. Is that why the children had trouble pronouncing her name? Is that why she had chosen Beret? She wondered now, with all her heart, what had become of her three beautiful sisters?

Then there was the intriguing matter of her father's silver talisman hanging around Raoulf's neck. What had happened to him last night after he had left the School? She then became scared as the fearsome visages of Wolves, Witches and Giants reared up in front of her before falling away, lost in a crashing wave of swirling smoke, gunshot and fire. What did Raoulf know of her father? The wheels of fate turned, tumbled, and with a quick, quiet click the locked safe of her heart opened. Although Miss Beret did not know it fully, not quite yet, Raoulf had achieved what had previously been considered impossible; he had, with the help of Janus and his fabulous stories, cracked the Rose code and simultaneously sealed their fates.

Raoulf beamed, for he knew that today Miss Berry would read them the best story ever for she was… Well, she was just so full of joy; so full of memory and pleasure, courage and smiles. It was a new-found love for all the children's faces looking up at her in hope, because for them the whole wide world lay ahead and fantastic future patterns were waiting to be drawn on their daring hearts and minds.

'My little darlings!' she thought. 'And you, Raoulf, my brave soldier. What have you done?'

For all of them, Miss Beret would be able to express and convince them of a love that never went away, not for all the departures in the world. Not faint hope, but Love's spiritual and abiding reality. This was her day, a special and perfect day, and nothing would stop her sharing her joy with the children. For in today's Story of Stories she would dig deep and enter with them into another exciting quest in the realm of fairy tale and wonderful adventure. Only Miss Beret did not know which one yet; could not guess which story she would tell at all.

Unfortunately for Miss Beret and the other infant teachers – Ms Applepip, Ms Cherrystone and Mrs Peppercorn – today was also the day on which the Headmaster made an ominous announcement in the morning assembly. After the usual round of enthusiastic piano playing by Mrs Peppercorn, accompanied by the off-key recorders and tuneless singing of the children, the Headmaster cleared his throat and declared,

'It is with much sadness that I have to inform you… that the School is to be closed.'

There, he had said it. In the end it was as simple and as difficult as that. A ripple of dismay ran through the stunned staff, whilst the children were only mildly fazed. Shuffling in their seats, looking around, they silently mouthed to one another as they tried to figure out whether or not it meant less homework and extra holidays. Billy Goat Plum grinned and nudged Raoulf.

'When?' asked the ever-practical Ms Cherrystone over the din.

Looking out at the sea of youthful faces the Headmaster suddenly felt old, sad and somewhat fatigued. 'As far as I understand,' he replied glumly, 'the School will be closed at the end of the Summer term.'

Thunderstruck, the teachers herded their pupils together and led them distractedly through the corridors to their first lesson. Ms Applepip's 'Spelling Bee' was a complete disaster, whilst Ms Cherrystone's class recounting of the times tables by rote was left entirely uncorrected as the children mumbled their way through the difficult 6's and 7's. Mrs Peppercorn's 'Quick Fire' question round on Danish historical rulers from the reign of King Cnut the Great steadily disintegrated into a farce, ending in factual assassination. Likewise, Miss Beret's rather shambolic class was making very little progress with the few yoghurt pots, tin cans and pieces of string that had been brought in. The children, as well as the teachers, were equally distracted and bemused.

Looking outside in exasperation, Ms Applepip was struck with a sudden moment of brilliance, an ingenious strategy that resulted in all the children being immediately sent on a premature and extended playground break. The children quickly ran off to play hopscotch, skipping and 'Ghost in the Graveyard' – a spooky game of tag if they could find Charlie Cartwheel to be 'it'. The classroom clocks were busily reporting the morning's chaotic activities to the Headmaster who hurriedly called a staff meeting in the hall.

'Yes, a car park and a new building project are in the offing. Of course I will do all that I can to help relocate you, but each must tend to their needs and look to their departure. The Mayor has made it quite clear what he intends to do…'

Here the Headmaster lifted up the Mayor's 'Closure Notice' and shook it in the air. The letter, deliberately designed to bamboozle, contained a series of unreasonable requests, difficult demands and conflicting interests.

'…Unless, of course, someone can stop him in time. I will talk to you all individually about the proposal and what you wish to do in due course. However, today must press on as usual. Time and tides, eh Miss Beret?'

Here the Headmaster stopped to beam at his ward. Miss Beret, looking rather dismayed, was feeling overwhelmed by the morning's unfolding events. So the kindly Headmaster discretely ushered her into a corner away from the other teachers.

'You must still hold your afternoon Teapot Tales storytelling session, my dear. I feel it's very important today for the children to imbibe their special tea, as well as for you to do your own emptying and tipping. For the sake of the children's equilibrium, pour into their cups a refreshing Darjeeling brew. Remember, different endings need new beginnings. Effects and causes, you know. Is the Mayor's "New Book of Joy" still on loan?'

'It is, Headmaster,' Miss Beret replied utterly perplexed.

'Then perhaps tell them my favourite tale: "The Stubborn Sea and the Feet-Splashed King". Or how about "Polly Coal and the Bubbling Kettle of Skald".'

'Perhaps "The Wittering of Twits and the Half-Told Tale" would be more appropriate?' countered Miss Beret abruptly.

'Ah yes! That was always a good one especially the characters of Twit Hooting and the Two Who Owl. Some stories are never too old for the re-telling…'

'Rather like "The Donkey, The Ass and The Goat of the Golden Mountain",' Miss Beret retorted.

'There's certainly an unexpected kick in the tale with that one…' he smiled. 'Of course, there's always the frightening saga of "The Hungry Birds and the Witch's Cake" or the cautionary account about "The Mole Who Dug Too Deep"…'

'But Headmaster,' interrupted an exasperated Miss Beret, 'what about the School?'

Miss Beret loved the Headmaster dearly, but she was positively flummoxed by his approach to this most serious of days. She could not believe the news. Having taught at the School for the past two years, it was the one place that offered stability in her otherwise out-at-sea life. Up until an hour ago she was having the most perfect of mornings. Now everything seemed quite hopeless. The Headmaster paused before looking deeply into Miss Beret's puzzled eyes…

'Of course there's always "Goat's Beard" – the final tale of tales. I hear it's abroad again and the timing might be ripe.'

This particular title startled Miss Beret.

'Why, I don't think I know that one. It's right at the end of the "New Book of Joy" but the pages are missing…'

'…As though a Giant's thumb had clumsily turned the page and torn them?' the Headmaster mused out loud as though in a daze of distant events and difficult recollections. 'Or perhaps pages hastily ripped out to swaddle a stolen baby?'

A deep silence fell between them until the Headmaster pulled himself back from his gazing at the past to look meaningfully at Miss Beret.

'Torn pages? A stolen baby? The missing story?' she replied confounded. 'Sorry, Headmaster, I don't understand.'

'That's the point,' the Headmaster continued, 'nobody knows "Goat's Beard" until its secret is revealed and then you remember it as though it was once told to yourself in your childhood and that you have known it all your life.'

'But Headmaster, how does that relate to me?'

'The "New Book of Joy" is on loan to us, but how did the Mayor acquire it in the first place? Where did the book come from and why did it seek you out? Perhaps that's the mystery that should now make you curious.'

'It is rather magical...' she mused.

'Indeed it is, my dear. If you inspected the book's cover closely you'd think it might have once been in a tragic fire or blasted by an unusual enchantment... and, according to the hands on my Rune Clock this morning, I believe a child has already found the key to the unlocking of a certain 'Forgetfulness Spell'...'

Miss Beret looked quizzical as the Headmaster paused to admire the palpable blooming of her Rose heart.

'Perhaps the book can help you further. Was it rescued, one might ask, or stolen? Trust in the children as I trust in you. They will help you fill in the missing pages. Just listen to them, for they know that some special day you will share your exciting story with them. Perhaps that day is today. Then you'll discover the untold aspects of your childhood waiting for you within the silence... Do you comprehend?'

'To be honest Headmaster,' replied a mystified Miss Beret, 'I'm not sure that I do. My childhood memories are so vague, but this morning I had a vision of my mother calling out my real name...'

'Rose Pink?' enquired the Headmaster.

'Yes... but how did you know?'

The Headmaster smiled. 'Until the spell was broken no one could speak your name or mention your past. It will take time to adjust to your awakening memories, but you now need to listen and trust your visions. Your mother did and that is why you alone of her daughters are standing here today.'

Miss Beret was taken aback at the Headmaster's mention of her mother and her sisters.

'My child, believe me when I say that you are not a forsaken Rose, but the one truly saved. It was all your mother could do in the most difficult and strangest of circumstances.'

Miss Beret stared at him, helplessly pleading for more information, but he seemed only to reminisce and drift further away.

'She did it all for the sake of love, my dear.' Then he quietly added, 'You get your special kind of survival and distinctive bravery from both your mother and your father.'

The Headmaster caught himself in his reverie as he glimpsed the ethereal forms of Mother Rose and Eirik the Huntingsman standing behind her; the strange harmonious unity of the two in their child standing before him. Encouragingly, he continued to explain...

'In my day, of course, "Goat's Beard" was called something quite different. "Old King Cloud and the Goat of Yester Yore" I seem to re-call, but that's many generations ago. My, my, how quickly Time passes and because it starts off so slowly it tricks you, then suddenly... bam! You find yourself old. Do you understand?'

Baffled, Miss Beret shook her head. 'Not really, Headmaster...'

'Soon it will be time for me to take my leave. You are concerned about your role and the fate of the School, but the truth is I cannot remain here much longer and cannot hold back the racing tide of New Times. I need to stand down and this unfortunate turn of events is my opportunity. I protected you once as a child in deep distress, but I cannot do so again. That which your heart was seeking, remembrance of events past, has turned and found you. Your future now beckons... and you alone can step into that.'

The Headmaster beamed in a self-congratulatory manner. He thought he had explained everything in a particularly clear and helpful manner, whilst a dumbfounded Miss Beret was left reeling.

'Remember, the answer is never the end, merely a question waiting to take you on further.'

Then, with a quick hop, skip and a jump, the rambling Headmaster turned away toward the other teachers gathered at the far end of the hall. Ms Cherrystone was flicking through a travel brochure engrossed in wishful exotic holiday plans. Ms Applepip was busy discussing her upcoming wedding arrangements with Mrs Peppercorn, who occasionally interjected with sage advice whilst practising some unusual chords on the piano. Looking extraordinarily like a flustered White Rabbit, the Headmaster reached into his waistcoat for his pocket-watch that dangled like a missing Star-Compass at the end of his fob chain.

'Good gracious,' the Headmaster asked loudly, 'is that the time? Heaven help us all! Ms Applepip, do you mind gathering the children back into the hall? I think I shall tell them the story of "The Fire Dragons' Tea Party" before lunch. After all, Dragons are so exciting and no adventure should be without one…'

So, events had finally come to pass. With the exception of his remaining interest in the lives of his secret wards, Miss Beret and Mayor Bear, the Headmaster was feeling tired and was becoming more and more detached from everyday School life. The thought of retirement, on full pension, was one he actually looked forward to. In fact, he felt somewhat relieved at the prospect of having less responsibility. The School could not go on living inside his protective bubble forever.

Much had changed during his time as Headmaster, former Mayor, and Mathmagician. He would stand down at the end of the academic year, whatever the School's fate, and write that 'Book of Secret Spells' he had always promised himself. Or perhaps travel whilst he still could. A last nostalgic journey back to the Old Hawk Land appealed to him – a one-way ticket to spend his final years conversing with the Fire Dragons. Plus, if the Headmaster had calculated correctly by glimpses into the Dragons' Star-Compass, the beginning of New Time was almost upon them. All the almanacs and calendars pointed to it. Until then he would simply aid the transition of the Sky Monk's 'Dream Plan' as much as possible.

Of course, he would protest Mayor Bear's decision to demolish the School and redevelop the site, and he felt particularly troubled on behalf of all his staff, the children and Town's remaining Fairy Folk. The question was – were they equally as concerned? And if so, then why not let them oversee the safeguarding of the School. It would be the natural conferring of strengths. At that particular prospect, the

Headmaster smiled wryly and left the hall to prepare for his epic storytelling session. Turning his head, he looked out of the window at the Statue surrounded by screaming children. The eyes of the Philosopher-Prince momentarily glistened.

Smiling, Little Star and Little Seed held onto each other's hands as they made their dreamlike descent. Unlike their sister Little Spark they were in no hurry, for they were still formulating their plans whilst falling through the Great Unknown. For them, consideration always came before reckless action. Could they aid each other in the unfolding of their desires? What were their secret wishes? They definitely wanted to help, but not at the loss of their own unique identities and expressions. Yet how could they be most of service?

Slowing their fall to give themselves more time to decide upon a course of action, the two sisters found they were steadily increasing in density, being wrapped in elemental matter and pulled by gravitational forces beyond their control. Being renegades with no guidance, they transmitted their situation telepathically to their surroundings and found uniquely different answers.

Little Star began to sparkle uncontrollably and was attracted by the Music of the Spheres, particularly by an a cappella ensemble somewhere left of the Milky Way. Twinkling like a three-dimensional snowflake she found she was twisting and transforming into startling geometric shapes and golden ratio holographic forms. Dancing across the cosmos Little Star reluctantly let go of Little Seed's hand and beamed her brilliance right across the sky.

'I rather fancy playing the saxophone,' declared Little Star smiling. 'Who'd have thought it – some light jazz?'

'Shine on,' Little Seed answered, laughing at her sister's audacity. 'See you back at Cloud Base Camp.'

Gracefully, Little Star pirouetted into position amongst the other members of the band, greeting musicians all. 'And remember to follow the guiding light.'

'I'll try. As far as I understand it's all in the swirl of dream-forgetfulness now...' Little Seed replied beginning to yawn.

'That's true. "To be born on the elemental side of life you must fall asleep to yourself. To return to spirit you simply must die",' quoted Little Star recalling a passage from the ancient Book of Law they had recently been studying.

Yet spinning in ever-forgetful circles Little Seed was no longer sure of the Whos, Whys and Whens. Even the Whatevers were slipping fast. They were now anybody's guess. As for the Which Ways and Where Fores, Little Seed simply trusted to love, luck and her own deservedness. She was at one with the Law of... Zzzzd's. Slowly, the deep sleep of enchanted princesses descended...

The Monk's projected vision of the 'One Dream Awakening' – shared by Seers, Healers and Grandmothers of Awe alike – was transmitted on the mid-Autumn Harvest Moon festival of the ninth month, old calendar, from the Sky City monastery. Abetted by the Star-Sandman, the 'One Dream' was trumpeted in by a smooth jazz band playing in the southern quadrant of our solar system. It told a tale of the 'Three-Hares-Three' seen dancing and boxing around the Moon, which was surrounded by a ring of woven hawthorn and overlaid by a circle of six-pointed stars as a crowning mystery.

The 'One Dream' spoke of May blossom (which you must never take indoors) that fell like snow, foretelling that a rose petal secret would descend on the mystical thirteenth sign of the zodiac, hidden between the months of May and June. It conveyed a message of chaotic endings and glorious beginnings new. In the shared dream, a wandering female minstrel, a timeless Princess with long golden hair, rose above a valley singing a song of yearning – a remembrance of souls lost yet still loved. It was a totem call to sleeping power animals across the land and to one soul in particular.

Yet amidst the looming conflict would the one needed to awake be able to heed the calling and respond? Soon all deadly fears would catch up with their owners for the fate of fairy tales entwined them all. Yet with age and authority, personal crisis and peculiar catastrophes often became more difficult to contend with. Now, the once purloining Flash Jack was just plain, plodding Peter with his shadow firmly stitched to his stocking feet – however itching for adventure they still sometimes felt.

Poor Peter, he of the unfortunate muddle-head. Beanstalks and faded roses were all that remained of Mayor Bear's faint memories in regard to his family… because he had systematically eradicated all thoughts of his deceased parents and forsaken sisters from his mind. Yet his fanciful pretence, daily disregard and thoughtless actions were merely a defence to keep the painful recollections at bay; they hurt too much otherwise. Underneath, his true wishes, hopes and dreams continued to diminish as the protective, positive aspects of the 'Befuddlement Charm' wore out. Silver linings and blissful conclusions were wearing thin as an expanding tonsure-like baldness and receding hairline both testified.

So, in a desperate bid to move forward, the Mayor turned his attention to the sanctioning of his official plans and the strategic distribution of his increasingly unpopular policies. With the assistance of Gunnbjorn and his gun-toting mates, pamphlets were handed out all around Town. Unhelpfully, the blustery West Wind whipped the pages up and scattered them everywhere. Sticking to lampposts, slipping through railings and whirling along pavements, the informative flyers flew into the air and into the faces of passing people and flapping pigeons alike.

How the Wind laughed, racing after the leaflets, chasing them down Rat-Cat Alley where it tore the screaming sentences apart...

"With due date sounded on September airs... to everyone with listening ears... a resounding remittance of Progress and its accompanying fears... with nine months' notice of the closure of churches and the ceasing of bells... the termination of Schools and the construction of new builds, car parks and municipal hells... warnings are herewith given to all those concerned – resist at your peril and get your fingers burned. Sundry players fearing the loss of jobs shall be restructured in accordance to the conventions and procedures of mayoral plans... blithering bureaucracy and bombastic barnacles, as necessitated in article nine of the policy for ninnies, nincompoops and nautical numbskulls... blah, blah, blah... with no sense of regret and the smallest of small print, you are now politely informed that... and those doomed to stand in the way of advancement and speed with the foreseeable loss of land and hat... etcetera, etcetera... replaceable you... that life will continue... sincerely ours..."

Hush-hush, lip-tight, the leaflet's proclamation slipped out of the Mayor's smug, self-satisfied, transacting hand and swept across the Land of Awe. Outrage! Word-of-mouth stitched up as a job well done, as rumours of education versus profit and loss scurried abroad. The partnership between the State and its People became more divided. Fingers were pointed and accusations abounded as the exhumed dust of carpet-swept rugs divulged their dirty secrets. Those in command refused to listen, learn or take responsibility and the People no longer accepted the things they could not change.

Front-page parochial news continually landed in the lap of the frustrated Mayor, who secretly hired several Zephyrs to cause local disturbances in a bid to divert the public's attention. However, the Zephyrs' freak, out-of-season ice storm and the inexplicable appearance of crop circles in the nearby Wild Fields did not distract the denizens of the Jutted Land from their rabid pursuit of mayoral accountability. Self-interest and exploitation raised their ugly heads as Gunnbjorn, and his hunting mob, turned toward the Dark Tower looking for affirmation and legitimacy of their rising hate. The Eye of Light responded and countered with rays of upsurging hope.

Yet however much the Mayor tried to make things disappear, people, memories and events would not go politely away. Beleaguered, the Mayor groaned as headaches became the order of his day.

Meanwhile, the biting, northerly winds brought news from the Lava Fields of Fire Dragons taking to the air, their winged shadows casting terror across the lands. Their scorching tongues of amber ash, and spray of sparking embers, heralded the much-predicted end of Old Time. In the Jutted Land of Awe, the Dragons lifted the lid on the groaning Casket-of-Dark-Secrets, whilst rays from the Tower of Light swept through the Palace ruins. Graves opened. Fear escaped. The evil of Giant destruction and the foulness of Witches rejoiced once more, as the stale breath of dusty faked sighs and filthy rotten lies slipped out of the Casket and crept across the land. In the hollows a new horror arose, as the torn truths of ripped out hearts crept across the Forest floor as maniacal savage murder.

The bells of Saint Hansel and Saint Gretel solemnly tolled, blown on the beating wings of passing Dragons who summoned the souls of old. The Sky Monk's time of Prophecy had arrived: a phase in the world where revelation would win and secrecy would hang its sorry head in shame. The Dragon's 'Spell of Quick Reckoning' began to reel all the Townsfolk in. In abeyance, the Two Towers shone their penetrating lights into the Lands of Ore, Awe and Yester Yore. Allegiances were to be tested. A war was pending and souls were no longer safe.

Unpredictably, the good people of Town hit back. The Fairy Folk, Girl Guides and members of the Women's Institute, under the direction of the Eye of Light, pledged their green and dextrous fingers, their knowledge of the knitting arts and sewing crafts, as well as their considerable jam-making and baking skills, to fundraising and increasing awareness.

On the steps of the Mayor's office a group of young single mothers, dressed up as out-in-the-cold penguins, performed a song entitled 'Paradise'. The song was a political reminder of the investment hazards and short-termism of Car P-P-P-Parks, unfriendly environmental planning and detrimental social thinking. Would 'Paradise' prove to be popular enough to capture the imagination of those on the street and pique the conscience of those presently in command?

The public demonstration was inspired by those who were there the first time around, that most unexpected of demographics – the Grandmothers of Awe. The ever-watchful birds had recently observed a host of cardigan-wearing Grandmothers, already in full Winter knit, tootling off to celebrate their Harvest Festival success. Soon their fabled 'Champagne Campaign' would begin, as the collective elderly women of Town returned to the promotion of peaceful hippy protest: of Sixties love, of longhaired, eco-friendly social awareness, of elbow power, of not-so-quiet placard and banner-waving revolution within the community. So the spiritual goats of Awe slowly gathered the people of Town together.

At the Hazy Days Care Home, the Grinnies, Grannies, Ninnies and Nannies were all huddled around a large glass-topped table drinking their morning coffee and nibbling their butter biscuits and cinnamon cakes. They were chortling delightfully over a letter they had received from an anonymous, wandering, female minstrel that Ninny Nanny was reading aloud.

'Well, I do declare…' interrupted Nanny Nine Toes, but what that declaration was no-one ever knew as she descended into a spluttering fit of coughing and giggles. Mable Fable rummaged through her handbag, carefully avoiding some coins and gems stashed away at the bottom, and took out an old-fashioned cough drop. Silly Tilly, who was dozing in a chair by the viewing window, gently roused and listened with interest. Squinting her watery eyes, Ninny Nanny carried on reading…

'…donating my services free of charge to the 'Save-our-School' crusade… in light of which I have written an 'Angel Song' especially for you to perform at Town's 'Ceremony of Carols'… and would be delighted to sing at any future 'S-O-S' charity events…'

'How wonderful,' they all agreed.

So it was that the coordinated revenge of the Grandmothers of Awe began to bubble under, aided by the Philosopher-Prince, the strangeness of birds, and the sharing of the Sky Monk's 'One Dream'. The beloved Grans and much-loved Nans did not care if it seemed that they had lost their minds, for they could still muster the will to care and had the energy for one last fight.

Poor Mayor Bear!

The ever-masticating cows could have informed the Mayor and the people of Town what was going on, for they had recently jumped over the new Frost Moon to view the unfolding Heavenly Plan, but nobody was listening to the silent grazers and sacred star-gazers. Few could speak or were interested in the monosyllabic moo and so, unfortunately, no-one bothered to ask them. Ignored, the cows simply continued chewing the grass and minding their daily udder business, whilst secretly thinking, 'Oh dear, but I told you so.'

Unexpectedly, almost magically, the charitable concerns of the Grandmothers of Awe swiftly rocketed and funds began to roll in. Unease began to descend on the Authorities of Awe as anti-establishment feelings continued to bubble and brew. The Town's former disinterest in parasitic parliamentarianism and fund-rich intermediaries grew into active dislike, particularly of the self-aggrandising Mayor. The Fire Dragon's promised time of 'No Status-No Secrets' was rapidly descending and everyone in the Land of Awe was being forced to empty their pockets in 'Heart Reckoning Account and Compassionate Recompense'. Ownership was all, avoidance impossible.

Embarrassingly for Mayor Bear, some Giant artefacts wishing to return home to their rightful owners began to misbehave. Some of his beans, long hidden under his mattress, started jumping again, itching for the stalking, whilst the Hand-Mirror of Truth was beginning to reveal more than anybody should. The Asylum inmates were beginning to wail and rise. So this was the way that the Mayor's world would end, not with a whimper, but with growing fear, disorder and the dreadful fallout of another big bang. Only this time it would be him caught in the implosion.

Ever since the Autumn half-term, Raoulf knew things were going to be different. One night, in a half sleep, he had heard his bedroom door click open and felt his mother's shadow stealing softly over him as she kissed his forehead. Bestowing her love in a final goodbye, Mrs Littlesøn whispered sweet dreams into her son's ear and a lullaby of such deep sleep that he could not resist, despite all his struggles to get to the wakened bedside shore. His mother meant so much to him, but she had cocooned him in song from which he could not escape. She had the power now to extract and emit sound to her bidding, but to what cost her personal happiness?

When Mr Littlesøn roused Raoulf the next morning he explained to his son that his mother had returned to collect a few things before leaving. She was moving to Slow, a small town by the sea not so far away, where she would convalesce. The coast was good for that. Looking out to sea, Mrs Littlesøn would rest in a place overseen by the Church of St. Silence in the ward of Mary and Jacob White. The spiritual sisters would watch over her for a time until she could fully control her new-found wings and trust her voice.

Mr Littlesøn told Raoulf that he could visit his mother when the weather was warmer in the Summer, and they would explore the pirate caves, diving off dinghies and rocks, and discover all the fun of crashing waves and windswept coastal ways. They could see each other whenever they wished, but in the meantime Raoulf would live with his father. Raoulf understood then that his mother would not be coming back to live with them; never again would they all be together. So, something eventually ended between his parents that had actually ended emotionally many months before.

Whether by force or her own volition, Mrs Littlesøn had released the Unscreamable Scream and now wished to keep others out of harm's way. Well, until she fully understood the forces operating deep within. She was fascinated by the strength of her wings and had learnt how to fly by throwing herself off the Asylum roof. Even tethered, it had been thrilling to unleash her Banshee and hover upon the swirling breezes. Occasionally the Ravens and Crows of Black Nest would circle by, cawing, and she would playfully sing and get on their nerves. She knew then that she could be happy, and after all her terrible struggle and sadness she deserved that.

In the meantime, Raoulf wondered what his father would do for Mr Littlesøn was stumbling around like a lost child. Suddenly, in the new pain of confirmed loneliness, he no longer understood what his life was about. Newly hatched Banshee and spell-tainted Wolf had come to a crossroads and in the final stare, the final screaming and howling, had taken different paths as best befitted their natures. It was the most difficult of decisions and Mr Littlesøn mumbled to his son that he was sorry,

'Sorry for the way things had turned out… sorry for not being around… sorry for leaving you to cope on your own.'

After that, few words were spoken between them.

So, as Raoulf watched his father trudge through the gloomiest of days, he sensed that everything was different now; that something had been lost forever. Raoulf came to understand that what is seen on the surface differs from what lies under the skin, that things are not always what they seem to be, and that if you had eyes to see and ears to hear you had to change your way in light of new thinking. Adjustment was necessary for survival – his evening in the Forest had taught him that. However deeply sorry for his parents' unhappiness Raoulf felt, he wanted both of them to be well and contented. If that meant not being together then they must separate like leaves that tumble away from the same branch of a tree.

Yet if Autumn had been the natural and necessary time of departure, then a cold Winter backdrop befitted the Littlesøn's new painful situation. Raoulf struggled to believe that there could be a different outcome for them all, and he felt increasingly isolated and sorry for himself. Even the infrequent visits by Billy Goat Plum could not revive his diminishing spirits. The weeks passed and circumstances changed for Raoulf and his parents. By the time of the Christmas holiday he could tell by his mother's letters that she was getting better in her recuperation, but for his father things were getting worse as the excesses of smoking and drinking took hold.

Mr Littlesøn spiralled down into hurt and aimless wandering. Letting go was the hardest thing he had ever experienced for he feared the wrath of the beast that lived within. He had a son to care for, but still he escaped to the mountains where the howling became more and more frequent, more and more desperate, more and more unbearable and out of control. Mr Littlesøn took to his motorbike and spent nights out with the Lone Lads. Unknowingly, he walked upon a cliff's edge. Janus stood by, imploring the Moon to save Raoulf's father from the madness of the deep Wolf-ravine. The Moon watched down, but for all her pity did not intervene.

Father and son roles were reversed. At night Raoulf would lead his drunken father to bed or cover him with blankets if he could not rouse him from his sofa sleep. Then he would wake his father in the mornings with tea and buttered toast before sending him on his grudging way to work.

'Come on, Dad. It'll be all right…' but neither really believed the sentiment.

Grandmother May visited regularly, but Raoulf withdrew himself to the imperceptible place of childhood's imaginings, as he tried to shut out the troubles of the discomforting adult world. He grew feverish and dived down into the feathery covers of his bed, falling into the childish place of unwellness. Pent up with pain, tears of unfairness filled Raoulf's eyes, whilst his unanswered wishes and unfulfilled dreams piled high. Discarded pillows, prayers and teddy bears littered his bedroom floor as his hopes for a happy family life were slowly stripped away.

As Christmas approached Raoulf's spirits sunk further and his disappointment swirled in the first settling snow. To everyone else the low-rising morning Sun felt good through the bare Winter branches. To Raoulf it was nothing but a raw, blue sky and a continuing sharp snap of an unwelcome 'Cold Spell'. He felt shut out from the usual cheer of Christmas so pretended it did not matter. He often wondered to himself – was he the only one not walking in a Winter Wonderland?

Meanwhile, Miss Beret missed seeing Raoulf – her valiant pupil who so loved her stories. She was therefore delightfully surprised to bump into him and his father at the Winter solstice 'Ceremony of Carols' in the Old Town Square. Raoulf was unusually withdrawn toward her and would not let her newfound happiness in, whereas the chance meeting pleasantly surprised Mr Littlesøn. His previous interaction with Miss Beret had been a hostile one – for she had berated him for leaving Raoulf forgotten at the School gates. She had questioned his responsibilities as a father, but what could he say that would not expose his lupine secret?

Now, desperately overcompensating, Mr Littlesøn apologised effusively for missing the recent end of term parents' evening. It had fallen on yet another Full Moon howling. Laughingly, Miss Beret brushed his faltering excuses aside, although oddly numerous fathers had also been absent that night. Mr Littlesøn was intrigued by her charm and naiveté, for was there not the faintest fragrance of fox emanating from her, similar to that which he had previously discerned, as if in a dream, one wolf-turning night three Moons ago? So, standing there in a moment of shared fondness for music, the Christmas tree of Town was lit and carols began to fill the frosty Square.

Then the collective Goat Grandmothers of Awe, now known as the 'Try-and-Stop-Me-Can't-Sing-Choir', gathered around the rest of the singers to chant a specially written grace-carol – an 'Angel Song' best sung by as many out of tune voices as possible. From out their champing mouths and croaky throats, strange melodies and hummed harmonies echoed around, yet somehow a charming sound was created. The song, combining with the vapours of warm Glögg and the choir's billowing breath, slowly formed into the ethereal shape of a shimmering Air Angel, which hovered joyfully above them.

Something deep inside Miss Beret stirred. She loved this cold time of year and the musky scent of Raoulf's awkward father seemed rather alluring. She felt somewhat intoxicated, yet bemused, by Mr Littlesøn's abashed and somewhat shabby outer appearance, whilst simultaneously thrilled by the majesty of his inner, turning wolf. It was an altogether odd concoction. After the carols they chatted briefly over glasses of mulled Glögg and cinnamon strudel, talking about Town's upcoming Yuletide celebrations. With its sparkling lights, the large Christmas tree loomed above them all, but the tree's presence only upset Raoulf further. He recognised this tree from the Forest and a pain shot through his thumb in sharp remembrance.

'Too many Christmas trees,' mumbled Raoulf, who was in no mood for festivities.

Raoulf pulled his father away, insisting that there was to be no Christmas tree indoors that year as he had, temporarily, grown to hate them. Equally, he had no time for carols or grace or strangely materialising Air Angels, for the sound of a Frost Giant being torn apart in the Icy Wastes, last battlefield of the renegade Banshees, now filled his ears. Miles away Raoulf could hear his mother praying. It was a terrible, eerie sound, racked with pain, emitted by the few remaining Banshees in commemoration of their solstice self-exile.

Hovering overhead, the Air Angel took fright at the sound like a fleeing ghost, blasting right through the trio standing below. Suddenly feeling somewhat cold and ill at ease, Miss Beret said goodnight and took her leave. The Angel followed Raoulf and his father as they walked home, floating like a cloud above them. The Angel's outline was like the vapour that could sometimes be seen rolling down the southern crescent of Fang Ridge – shimmering and misty. Feeling somewhat despondent, Raoulf tried to ignore the Angel and forget all about the dreary concert and upsetting tree.

Overnight, a freezing frost swept the Jutted Land, chilling the air and covering the ground with white. Raoulf awoke to find the ice-covered body of one of his pet rabbits, which only helped compound his misery and sense of unfairness further. His father helped dig a small grave in the hard, bare earth at the bottom of the garden. After a brief burial ceremony, Raoulf went to the Fir trees and angrily snapped off a small, low-lying branch. He plaited a wreath and made an effigy out of torn twigs to place upon the grave. Raoulf felt truly alone. As he scrunched heavily over the frozen grass back towards the house, the Air Angel from the carol concert appeared and floated alongside him.

The Angel told Raoulf that he had come to stay for a while, until the Spring, and would live in the tree house at the bottom of the garden – if that was all right with him? Shrugging, Raoulf said yes, but he in turn mentioned it to his father who was at first bemused by his son's story. Like most parents, Mr Littlesøn believed that all children had imaginary friends, whilst he knew for a fact that some of the older boys had real, inner, animal fiends to contend with. So his father did not mind how his son spent the short Winter days, as long as he was pleasantly distracted and coping. The rest of Raoulf's problems were left for his Grandmother to deal with.

Yet as Mr Littlesøn continued to frequent the bars and places of Christmas festivity he became more and more aware of a kindly talkative presence, which often over-shadowed and sat next to him. The Air Angel easily slipped away from the Winter-fuelled despair of the son to that of the lost, drinking father. The Angel explained to Raoulf that supporting his father was important for the hatching of future Easter Eggs and the benefit of all. Raoulf comprehended little of what the Angel said, but he could see that his father was happier, less lonely, so he simply upped thumbs to show that he understood and was all right with the situation.

For Raoulf, Christmas meant little but dawn mists, drawn in days of darkness and early evening chill. Familiar absence and unwelcome change were upon him, although he still enjoyed spending time with his Grandmother, who made him porridge with honey and told him tantalising tales about a land she had once visited called Yester Yore. Raoulf learnt that his Grandmother, in her prime, had been the best knife thrower in a travelling circus. It was there she had met his grandfather who had been the human target in her wheel-turning, balloon-popping act of the 'Fantastic Impalement Arts'. They were all rovers by nature so there had been no question of settling down and that was where Raoulf's father had grown up – with the wandering circus gypsies.

Meanwhile, Mr Littlesøn welcomed the companionship of the Air Angel for it was a way of passing time and practising a new type of communication and friendship; a fresh and safe approach to answering questions of uncomfortable feeling and truth. It was a useful solitary practice, for as he slowly responded to the Angel's questions and viewpoints he became aware that he was not alone in his predicament. Consequently, Mr Littleson started looking beyond the swagger of motorbike escape and the prolonged drinking bouts with the Lone Lads at their tired 'Camaraderie of Crocodiles' haunt.

It was then that Miss Beret's fox-like curiosity came to sniff out his intriguing wolf-scent. Suddenly, for the first time since her Europa travels, Miss Beret started to enjoy her newfound self. Together they explored Town's Christmas events, carousing with the crowds of the local music scene. Christmas and the New Year passed quickly in a swirl of social activity and fun. Then, an unexpected snowstorm from the bitter North descended; a battering, South-sweeping blizzard which encased the Jutted Land, separating families and killing many. Encased in snow and ice, everything stopped.

After the significant storm-delay, the Folkeskole's Spring term eventually started, but a month later than usual. Reluctantly, Raoulf trudged back to School only to find the kind tutelage of the Winter Pink Rose, Miss Beret, in full bloom. She was back with her little darlings and she had discarded the small blue pills. Once more he began to enjoy her daily reading of the terrifying Lost Stories. Time slowly moved the early, frost-hardened months of the year on. A thaw began. Elsewhere, Mr Janus Woolfe and Mayor Peter Bear began a series of difficult meetings.

'I've come to return this,' said Janus placing the large illustrated "New Book of Joy" upon the Mayor's desk.

'Ah yes! The "Book of Horrible Stories for the Correction of the Childhood Condition",' the Mayor replied wryly.

'The book has many names and uses,' Janus re-joined.

'But best to sort the nippers out whilst young and still malleable, don't you think?'

'Sort out!' Janus snapped, watching the Mayor wandering purposefully about the room. 'Perhaps the book would be better off in the library than in your private collection.'

'It is a regular loan, you know. Just one of several special gifts lent to the people of Town…' said the Mayor pleasantly.

'Of course, very generous… and the Headmaster thanks you. But it's funny how the origins of such items can be conveniently forgotten…'

'Meaning?' enquired the Mayor abruptly.

'That truth can be distorted and artefacts manipulated for personal gain,' Janus replied simply.

'History lost in the re-telling, whilst progress tramples over the customs and beliefs of your Old Wolf Way?' the Mayor retorted.

'Perhaps,' said Janus. 'Is that what you're doing?'

Ignoring Janus's question, the Mayor blithely continued, 'You see, we can't always agree with those who dedicate themselves to governance and power. Particularly those of a certain generation with old, aching, complaining bones…'

'But someone has to make the tough decisions on our behalf…' Janus mumbled sarcastically.

'Precisely,' said the Mayor manoeuvring around his large oak desk toward a Golden Lyre sitting in the centre. He casually stroked a pen against the strings. An enchanting ringing suddenly filled the room.

"Lie and die," the Lyre sung. "Life is often over before it's begun."

On hearing the bewitching sound the truth of Janus's inner wolf rapidly began to surface. He clenched his fist and bit down on his lip to stop a rising howl from escaping. As he did so he tasted blood and a faint underlying scent of aconite – the toxic bane of Fairy women, snow leopards and turning-wolves alike. Cleverly concealed, it was wielded on visitors as part of a protection ritual – the Sky Monks' herb lore used for clearing unwelcome guests from any ground. Just one of many things Peter had learnt in the monastery.

'If that is everything Janus,' said the smiling Mayor gesturing nonchalantly toward the door, 'I believe you know the way out.'

Janus leant forward on the desk, his weathered hands and thick bulging veins on the verge of wolf-changing. Spit frothed from the corner of his snarling mouth. His blood boiled, his body ached, but biting the heart out of this dismissive man was not his job. No, the Headmaster had made it clear to him that was not The Way.

'Aid only the Monk's 'One Dream Awakening', Janus,' the Headmaster had warned. 'Keep your own power struggle out of it. You cannot use dark desire to do good here.'

Janus listened to the Headmaster's guiding voice instructing him not to be provoked into doing something regrettable. Resisting the urge to strike, he braced himself against the desk, breathing deeply to calm his inner conflict.

'Your self-possession is almost impressive,' retorted the Mayor, 'but please enlighten me, were you speaking of some self-confessed higher awareness and spiritual point of view – or just acting out old ideals under the instructions of another?'

Bristling, Janus said nothing.

'Now, now… don't be shy. You're most welcome to stick your paw in where your jaw won't go,' the Mayor taunted. 'Cynicism is so soul-destroying, or would you still have me believe in the rule of your Old Wolf Way?'

'You pompous ass!' Janus snarled at this powerful fool and unknowingly dichroic man standing before him. 'The Old Way is patient and waits for all to cross its mighty river…'

'Unlike you, my hot-headed friend! Patience was never one of your greater gifts. Am I to be your next sacrifice for the dark?'

'I'm considering it,' Janus countered baring his teeth, 'but I'm not feeling hungry right now.'

'A threat, Janus, is that what you're reduced to?'

Janus smiled whilst looking the Mayor up and down. 'Plump, but unappetising. I doubt anyone would miss you.'

'Gunnbjorn would hang and gut you if you touched me, and then what would your Moon Crew do? How long would they survive roaming the forest without you? Are they still misguidedly wondering when the curse will break, or have you found the gumption to tell them the truth?'

'Nobody knows the answer to that...' Janus faltered. 'Not even the Headmaster.'

"When the dream breaks, and shadows flee. That is when..."

The Mayor rapidly interrupted the singing Lyre. 'But what about you, Janus? Is this your final stand as the valiant Nordic Silver Wolf who once famously brought the Screech Queen and the Frost King to their knees? Or are you just another decrepit, failed follower of the Mathmagicians seeking salvation? Go on, tell me, are you still happy under the Headmaster's leash – Ulfhelm?'

Janus growled to hear his detested pet name spoken. 'Some of us operated from the inside.'

'Turn Tails often say that, but I'm intrigued... How did a life of being caged on behalf of the Mathmagicians' cleansing purge feel?'

Janus fell quiet. 'Perhaps the curse will never lift, but they can still live full lives without it destroying them or their families...'

'But it was never a possibility for you given your own twisted bloodline. Abandoned offspring of an uncaring Sorceress mother... just what the people of Town need!'

Momentarily, the room fell silent as the two men glared furiously at each other from opposite sides of the table. Slowly the Mayor continued,

'How long do you think it will be before you and your alleged saviour can turn this mess around?'

'As many Moons as Nature takes,' Janus countered.

'Really, Janus?' the Mayor asked incredulously. 'No plan, just another series of blood crimes and night terrors, waking up to find more dead bodies beside you. Old age and a weak stomach – is that why you're here? You must be fed up counting the carcasses on the monthly death watch by now.'

'Don't talk to me about death,' spat Janus. 'You've seen your fair share of corpses too. Remember the Sky Monks saying...'

'What! That "the jaws of death can be deeply unfortunate when they bite unexpectedly, but merciful to those in great pain".'

'Damn right!' retorted Janus bearing his fangs. 'But somehow you survived the catastrophe that befell your family, yet no-one ever truly knew how. Cat still got Jack's tongue or are we back to the brother who sold his infant sister to the Giants?'

'How dare you,' exploded the Mayor. 'Events happen. Realities get broken. You of all people should know that...'

'But you were given special protection and carefully guided for years. Now look at you – poor muddle-headed Peter! Was it really all to no avail?'

'Perhaps you regret not killing me when you had the chance on the way up to the monastery?'

'I should've let the Trolls finish you off,' Janus snarled, putting his face close to the Mayor. 'Or were they in your pocket too?'

'You think you're so formidable,' yelled the reddening Mayor wiping the spit from his face, 'but I'm afraid you're just an old paper tiger, my friend. Any amnesty formerly offered to you in the name of the Headmaster is duly rescinded. I don't want to see you in my office ever again.'

'Gladly,' bawled Janus.

'Now get out of here,' the Mayor said venomously hovering over the Lyre. 'And take that wretched book with you. Send it back when the School is closed along with your letter of resignation.'

Picking up the book from the Mayor's desk, Janus thumbed through the leaves and let the cover drop open at the back. 'How those torn pages must haunt...'

The Mayor erupted at Janus's calculated remark. Only the Giants and he knew what had actually happened to the missing pages of the "New Book of Joy" in which his youngest sister had been swaddled and carried away.

'End your suffering, brother Bear,' said Janus reading the Mayor's tortured face, for he knew only too well the agony of defeat and thwarted battle plans. 'Sacrifice your pain and let Life renew you.'

'Don't preach to me about suffering, Janus. End your own, for it has just got considerably worse.'

Furious, the Mayor slammed the door shut behind the departing silver-haired man and leant forcibly back against his desk. The Golden Lyre accidentally reverberated and the final words of Lone Silver Wolf, combining with the enchanted music, echoed overpoweringly in his ears. Unlike Raoulf, desire and cunning, not fear, were the Mayor's ultimate obstacles. The Lyre, in its haunting strumming, was quite clear about this.

'Good morning Raoulf,' said Mr Littlesøn throwing open the bedroom curtains. 'Rise and shine, it's a beautiful day...'

'Morning dad,' mumbled Raoulf as he slowly rolled over blinking his eyes and burying his head back in the pillow.

'Up you get sleepy head. We have a visitor waiting downstairs… Get dressed and come down. There's something we want to talk to you about…'

So it was, one pleasant Spring morning, that Raoulf awoke to the arrival of an unexpected guest. As Raoulf dressed, his father sat on the edge of the bed, awkwardly informing his son that the visitor might possibly be calling more often, and perhaps even start staying over at weekends.

'We've grown rather fond of each other…' Mr Littlesøn muttered. 'Really, we've got a lot in common… music, mountains, motorbikes… exploring the forest and the travelling road…'

Whilst his father went on explaining, a bemused Raoulf pulled on his favourite blood-red sweater – a colour he had grown to love.

'You must understand, son, that she's not here to replace your mother… but I hope we can all join forces and get along… and be happy…'

Raoulf smiled at his father's embarrassed rambling, whilst his brave heart and scarred fingers remembered that he had once given away a Rose of Pink for a reason. Somehow Raoulf knew that somewhere around the corner love waited for them all.

'…And if you have any doubts you must say so… We'll try to answer any questions truthfully and you must try to be honest about how you're feeling…'

What his father now spoke about was far easier for Raoulf to understand than Mr Littlesøn realised because he loved Miss Berry already – she who smiled at him and read to him such wonderful, scary stories. So it was, against a backdrop of such childlike Winter trauma, that an unforeseen and delightful Spring change occurred.

Miss Beret arrived at the Littlesøn's home that morning looking more vulpine than usual, well… more so than her role as infant schoolteacher allowed. She winked at Raoulf as she tapped the side of her nose and whispered,

'Long runs the fox, Raoulf, remember that… long runs the fox.'

Raoulf nodded at her words, which sounded just like one of his Grandmother's sayings. Then he took Miss Berry by the hand and showed her around the house. He particularly liked showing off his bedroom, which he had called 'The Sunshine Playroom' because of the bright daffodil colour he and his father had recently repainted it. The warm light that filtered through the thin, butterscotch curtains aided the somewhat streaky yellow effect that held the promise of Summer, and brighter, sunnier times ahead.

Meanwhile, Mr Littlesøn went to make coffee, smiling and humming a few bars of an obscure song called 'The Secret of the Hanging Tree' – a song passed down from his father and the other circus travellers…

"One rune too many, stolen for you,

Your face in the rain, blinding my view,

Raised up on high, cast down in pain,

Lord Odin, on top of the sky world again…"

Mr Littlesøn was bemused by the seeming ease of it all between the three of them. The past few months had been a difficult time, but he was pleased to see how excited his son was at showing Miss

Beret his rickety tree house. Raoulf had named it, 'The House in the Trees Where the Moon Shines in,' which nestled at the bottom of the garden in a hug of strong branches. Raoulf even revealed to her the secret password to gain admittance, which only he, Billy Goat Plum and the other Radio Boys knew:

'The caught kite flies high in the branches…' Raoulf whispered.

'…But never moves,' replied Miss Beret, proving yet again that she was definitely one of the gang.

Miss Beret remembered that particular story being told to her by the Headmaster. It was a curious tale about a wizened Oriental circus owner who performed astonishing magical tricks, whilst revealing marvellous mysteries and profound truths through a winding maze of distorting mirrors. Part of the act involved an accomplice strapped to a kite who hovered high above the crowd until, one day, the assistant unfortunately became entangled in a tree allowing the fabled dancing fire-horse to escape. The only way to release the kite was to cut the string and shake the tree. Unfortunately, the kite had soared off into the distant mountains with the assistant still attached. According to legend, that is how Sky City had come to be founded.

Yet how Raoulf had come to hear of that story Miss Beret did not know, for it was not one of her daily tales. In fact, it was the Air Angel who had told Raoulf and the Radio Boys in one of their recent tree house gatherings. The Angel also informed them that the Moon was very sorry for all the past things that had been done, but could not be undone. That night the Moon had shone down on them and the Angel performed a candle ceremony to bless all the lost fathers and missing mothers in a bid to say thank you. Promises were made that night to the Radio Boys that things would be different, that changes were afoot for the better. And they were.

When they returned to the house Raoulf took from out his play box a ball of sparkling wool, which he called 'Glisten-the-Good'. Spinning faster and faster he ran around the room like a whirling demon, threading his yarn around the upright legs of his father, Miss Beret and the furniture as he constructed the outline of his adventure through the Forest to his Grandmother's cottage. He even tried to ensnare Olaf the snow cat who, on seeing Raoulf's rapid advances, had escaped to the safety of the stair landing and was now grinning down upon them.

Toppling towards each other, Miss Beret and Mr Littlesøn laughed at being caught up in the boy's tangled web. Looking briefly into each other's eyes a promise was made there, in that moment, which was not there before. So a smile and a tacit recognition passed between the two adults and a new kind of joy emerged that day. It was as though the Sun had finally come out breaking over them all with its warm, golden rays.

Neatly and quickly, Miss Beret stepped skilfully out of Raoulf's woollen web and took control of the situation. Catching hold of the spinning boy, she steadied him until she could gently guide him back out into the garden. Collapsing upon the grass Raoulf gazed up at the puffy-white clouds. Ever since the encounter with Little Spark he could sometimes see sparkling orbs floating gently in the air, drifting in the spaces in-between. Miss Beret observed Raoulf's preoccupied staring and wondered if he was hyperactive, sensitive or a true recruit of the Crazy Crew? Fortunately, her thoughts were distracted as coffee, biscuits and lemonade were served. It was then that she suddenly sensed that she was happy. Miss Beret felt good.

Ninny Nanny and Grinny Granny, two shrunken alopecia dwarf women, sat by the large bay window in the worn, comfy chairs recently donated to the Hazy Days Care Home. Chatting merrily away, they occupied their fingers and their time by diligently crocheting colourful squares to contribute to a charitable patchwork quilt the Old Goats of Town were all working on. Seated alone at the mahogany drawing-room table, an exasperated Nanny Nine Toes was squinting at one of several remaining sky-blue pieces that refused to fit into her jigsaw puzzle. She did not realise that she had been sabotaged – certain pieces having been strategically removed, whilst pieces belonging to another puzzle had been secretly added.

The culprits, Tripsy, Ditsy, and Tipsy (not triplets, but the last surviving sisters of sextuplets), were gathered in the adjoining games room with some of the other residents. Snip, Snap, then Bonkers Conkers, Unpicking the Knitting, and marble rolling were always followed by Happy Families and a card game where matches were swapped later for cafeteria contraband and other, more exciting, illicit goods. Oh, how the old dears all loved their coffee mornings with the other ladies of the 'Congregation of Gently off their Rails and Rockers Folk Society'. Peace and quiet, tittle and tattle, spittle and rattle tales, all was harmless gossip and fun between the whiskery women with whiskey-nip hipflasks, brandy-snap thermoses, and those gambling souls awake enough to be playing gin rummy.

Meanwhile, feeling somewhat defeated by her ill-fitting jigsaw puzzle, Nanny Nine Toes turned to Mable Fable to ask for assistance. However, her friend was standing behind the flock curtains peering apprehensively out of the window, staring at the birds swooping above the lawn.

'Are you all right, dear?' asked Nanny Nine Toes. 'You seem rather perturbed.'

'I think the birds are following me...' Mable Fable replied. She then got into a right two-and-eight explaining how she had found another sixpence baked in one of her Swan-shaped pies. She also swore blind that a Swallow had dropped a bright blue sapphire in her dough whilst she was kneading her daily Rugbrød that morning.

Eavesdropping from her comfy chair, an intrigued Ninny Nanny was certain she had got it wrong. 'A Swallow, you say. Are you sure?'

Grinny Granny grinned and winked at the others.

Mable Fable nodded her head. 'Yes,' she said sourly.

Gurning, Ninny Nanny blinked her disbelief. 'The bird sang you a song and gave you a silver sixpence? Are you sure?'

Mable Fable pursed her lips. 'Yes,' she confirmed dryly.

Ninny Nanny rolled her laughing, watery eyes... 'And brought you a sapphire? Are you sure?'

'Yes,' snapped Mable Fable becoming increasingly irritable with her friends.

All the women looked at each other as they shared the same thought, 'Senile old goat.' Then they all burst out laughing. Hooting and cackling away, they nudged one another and took a quick sip from their medicinal hip flasks. Mable Fable was furious. So, in the face of all this decrepitude and incredulity, she opened her handbag, removed her lace handkerchief and reluctantly revealed a blazing blue sapphire that once had been a Statue's eye. The sixpence, alongside an assortment of other bird-delivered coins and gems, she held back for her own rainy day fund.

'See,' she said brusquely, 'I'm not going mad.'

As nominated treasurer to the recent 'Champagne Campaign' and 'strange going-ons trust', Grinny Granny clutched a large handbag with the year's takings harvested by the birds and distributed without warning to the Grandmothers of Town. Now, to their astonishment, a sapphire had been delivered. Something bizarre was going on with their feathered friends, but what did it all mean?

'Oi Nin!' said Grinny Gran, gently elbowing her dozing friend awake again, 'I think we'd better investigate. I've got a hunch this bird stuff might be important.'

Speaking mainly goat, the birds' excitable twitter was getting lost in translation, yet there was one among their elderly number who understood the birds' meaning.

'They need help,' explained Waltzing Matilda as she glided by in her crystalline slippers and gossamer robe. 'It's something to do with a dream… and a fight, a good fight. They want us to organise a rally.'

So the Old Goats of Awe established a fighting fund, which instantly grew as a quick collection of coins and notes left forgotten in the bottom of handbags, and found dropped down the back of sofas and armchairs, produced some surprising and pleasing results.

Later came the selling of eco-cakes, herbal curatives, and a range of homemade marmalades and vodka-infused jellies and jams – which proved to be very popular. Across the Jutted Terrain, the Forest Drums were sounding again. Flash-mob sing-a-longs and merry knit-athons, poetry recitals and spontaneous dance, became the disorder of the day. Loopy-Lou Grandmothers all joined in and formed the now infamous 'Singing Nannies and the Knitting Knit Twits.' Interest, eyebrows and more money were raised, along with elbows, whisks and wooden spoons, in a friendly cake cooking competition held in a nearby field.

The accumulated assortment of gems, ancient coins, and precious leaf were promptly taken to Jakob the elderly Clockmaker and Silversmith who ran a Pawnbroker shop in the Old Town. The Nans and Grans found him sitting in his office reading an article – 'The Correction of Clock Faces' – in the Mathmagician's 'Timely Considerations' quarterly magazine. As a good friend of the Headmaster it was his job to annually examine and repair the intricate mechanism of the Folkeskole's Old Norse grandfather clocks.

Handing over their assorted treasure, cash was readily released to the tenacious Nans and Grans, but Jakob's spidery eyebrows drew together in a concentrated frown. He recognised the source of some of the treasure from the Statue that had once occupied the central square facing his shop.

'Hhm,' he thought, 'time to visit the Headmaster.'

Meanwhile, an affordable, ethical lawyer was brought in to issue the first injunction against Mayor Bear. On a suggestion by the Headmaster, who had gleaned it from the birds, the lawyer made an initial search of a dilapidated cupboard locked in the basement of the Old Town Hall. This led to the discovery of a mediaeval atlas, some faded rune stones used as seals, and a handful of dusty scrolled documents that heralded back to King Gorm the Great. These deeds of provenance – decrees, symbols, and maps – contained principled by-laws protecting the common land that surrounded Town, as far as the Fang Ridge Mountains in the North and reaching down to the rolling plains of the Southern borders. Interestingly, certain scrolls seemed to have been re-draughted, possibly by the Mayor himself.

There was some unusual wording in the matter of mountains, forests and Wandering Ways that entitled the Folk of Town to a commission regarding hunting rights, fishing permits and building permissions. Yet where these missing common payments and funds were, nobody knew. Lying in the bottom of some hidden community chest gathering interest for the general good or embezzled by the cash-guzzling Mayor? More curiously, the lawyer discovered a set of deeds to an ancient, long-forgotten castle. The Palace estate and its treasure was signed over to the control of the Mayor – 'as power of attorney in perpetuity' – unless an unlikely lost heir, most probably a daughter, laid claim to the whole of the Land of Awe.

Probing, the lawyer took out his investigative trowel to scratch the surface and dig a bit deeper, as there seemed to be some shaky foundations to the legal layering of this peculiar Jutted Land. Mayor Bear was not best pleased with the lawyer's proceedings and findings, whereas the Headmaster was secretly delighted and the twittering birds hopped up and down elatedly on their branches for days. Unfortunately, in his undercover rummaging amongst the Mayor's cupboards one afternoon, the lawyer accidentally stumbled upon a pair of strategically placed Seven-League Boots. Alas, just as evidence mounted and fingers were ready to rise to incriminate, the lawyer, the boots and the deeds of provenance all mysteriously disappeared.

The Trolls dwelling under the small arched bridge in the Fang Ridge Mountains were bemused to receive such a tasty present, but their squabbling soon led to the clever lawyer escaping, chasing leagues in leaps and bounds as though astride an invisible winged horse. The Air Fairies in charge of the boots were having ever so much fun, to see such a learned man bounce on his bum.

As for Little Seed's own drifting situation, she could do nothing but go with the universal flow, for she was well out of the Cloud Elders' transmission range.

Time had taken on a slower turn in support of her mission, yet as to what that actual mission was remained uncertain. No blazing trail for her. Drifting between wake, sleep and dream, Little Seed gently descended toward the Earth Lands, growing plumper and rounder by the minute. Yet she could not tell which way up she was, for her shape and size were ever shifting.

First, she was cherry-like with a single stone. Then, she became more like an apple core, star-shaped with five seed pockets. Next, to her bemusement, she found she was rotating and heart-shaped, covered in pips on the outside. Looking down at all the active lovers as she fell through the night sky, Little Seed felt more gooseberry then strawberry as she filled up inside with more seeds and pips than she could possibly bear. She felt ripe, full of goodness and fit to burst until she had become like a pomegranate. Unable to see where she was going she had to trust in the guiding light, veering like a soft kaleidoscopic sphere in a mingling of oh so much fleshy, fruity fun. Falling through the universe, what was she to become? Unlike her sisters, indecision and imprecision were qualities of hers, so she simply trusted in her loving heart.

That was when Little Seed, caught unaware, hit the aluminium factory roof, plunged down the central ventilation shaft and exploded like a starburst. As she did so, a million tumbling seeds went flying through the air. She was momentarily everywhere, whilst dispersing her pips and seeds both here and there. She seemed to be caught in the middle somewhere between beingness and bliss, but could not be sure in her continual sporing diaspora. She could not remember when she finally lost consciousness, but like a fine, dispersing mist she coated everything in sight and was absorbed.

For Little Seed it was as though she had fallen asleep again for a thousand years, resting on a pea-less bed fit for a Princess, ankles delicately crossed, waiting for a charming Prince – perhaps a midnight admirer or a stranger's kiss – to awake her. As she dozed and caught up on her beauty sleep, sunbeams fell gently through the window and onto her countless seeds and fruit. Then 'Oh!' something wonderful happened as she rose in a second multitudinous ripening. Over and over, rising and rising, so no surprising then, when, several months later all over the rejoicing Jutted Land...

The Apple and Eve Organic Pregnancy Agency wished to recall some of its products. Detective testing kits, where the pink and blue indicators were the wrong way round, and faulty contraceptive pills were blamed. A hitherto unknown ingredient was considered the culprit, but as to the infiltration process, no-one yet knew. No activist had come forward to claim the act, yet talk of compensation had begun between the bankrolled pharmaceutical companies, the Mayor and those many pregnant individuals involved. Nightly activity, both in the bed and in the wood, continued in their regular fertile phases and Moon-monthly cycles. At Nature's loving behest everybody joined in.

Ninth months had passed since Little Seed's initial pollination which now resulted in a collective maternity swelling – a community of waddling mothers awaiting group birth. So babies began popping out all over Town. A girl here. A boy there. Then mischievous rascals were bursting out everywhere – often in twos, threes and fortuitous fours. Far and wide the deafening sound of shotguns blasting was heard, announcing quick weddings, whilst others talked of Unwanteds being hastily put down. The zoological garden was affected too – cute kittens, cheeky chimps, cuddly koalas – even a couple of gay penguins were taking to motherhood as there were a myriad of eggs and chicks to be looked after!

So it was that a whole new generation of rambunctious babies were born unto Town and the Land of Awe. Thanks to Little Seed, those incoming soul-children with a secret sparkle in their eye arrived on an unforeseen, splendiferous wave, infiltrating society with new notions of love, merriment and encompassing spiritual madness. Meanwhile, the subversive 'Singing Nannies and the Knitting Knit Twits' had a second surge of success, now as Great-Grandmothers, so beloved were they by avenging agitprop crowds and adoring grandchildren throughout the land. The royalties rolled in, enough for a second injunction and a search party, which brought further difficult questions for the Mayor to answer. He was beginning to buckle at the knees whilst the Old Goats, it seemed, were ransacking his bees and disappearing with his honey.

If the opening of his Rose heart remained unheeded, it was purely to do with the direction the Mayor's somewhat scheming mind and pilfering fingers had previously set. Over the years he had grown strident, placing a large marble angel on top of the Town Hall building proclaiming his office's commitment to: "Progress". There was no escaping from it, so why not embrace it and mould the shifting times from in front, benefits of position included of course. Yet the allying forces of transparency and accountability were all very well when discussed in the political abstract, but when scrutinising beams from the Towers shone directly upon a particular individual, secrets had a nasty habit of popping up unexpectedly. Consequently, the hidden skeletons rattled and danced in the Mayor's closet.

As Jack Rose he had loved his family, but his knotted past made it all too difficult for muddled-headed Peter to undo. As for the fate of the school, perhaps it was one of the few enchanted places still standing, yet progress was progress and the doors were closing in upon Fairy Folk everywhere – for the World it was a-changing.

So at last it became the day of days on which the Sun and the Westerly Wind decided to have a game. It was an age-old favourite of theirs – how many hats, caps and beau chapeaux could you dislodge and remove in a single day? Not any day, but a day precisely chosen and a location specifically selected and adhered to. The Sun and the Westerly Wind were perusing an old sailor's map trying to decide upon a suitable setting when a passing Swallow, under the instruction of the Philosopher-Prince, dived down from on high and pecked at a particular spot. Seemingly, it was an ordinary town called Town on the dawn of an extraordinary day.

Well, by High Noon, it was neck and neck in the war of hat removal. Faster than fingers of quick-drawing gunslingers, hats, caps and the bonniest of bonnets were either removed or pulled tighter around the owners' heads. The Westerly Wind had made a great start earlier that morning having blown right along the High Street into the Park bandstand, removing all the musicians' boaters in a single bluster. If their hands were not busy playing their instruments, there was flapping sheet music to be held onto and music stands to be kept from toppling over. It was a clever move, but the midday marching band carried on playing regardless of any surprising gust. However, a second, sustained blast meant a clean sweep as all their bearskins tumbled away!

The Sun, on the other hand, had simply got up late and was gently increasing its hazy warmth enough for the entire population of Town to remove their hats voluntarily, as they cooled their overheating heads. But some had now swapped their beau chapeaux for more ordinary straw hats and peaked caps, making it difficult to tell who was who. The additional use of handkerchiefs, headscarves and parasols made it hard for the birds to tell who was actually winning. As over-seeing stewards of the 'Hat Game' they were trying to complete the head count, but had become somewhat overexcited.

Whilst contending with the day's soaring temperatures and salty sea breezes, the birds' feathers and brains had been quite whooshed about.

So it was that the Sun and the Wind agreed to start again. They settled on the notion that, in the end, it would come down to the concluding count of one particular person – an odd, slightly rotund chap with a funny triangular hat wandering around muttering to himself at Town's late May Day fete. On closer inspection, the Sun and the Wind discovered that the fete was being held in the schoolyard by the local community in an attempt to raise awareness and additional funds to help 'Save-our-School' – or so several large homemade banners declared.

A fake Village Green had been constructed in the old triangular style with a pond at one end where you could water your dogs and take your ducks and pine martins for a swim. There were food tents, tombola events, and white elephant stalls everywhere. Assorted drinking Townsfolk were congregating in cliques, particularly in front of the inn with the mediaeval façade – the 'Slippery Plank Saloon.' From above, the judging birds' perspective of the two views of triangles – that of the Village Green and the Mayor's Tricorn Hat – afforded the perfect target for the hat-removing game to continue. To help matters further, a brightly coloured sash and a glinting chain of office, which settled cumbersomely around the Mayor's shoulders, encircled the inner triangle creating a perfect bull's-eye.

Thus, the wager between the Sun and the Westerly Wind was underway with a renewed vigour. Who would have guessed that poor Mayor Bear, in all his civic regalia, was going to be candidate elect of the elements and of the birds' deciding vote? The Mayor not only became an official target for the Sun and the Wind, but also for every person in Town – whether young or old, fair or foul, butting goat or belligerent ram! His face-cheeks were ruddy and ripe for the pinching from every mother that passed by holding a gurgling baby (and in the Mayor's opinion there were so many blasted mothers passing by holding blessed babies!), whereas the Mayor's butt-cheeks were ripe for the kicking from every idiot that passed by with an opinion (and there were so many idiots passing by with unsolicited blessed opinions!). Everyone, except Mayor Bear, seemed to know the score:

'Offenders and nincompoops – come one, come all;

For the dunderhead egg-pelters are having a ball!'

Close by, Gunnbjorn's rifle range and shooting galleries were doing a brisk trade with wolf tails and fang totems tied to fast moving tins. The gunmen roared and laughed as they pulled their triggers and shot the tins to smithereens. Some had even brought their own guns especially for the occasion. The 'Build your own Bear' tent run by the temperamental Girl with the Golden Locks was well intentioned but mainly empty, as was the 'Weave your own Wolf Wig' stall run by a man who looked extraordinarily like a vengeful rear-end of a pig. Skulking at the back, gathering in packs, gangs of motorbike Wolf Men lent on fences, shifting uneasily.

Meanwhile, the Headmaster sat outside his red-and-white striped tent with a sign above his head that stated:

"Touch the Door Knob and visit your Dream Destination –

(no refunds for disappointments)."

Unfortunately, it was attracting rather a lot of the wrong kind of attention. The innocent few were disappearing in a puff of smoke and going Odin-knows-where, whilst less desirable others remained unmoved, as the beams from the Towers of Dark and Light locked in dispute as to the assignation of fears and dreams. Neither side, it seemed, wanted to take certain individuals, and even the usually patient Fairies were becoming fed up with the stalemate.

The Door Knob Fears and Goblins were rather disheartened by that year's cache of children, and had grown bored sitting around the same classroom for so long. Wishing to flex their military muscles they had visited the Headmaster one night whilst he was soaking in his bath, asking if they could contribute to the May Day fete's hokum. The Headmaster, taken unaware and a little afraid, slipped further down into the mountain of soapsuds.

'Yes, of course,' the Headmaster had glugged brightly from the foamy depths, 'the more the merrier. It's all in a charitable cause, so return trips must be guaranteed to all those wishing to come home.'

Secretly, the Headmaster thought it would be good for the unruly Fears and Goblins to exorcise any pent-up emotion and untoward feeling they might be harbouring toward the School staff and children.

Now, in a moment of brilliance and madness, the Headmaster came to a cunning truce with the Door Knob inhabitants and the Two Towers. A rescue team of selected Fairies and infant teachers were waiting in the woods armed with magical strategies for those vanishing folk who were stuck wishing to return, and those trying to remain lost – rogue runaway plans, emergency escape routes, and alien-reintegration programmes being the most popular solutions. It was a risky business as there were fears, enemies and dark Dream Worlds lurking everywhere, but so far everyone seemed to be keeping their cool and having fun – all, that is, except the blinking Two Towers who could hardly ever agree on appropriate destinations and could never settle on a suitable compromise. The Headmaster had ruled out the tearing of people in half.

Phew! Mayor Bear was growing increasingly hot under his pinching collar when a sudden icy-breeze blew down the nape of his neck and chilled the sweat along his spine. More than anything he simply wished to remove his Tricorn hat and mop his balding pate with a handkerchief. Somebody nearby giggled. The Mayor frowned. His ego was stern in such matters as misuse of magic for frivolity, particularly when he was not the one at the helm. However, he managed to control his rising temper and anchored his steely will in the heels of his Seven League Zip Boots. He needed to take a firm stance. There was no room for stuff-and-nonsense in the matters of pomp and civic duty that he had to execute this afternoon.

Yet the portentous encumbrance of the mayoral chain and his Tricorn hat, combined with the difficulty of the announcements he had to make in regards to closures of Schools and withdrawal of maternity benefit and child support, began to weigh heavily on the Mayor. Poor Peter! He rapidly stuffed his nifty thoughts of escape away, and turned to the dismal and awkward problems at hand. Mundane matters were the order of the day and personal views often needed shielding, particularly if there were any passing Fairy Folk with a touch of telepath or Banshee in their blood – rare, but not unheard of in this crazy, mixed up Land of Awe.

Once more the Mayor felt an unwelcome nudge as something drifting in the Westerly Wind deliberately tugged at the corner of his Tricorn hat. He did not always trust a breeze for it could transport you anywhere when the Elemental Forces were at work. He believed the leaves on the surrounding silver birches were tinkling with laughter. Zephyrs, if he was not mistaken. Tricky! He had recently rid himself of that pesky lawyer by using the Zip Boots and he knew the

Air Fairies would soon return demanding payment or favours – just surely not today.

As the Mayor looked around, the Trickster Birds from the Forest of Thirst flew in. Perching in neat rows, the Ravens from Black Nest looked like attendees at a church funeral, but whose wake would this turn out to be? They were blinking at him disarmingly, shivering his blighted timbers! Now a marauding gang of mercenary Castle Crows from Obsidian Lake were joining the Ravens. He recognised them because he had used their lookout services himself, rewarding them handsomely to cover his former cloud capers and helping to ditch the Shadow Witch when he was purloining a map of hers hidden in the westerly turret.

Continuing on through the stalls, the Mayor passed by a particularly distorting 'Maze of a Thousand Mirrors'. His Tricorn hat made him look fat in the face and ridiculous. He was beginning to feel rather over-stuffed at his not insubstantial bulging corners. Curse it! Now even his blessed Zip Boots were beginning to pinch. Somewhere in his mind he longed for a life far away from the ambition of it all. Steady on! One simple desire instruction and his wish-itchy feet and Flying Boots would be off. Awkward when he needed to deliver a critical speech and put the final nail in the School's coffin.

Superficially nodding, smiling, and waving, the Mayor walked amongst the gathering crowd clumsily clutching the pages of his speech. Gnashing their teeth, the gathering multitude were audibly mooing and braying their discontent. He felt the growing hostility of the Townsfolk as they jostled about him, jeering and snarling. Hemmed in, Mayor Bear felt more and more isolated from those surrounding him. Events began spiralling uncontrollably when a gust from a passing Zephyr tugged the pages out of his hand.

Then, from out of nowhere, the Headmaster darted by in pursuit of an invisible whizzing Fear, desperately trying to avert a major fingerprint catastrophe. As he ran he picked up a page of the Mayor's speech and waved it in the air, calling out something that was whipped away in the laughing wind.

'Looking forward...'

But to what? Mayor Bear scrabbled around on the floor trying to collect the surviving pages that had not blown away or been trampled underfoot. Smiling, the Sun quite simply beamed and beamed and beamed.

Meanwhile, Granny Goat Gruff was having a very strange day. Ever since the dawn Fire Cockerel had crowed her awake she had felt out of sorts. Now she was in a cantankerous mood having put her hat on as often as she had taken it off in the strange battle between warm and windy weather. So, if this was not the perfect day to have half a mind to tell the incompetent and corrupt establishment what she thought of them, then she did not know which day was. As to the mystery of where Granny Goat Gruff had put the other half of her mind – the less coherent, more affectionate side – well, she just could not remember. Her old man, Grandpa Joseph, said she must have left it locked carelessly in a dresser drawer somewhere. The clue was in his loving answer. Over twenty years had passed since his death.

Fortuitously, Joseph had enough far sight to see his own demise whilst knowing that his wife had one final task to complete. Funny, some old birds were tough like that – resilient and unafraid to be left out on a long wing and a prayer in their end of days – whereas certain rams and billy goats were often more fragile and left life early. Joseph had surmised correctly the reasons for her survival and his early departure from life. There was just enough spirit left in his wife to complete her speech, turn the crazy birds and silly goats of Town around before she ultimately fell silent and gave in to becoming a happy phantom. If only the Other Side would have her, that was. If she could speak purposefully and find her power and peace, she would take that elusive quality of tranquillity with her into the Afterlife once and for all. Really, what had she left to surrender but her wilfulness used for the good?

So it was that one warm, sunny afternoon, just before he passed away, Joseph had skilfully locked the other half of his wife's drifting mind away in a drawer where she would never look – thus safeguarding the emotional part that loved him so much. He figured she would not miss him half so much if it was tucked neatly away and that would help her survive the remaining years she would outlive him. He had seen that part of her innocent mind wandering dreamily, and somewhat carelessly, across the room to the window to investigate the wonder of sunlight sparkling on overly cleaned glass. She had been in a childlike reverie at the time.

In the half mind left to her, Granny Goat Gruff had devoted the rest of her life to the tending of her garden and the feeding of the birds she loved so much. That, alongside the whiskey, whist drives and some form of annual charitable good-deed, would always put her at the social heart of old age. In her own steadfast, dogged, argumentative way, she liked to help other people... whether they wanted to be helped or not.

Today, Granny Goat Gruff was booked to sing along with the other Grandmothers at Town's May Day fete. Then she was going to settle down to a right good heckle with that idiot Mayor. Closing the

Folkeskole! Whatever next? Did he not know it was a special place, built on an over-cross of two very potent ley lines? Blessed it was. Why, she had been sent there as an orphaned child of Ore after the Dark Wars. It was where many a friendship had been born, idling away at the back of the classroom. It was where she had met Joseph as a young boy. The School would have to be rescued and she was just in the mood for championing such a cause.

After that, not that she knew it, Granny Goat Gruff would celebrate her last ever night. She would not follow her usual routine of going to bed early, but instead would stay up late with a bottle of her favourite 'Ild Vand'. Then, she would fall asleep forever. In her dreams she would be welcomed back into the embracing arms of her old man Joseph, where they would begin to plot the next Ten Thousand things to do together – a dream place she would never have to leave unless she wished to. He had a few ideas already prepared that he wanted to share with her. Assuredly, after today, Granny Goat Gruff would never awake to the violence of another cockcrow from the damnable morning Fire Cockerel.

'Aitchoo!' went Raoulf, hastily covering his nose and mouth with both hands whilst being propelled backward in the force of the blast.

Raoulf was having a laugh and all kind of unfathomable joy on this most wonderful day of days. He had already sneezed outright at least four or five times, but who was counting. To him it was simply pure, unadulterated fun, probably the result of too much candyfloss tickling his tongue and toffee apple sticking to his nose and chin. As a result, his whole body was electrified by so much sugar and so many sneezes. Plus he was overexcited by all the surrounding sound and colours of the stalls and gathering strange people, so much so that he started yelping and barking whilst running around.

Something in Raoulf's blood brought out the best and worst in folk and their comments,

'My, my, blessed me! What a young whippersnapper you've turned out to be.'

To Raoulf, the whole day was simply another marvellous adventure, just like the one he had recently spent at the Big Top with his Grandmother. Watching tumbling clowns juggling chain saws, and blindfolded trapeze artists leaping on and off the backs of fast-moving motorbikes, had been both thrilling and scary to watch. At times he had hidden behind his Grandmother's cape. Grandmother May had loved the outing too, reminding her of her own crazy, knife-throwing circus days. Now, Raoulf ran around the stalls howling up to the sky...

*'Blood of Banshee, howl of Wolf,

I am here,' cried Little Raoulf.

The Westerly Wind whipped up his cry and, spreading it eerily thin, carried it across the fete to all those who had ears to hear and to one who stubbornly refused. Those in the know nodded. So, it was true. The strange blood of the mother ran within the boy. Those spell-infected with paws and guns shifted uneasily looking for any excuse to spark off.

Today, however, soft bouncy castles and trampolines beckoned those who were young at heart like Raoulf and Miss Beret. With the aid of the helpful Air Angel and his misty vapour, the ghost of Cartwheel Charlie was somersaulting around the schoolyard for

THE LAND OF BLISS

everyone to see. His Grandpa stood close by enthusiastically waving hello. Together they had discovered the whereabouts of Snow Rose living in the Cloud Lands, and she had graciously shown them a way that meant they could return to the Folkeskole with the help of the Door Knob. That was when she had recognised Jack, her brother, parading around the fete dressed cumbersomely as the Mayor.

Meanwhile, oblivious to events, the Mayor was still feeling decidedly hot and bothered. He was not in the mood for succumbing to fun and now he had that young boy's unnerving howl ringing in his ears. Nor was he feeling up to being the sporting back end of the pantomime cow or being paraded like some bouffant, bloomer-frilled, painted dame, which is what a lot of the unfriendly onlookers were secretly thinking and hopefully wishing for. The Townsfolk were simply fed up with corrupt politicians and their slick smiles and oily ways. Merriment and topsy-turvy entertainment were the very point of May Day madness but the Mayor was having none of it, as he struggled with the portentous absurdity of himself. Not only was he on 'hat holding' duty against the beaming Sun, but 'wig alert' against the blustering Wind as well.

The Mayor wiped down his reddening face with his sweat-soaked handkerchief and tried to smile at everybody that passed. But well-wishers were few and far between now. Even Gunnbjorn and the hunting lads were ignoring him, not wanting to be caught in the ugly groundswell that was steadily rising. Coloured sugar, crazy tobacco and homebrew alcohol were all taking effect, and folk were becoming more and more carefree and dangerous. The Mayor started to believe that the wellspring of his luck had truly run dry, Heaven knows how or when. He did not understand that he was spinning the wrong way in the Sky Monk's recently cast 'Vision Spell' – part of their invocation of the 'One Dream Awakening'.

With so many forces of friction rubbing against him, the Mayor was becoming increasingly fractious, unable to access good humour or lightness of spirit.

'Aaaaaaah, Eeeeeeeh, Iiiiiiiih, Oooooh, Uuuuuuuh!'

'Odin above!' thought the Mayor as his ears pricked up in dismay, 'was there some creature in distress?'

The penetrating sound was not dissimilar to the boy's alarming cry heard only moments ago, but this time it was closer, higher, shriller. Silly him! He was merely passing the podium where those cranky, croaky old souls were singing knees-up songs of yesteryear, only this time infused with lashings of alcohol and surplus bonhomie. Yet this particular voice was strikingly different, pricking his eyeballs and prickling the hair on his ears and the back of his neck. Whatever next; surely not more unwanted bedlam, commotion and hullabaloo? The Mayor feared it was one of the demented escaped from the Elysium Asylum, and he had been through enough for one day without having to account for those strange inmates.

'...Iiiiiiiih, L...Oooooh, Y...Uuuuuuuh!' sang the captivating woman with the long golden hair as she practised her arpeggios and warmed up her piercing vocal chords.

Then, striding centre stage to sit at her harpsichord, the Beltane Belter, that singer with the touch of royalty in her blood and Stradivarius magic in her voice, started doing something rather drastic to the Mayor's nerves. Shredding them! Not only that, but compounding the matter by jumping up and down, cheese grater in hand, making indecipherable sounds that alarmingly plucked at his senses. Was he really experiencing the delight of the 'Music-of-the-Spheres' as suggested by the nearby poster? Quite frankly, the Mayor wished the Beltane Belter would stop singing and that the vociferous unwanted cats she dragged with her as backing vocals had been drowned at birth.

Yet all the while, the struggling Mayor tried to keep his composure, smiling at the gathering congregation who seemed enthralled, positively bewitched, by the bat and the bird in the Belter's beguiling song. As the lovely Lady sat at her harpsichord singing songs about numbers, circles, and the endless spinning of spinning wheels, her long flaxen hair danced about her with a hypnotic Medusa-like life of its own.

'Not what 1 was, but 2,' warbled the Princess playfully. 'As between the 2 and the 2 of 2's lay 3…'

Really, was there a third way? Why else had she followed it with such a sacred sounding 4? What possibility for the Mayor an opening new door? The Beltane Belters' unusual polyphony presaged a change and now she was beginning to hum and strum the strings of her harpsichord in multiple primes. Add, subtract, multiply, divide; what fresh hope for him in the equation of Life?

'Here comes the rare 9 of 9's,' sang the Princess, 'how divine.'

As the Mayor continued to watch the golden-haired singer perform, there seemed to be something almost Timeless about her, but surely that kind of magic only belonged to the Fairy Godmothers of old to bestow; that and a certain missing miraculous Turtle Egg Tide Turner. It was obvious to him that she had no idea of who she truly was and he intended to keep it that way. He would not be as easily beguiled as the surrounding happy-clapping multitudes. Accordingly, the Mayor steeled himself further against the burden and brunt of this most difficult of days – so little did he know about approaching cloud joy and the oncoming prick of his Rose.

'Aa… Aa… Aaitch…choo!' Raoulf spluttered and giggled.

'Oh, that boy and his annoying, ridiculous sneezing!' thought the Mayor grumpily. 'How many times was it now? Five or six?'

In the Mayor's perturbed mind the pages of a storybook were beginning to turn, as awakened memories and childhood nursery rhymes fluttered about him. How did the verse go? Was it not five for silver, six for gold, and seven for a secret never to be told? No! That was not it. That particular rhyme concerned magpies, not sneezes, but why-oh-why was he thinking of such absurd infantile things? That was a time he did not wish to remember. Lilting lullabies, soothing serenades and cradle-side crooning must be resisted for they were a form of innocent incantation that informed his childhood. Suddenly, all around, there was the scent of rain-drenched roses; a bombarding sense-memory of his family's rose garden hanging in the air.

'A… Aa… Aah…' Raoulf stopped in a suspended half-sneeze which balanced between the tip of his nose and the edge of the Mayor's nerves. According to the counting birds it was six-and-a-half sneezes, for even now there was one caught between the surprising spasm and the rewarding release. Was the boy's nose somehow sensing the pervading scent of roses too?

'Blast it!' the Mayor cursed out loud, but he instantly regretted his cussing as he became all caught up in himself. People were watching and listening with close interest, scrutinising his every move. Yet still the voices in his head continued, speaking in babble tongues of Yester Yore and the far northern countries. Was the protective enchantment of Giant relics waning? Were the days of the

aging magical folk of Town running out as he had predicted –
including his own?

'…Everything for the roses of L-oooooooo-vvv-e,' wailed the
golden-haired Princess, expressing all of the shared joy and sadness
of relationships past, present and future. The Beltane Belter was on
great form today.

'Good grief!' thought the Mayor. 'Of all the blessed songs and
aching heart-chord reminders – why this one?'

To escape the Beltane's localised caterwauling, Mayor Bear let
himself momentarily slip into a reverie of elsewhere. In an instant,
Flash Jack was once more in league with his Cloud Boots. They had
not lost their zip! Immediately, a few loyal Air Fairies, and some
mischievous opportunistic Zephyrs on the make, were right by his
side encouraging him on to fly further. They remembered their dear
old friend Jack from his youthful days of daring Giant adventure.

'Follow,' they said, 'fly away with us. Forget the Sun and the
Wind and the people's fuss.'

Momentarily suspended between cloud and land, the agitated
Mayor floated nervously looking for a way out. Unfortunately
inspiration eluded him and, as his heels clicked together, he found
himself standing back whence he had started. Returning with a jolt,
the Mayor's toes curled in his boots and his slamming heels sent a
shuddering ache all the way along his spine and up to his over-heated
head. Tilting his hat and mopping his brow, he hoped no-one had
noticed his teleporting reverie. Split seconds were like that! Yet still
he had not managed to escape or collect his cool.

'Oh my!' cried a woman. 'Ooh! Ooh! Oh!'

'Now what in the blue blazes is going on?' thought the Mayor.

The commotion was coming from a member of the group of very pregnant women standing near the Statue, one of whom seemed to be going into labour. Hoping to be able to present himself in a positive light, the Mayor bustled through the crowd pretending to help whilst grumbling away,

'Damn that failed contraception programme.'

The Mayor knew he must follow that company of menstrual mistakes up and further discuss the 'Whims and Strange Acts of Odin' get-out clause with the insurance companies. Now, though, he had to keep calm and collected. In discussion with the Apple and Eve Organic Pregnancy Agency, the latest statistics from private research were up his sleeve – massaged results, non-committal rhetoric and evasive answers to demonstrate his ongoing care and responsibility to the community. Unfortunately for the Mayor, that was one of the many pages of his speech that had been lost in the surprise gust of wind.

'Blow the bothers away. Let them come back another day,' sang the Air Fairies as they lazily sat astride some passing gulls winging towards the coast.

Once more the Mayor's pinched, hot toes twitched. It seemed such good advice and the Jack within would have been off in a shot, shooting the blustering breezes.

'Birds of a feather travel better together,' called the Zephyrs using their sparkling ice-daggers to cut holes through puffy-white clouds on their way to Angel's Landing.

'Be carefree and kind,' chorused the Fairies. 'Release yourself from your human binds.'

As the Zephyrs and Air Fairies tore through the blue with their cheerful dare, zipping brightly through the sun-scorched atmosphere, vapour trails emerged behind them like runic skywriting. They were laughing at the Mayor with renewed vigour when the Westerly Wind gently tugged once more at the corner of his 'Good Fortune' Tricorn hat. He must not lose that or all of his protective providence would be lost in one blast. Yet what on earth was he going to say when the time came to take the platform and make his speech? Could he really save his day? General proclamations on 'progress' and 'people' were not going to cut the mustard with this quarrelsome crowd. Visions had to be clear, plans precise, and budgets needed to add up.

Now the Mayor became flustered: caring for children, concern for Schools, preserving Forests, and discussions involving Townsfolk – the old and the young, the wolf and the gun – were priorities beyond his notions for social improvement, his precious magical resources and the gold reserves he had stolen from the Palace. Fostering! Perhaps that was the answer to Town's unexpected maternity crises, but who would have the strange blighters? After the invasion by the Cuckoo Cloud usurpers, any notions of simply dumping the unruly mothers and unwanted brats in the neighbouring towns of Wife and Mid-Witch would have to proceed with caution. Beleaguered, the Mayor felt fatigued, whilst secretly fearing he could no longer trust his thoughts or control his tongue.

At the back of the fete the Mayor could see the gathering pack of bikers grow bigger – all followers of the Clan of Janus. Leaning on fences, the jeering wolf-men seemed harmless enough in the afternoon sun, despite their argumentative demeanour. Laughing away, the Lone Boys drank and smoked whilst talking to the mangy menagerie of other whiskery men, and wolf-whistled the passing musk-interested women. Indeed, the Lone Boys were simply enjoying the company of goats, plum-pudding women, crows and other oddly behaving birds. Yet where was that irritating man who had been such a frequent thorn in his side?

'Janus!' the Mayor muttered away to himself. 'If anyone was to blame…'

Here the Mayor's thoughts turned hastily and nastily to the menace of Mr Woolfe, who had thwarted him on so many different occasions. Always snooping and prying on pretend visits at the behest of the Headmaster, Janus had recently come to him demanding the woodland 'right to roam'. The Headmaster wanted the freedom of the Forest protected for all – spell-infected or not. Fairy Folk must be able to wander freely, especially the gun and wolf turners. But for the Mayor there was always the risk that such wanderers might discover the truth about the briar-bound castle left to crumble and rot. The Headmaster and he knew that the turrets were not church spires, but a Palace of medieval mishap and sorcery rotten; a fertile place of gold, artefacts and mirrors best forgotten.

Up until now the entanglement of local history, superstition and ghoulish Forest tales had suited the Mayor, but it required a lot of juggling and spinning of plates, whilst remembering the different deceptions. Part past muddle, part past lies; what was the true meat in Peter's pretend pies? Like his hair, his natural gifts of laziness and luck, alongside the Headmaster's gifted silver linings and charmed conclusions, were wearing thin. Perhaps that was why all manner of fairy creatures had been summoned to witness the Mayor's public flogging. Garrulous tongues, pecking beaks and champing mouths were simply conduits for the humiliation poised on the assembled Townsfolk's clucking minds.

Yet still the Mayor clutched at his house of straw, steadfastly believing that allegiances and outcomes could be easily swerved, severed and swapped – especially for the right price amongst those creatures that sought the best of the self-serving deals. In the realm of Turn Tails, Renegades and Rascals, hired scapegoats, curs and cutthroats were always useful in maintaining a position or procuring a downfall. People's problems were simply events for those in power to resolve and take credit for, whereas truly – there was to be no governing of the Fairy Folk at all.

Elsewhere, events in the 'Door Knob and Dream Disappearance' tent had taken a shambolic turn for the worse – a disaster that even the Headmaster was finding difficult to contain. In their dispute and struggle for control, the Two Towers ongoing battle had turned into a dangerous game of chess. Used as pawns, unfortunate participants were being strategically placed in all kinds of peril and predicament. The Goblins, Fears and Rescuing Fairies were having a field day.

Thus, in an attempt to conclude the question of who would win in the eternal clash of Dark or Light, the Headmaster suggested that a new approach was necessary – one that required tactical thinking, an acquired target and practical application. So, at last in agreement, the Two Towers turned their beams onto the already besieged Mayor, who immediately felt exhausted and completely overwhelmed by their assault. It was all leading to a final silent, but screaming point. Was this then to be the end of Mayor Bear?

Slowly, in preparation for his speech, the Mayor started making his way up the small wooden steps to the side of the stage, desperately trying to organise the remaining pages. He did not wish to suffer the same fate as the unfortunate Hansel and Gretel – of being torn to pieces and fed to a devouring enemy. Would that all depend on his correcting stance now? His destiny stood clearly before him based on the choice of words in his forthcoming speech. How on earth was he going to get out alive? Perhaps he, like the two lost children, would be better off dead? He must doff his hat before he lost his neck and head.

'Don't be afraid,' sang the songstress with the lilt of a Lark. 'For awakening remembers and heals many a heart...'

Was the Mayor no longer an ugly duck just down on his luck but an emerging swan? No, he did not think so. Whilst invisible spirits like the Cloud Littles lived on in the Inbetween Lands, the Family Rose were deceased – lost and long forgotten. However, even now, someone in the horizon's distance was reaching out to greet the Mayor, hurting his heart, yet giving him courage. From above, in the cloud line of sky, some form of greater light was descending. The Sun, the Wind, and the Eyes of the Two Towers all joined in, beaming their presence, which only resulted in making him hotter.

Standing ready, the now sweltering Mayor looked out at the surrounding crowd, whilst his painful past and hoped for future all collided in a swirling kaleidoscope of Time around him. He wondered if it was his myopia or purely his growing sense of stage fright? Perhaps it was a much-needed change descending. Just like the sneezing boy standing at the front of the crowd reaching up for the charming woman's hand, the Mayor was not lost but found. Was this simply the moment of his eternal Now descending?

So it was that the bewildered and uncertain Mayor slowly moved centre stage.

Reaching up for Miss Beret's hand, Raoulf felt wonderful warmth pass between him, her and his father. At last, he felt safe and happy. He also felt able to think more clearly about his mother who had found her own coastal contentment. He loved her so and would see her again soon in the fast approaching Summer holidays. For all the grim months of snow and letting go, it now felt easier for Raoulf; more evens and not so at odds at all. He turned his attention back to the man with the funny triangular hat standing on stage. Whatever he was trying to proclaim was definitely for the grown-ups.

'Silly old sausage,' Raoulf thought, trying to hold back a seventh sneeze. 'I'd rather be watching the tumbling clowns back at the circus.'

Miss Beret squeezed Raoulf's hand as they looked up into the sky to watch the circling of Swallows, swooping and diving in figures of eight and eternal delight. They both smiled and laughed at the aerial spectacle. The Mayor looked up at their sky gazing, yet from where he was standing on stage the sinister Birds of Black were still gathering. Further in the distance a small white cloud in the shape of a palm tree drifted aimlessly across the sky. The floating Cloud Land of Bliss was returning. For some, the sparkling cloud held the thought of a dear friend and their memory, for others it was under such signs that pirate's buried treasure was found. For one it housed the possible refuge of a long-lost sister – a daughter of the divine. Where now the drifting abode of Snow Rose? Perhaps things were turning out nicely after all.

As the Mayor began his speech, Raoulf quickly became bored and began to run about. He was too caught up in his own private world to care what the Mayor was saying regarding the closure of the School. However, Nanny Goat Gruff, just back from singing support with the 'Huff-and-Puffs', was exercising her not inconsiderable lung capacity at the Mayor. Smoking twenty a day helped her rasping voice with a texture like leather – she was certainly giving it her all.

'Are you insane?' roared Granny Goat Gruff.

'Inane,' Grinny Gran mumbled under her breath.

'Asinine, more like it,' muttered Nanny Nine Toes.

Nearby, some wolf-men cheered in support and so the 'boycott-the-Bear' rant of goats, hens and wolfs started to kick off noisily.

'Bumbling buffoon,' thought the perspiring Mayor fumbling with the few remaining pages of his speech. 'What have I done? Who is it that I have truly become?'

'Be ye proud,' said the Sun.

'Be ye not proud,' said the Wind.

The Mayor's thoughts were caught mid-stream as the conversation passed between the two elemental friends. There was no getting around the Sun and the Wind, but why were they being so tricky?

'Do you still fear my heat?' asked the Sun.

'Or the fury of my gale?' taunted the Wind.

'Aa… Aah… Aitchoo!' went the boy's unexpected and startling sneeze as he catapulted backward and tumbled right over.

So it was that the uncontrollable seventh sneeze, the sneeze of all sneezes, escaped from Raoulf's nose. It was as though a feather of a passing Air Angel had deliberately tickled him, as though a Zephyr had flown down upon the Wind's laughing breeze and brushed unexpectedly against his surprised nose, as though somebody's life depended upon it. Then the pregnant woman let out a primal scream, gave one final push and dropped her bonny load right next to the Philosopher-Prince. A Swallow Chief sat on the outstretched fingers of the Statue's hand, observing the colourful bustling scene. Above, a large Hill Hawk hovered ominously.

Miss Beret pulled away from Mr Littlesøn and Raoulf saying she would be back in a moment, for she had just made a decision to have a tattoo. Not for her a Black Crow rising or a Bluebird swooping, but a life-size Swallow diving over the top of her left shoulder directly toward her Rose-cossetted heart. The prospect of needles and bloodening intrigued Mr Littlesøn so he followed her, dragging a bemused Raoulf behind him.

'Can I get one too?' asked Raoulf.

'No,' said Mr Littlesøn firmly. 'You're far too young. Besides, it hurts…'

If Raoulf was momentarily disappointed he did not mind too much, as he was busy having so much fun. Anyway, sometimes that was what grown-ups were useful for – keeping you safe and saying no. But it was a bit tiresome. So Raoulf opened his arms wide and zoomed off like an aeroplane around the pink-and-red striped candyfloss machine next to where the toffee apples, thumping bags and boxing-balls hung. Flying around, Raoulf shouted out that he would like to go and hit some peeking moles back into their holes. Running without looking, he bumped straight into the legs of somebody large and grown-up.

'Oops, sorry' said Raoulf, looking up to see who it was getting in the way. 'Oh hello, it's you…'

'Hello to you too,' replied Mr Woolfe looking down at Raoulf, smiling. 'Playing planes are we? Flying off somewhere special – into battle?'

'Yes,' Raoulf nodded, bemused. How was it that Mr Woolfe always seemed to know what he was up to? He seemed to have an uncanny knack for that – knowing what was going on underneath. Raoulf furrowed his forehead and pursed his lips in a pensive manner. For a moment he was rather wary of Mr Woolfe, but then decided to fly on by. Some mysteries were best left unmasked. Janus walked beside them, grinning.

Miss Beret decided to design the tattoo of a Swallow entwined with roses herself, and had the preliminary outline etched in henna. Mr Littlesøn thought it looked striking. Whilst waiting, Raoulf had his face painted. He had chosen to be a tiger.

'Raahhh!' roared Raoulf growling and clawing the air as he dragged everyone along to watch him bash the moles back into their holes. He explained to Mr Woolfe that the moles were emerging Goblins, Witches and Trolls, which he liked to bludgeon back into their burrows and dingy hovels.

'That must be thirsty work, even for a brave soldier. You must be in need of an ice-cream…'

'Yes please. Scary tigers need lots of ice-cream…'

'And very frightening you are too,' said Janus jumping a step back in mock fear. 'Perhaps it's time you joined the Forest Brigade.'

Smiling proudly, Mr Littlesøn pulled Raoulf close and ruffled his son's hair.

So it was that Mayor Bear was having his breakthrough at the very worst possible moment, all things being considered. His head was hot, his hands were sweaty, and his whole body was tingling uncomfortably. On the nearby music stage, the remaining singers were building up a storm, pushing their finales on to a deafening crescendo. But as they sang aloud their glorious choral rapture, bleating out the joy of the Old Way, the Mayor's soul was set in further strange motion. His heart was fluttering and his mind was trembling upon the music. Mayor Bear was visibly shaken to the core by the combined force of the singing, the sneezing, and the aggravating dissenting crowd.

In his youthful innocence, Jack Rose had been easily mesmerised by enchanted treasures and the promise of gold. As the grower of beanstalks, he had subsequently turned Jack Flash, thief, goliath tracker, and collector of gems, fortune and relics alike. After that he had been changed into plain muddled-headed Peter. Yet in reality, the Mayor was not any one of these old guises. Most importantly, he wished to be different now, to grow into someone new; to be someone happier, like that woman in the crowd with the sneezing child whose wonderful smile had reminded him of an opening rose.

Today, the Sun and the Westerly Wind were here to aid the Mayor's decision and seal his fate. Around him, the crowds' pecking beaks, shuffling feet and simultaneous clicking open of handbags by the Grandmothers of Awe resulted in further disturbance. The Sun blazed, and the sudden dazzling of light on the accumulated shiny gold and silver-leaf, sparkling gems and glittering coins blinded the Mayor's eyes. Jakob had exchanged the Statue's pawned items of former glory for Dragon gold obtained from the Headmaster, who had returned the treasure to the Grandmothers of Awe.

'The birds gave it to you for a reason,' he said.

Yet, of all the various startling events surrounding the Mayor, it was the expelling of that seventh sneeze erupting from a boy's nose that had somehow broken a restricting seal and heralded his end. Something inside had snapped and his world now began to shatter about him. His hitherto unexpressed grief started to well up. What had previously been masked by conflicting desires, now broke over him in the unravelling of memories, shameful mistakes and life's just making do's. Coming home to himself, the Mayor arrived at his Rose heart to find its petals tightly closed. His heart spasmed and ached, for he missed his family so very much.

Then, like a calling, like a falling, like an unwelcome surprise, the Mayor began to panic. If only he could soothe his temples, clear his airways and stop the constricting pains in his chest that were making him so breathless. He wanted to sit down, take off his pinching Jack Boots and have a nice sip of his favourite 'Reyka' moonshine. Although at this point, any sort of medicinal drink or balm would do. Overwhelmed by emotion and the events of the day, the Mayor suddenly felt faint and giddy. It was time for his leap – if not of faith then at least avoidance of an untimely death.

'What is your answer then, my dear friend?' asked the Sun kindly.

The Sun beamed whilst the sea-kissed Westerly Wind blew a breath of fresh air over the Mayor. Once more the fragrance of roses descended upon him. This was a gift from the Rose of Snow, she who was only gone so she could be ever present for the good of all. She had forgiven her brother Jack such a long time ago because she had accepted her fate – safeguarded in a secret cloud where the Giants had raised and adored her. Yet Peter still blamed his younger self for her vanishing and had held his infant sister out of his heart by the confusion of his mind and the dishonour of his feelings. Now, Snow Rose simply radiated her gentleness down upon him like so much cloud blossom and blessing.

As the pressure mounted on Mayor Bear his knees buckled beneath him. He felt claustrophobic and sick as his stomach knotted. All the past things he had held onto – all the unnecessary restrictions of cumbersome fear, power and survival – started to release and tumble away. In a terrible, trembling moment of silence his memories plumed like dust and ashes. So, in full view of a jeering crowd, the Mayor collapsed upon the stage, grasping at his tightening chest and ailing heart. As he fell he could see the smiling face of his youngest sister in the cloud above, not lost, just forgotten and held at bay.

A moment of quiet descended and in the pervading silence the grace of a single falling petal from Snow Rose dissolved about the Mayor. At last, unexpected joy was here and he was ready to receive her peace.

Like an exhausted, broken child, the Mayor lay upon the wooden boards staring out at a sea of confused and concerned faces that now gathered around. For the first time in ages he felt safer curled up on the floor than standing up in confrontation. He wondered if he could rest there forever, surrendered in a cocoon of silence and peace as the world and its worries ebbed away. Blinking slowly, he gazed up into the firmament above watching the wheeling Zephyrs and Air Fairies race away into the great blue sky and toward the Forest. The much hoped for chance of change was here at last and the Sky Spirits would be the Mayor's heralds. In the distance, the medieval bells of Saint Gretel the very good and her brother, Saint Hansel, rang out together…

'Love knows injury,' sang St Gretel, 'but still she sweetly sings.'

'It is forgiveness freely and fully given,' sang St Hansel.

'And gratefully received,' mumbled the Mayor lying trembling, curled up on the stage.

'It is received,' confirmed the Palace bells echoing out to inform the Mountain Monks in Sky City. Instantly, their pealing filled the awakening wood, which understood the Mayor's change of heart.

Around the Mayor was a quick scrabbling of feet and a helping of hands as the Townsfolk cushioned the head of this fallen fool. He had almost dropped off the front of the stage in his sudden collapse. What was he thinking trying to step off the edge like that? Where did he think his Zip Boots would take him without the utterance of a command? For a moment the holding-their-breath crowd eaters and the berating-the-Mayor pack beaters, as well as the crowers, the gloaters and the fur-tufted men, all thought they had failed; yet the shedding of a single rainbow tear from the Mayor's left eye marked victory.

Slowly, Mayor Bear started to remember where he was, thanks to the aid of Nanny Goat Gruff's smelling salts and a quick sip from her hipflask. Coming too, he felt shiny and new. Perhaps he could not create a happy ending or a Rose paradise, but it was still within his power to save the School from being a car park and help free the Forest from the final taints of an ancient Witch spell. He should. He could. He would.

The Mayor, simultaneously Jack Rose and Peter Bear, was truly sorry for taking so long to realise himself, and in the shedding of a Sun-twinkled, glistening tear those around could see that. With the help of Granny Goat Gruff the Mayor slowly raised himself to his knees. With a shake of his head the Mayor apologised to the crowd as he remembered the recent pain and turmoil within his heart.

'I most humbly apologise…' the Mayor insisted as he waved people's help away and slowly hauled himself up from the floor, '…but I'm fine. Truly I'm fine.'

Here the Mayor let the few remaining crumpled pages of his speech fall from his hand. Everyone watched as they were carried away on the lightest of Zephyr breezes. Good riddance. What had he been thinking!

'And, of course, I thank you for your help regarding the error of my ways. In return I promise you this…' The Mayor paused to catch his breath. '…There will be no car park on the School site.'

Everyone in the crowd cheered, and in reward a hundred handbags containing the accumulated treasure from the selling of sewing and songs, cakes and jams – as well as a large red ruby, flakes of gold and silver-leaf, and two sapphires of brightest blue – were quickly thrust forward. Amongst the hoards of handbags were further offers of generosity and help. Formerly, such wealth would be food for the Mayor's greedy self, but now the glinting fortune was seen as funds for sharing and goodness. After all, who had not done such selfish things for a glittering sapphire or two in their past!

Feeling slightly lightheaded and decidedly dishevelled, the Mayor stood centre stage brushing himself down, as an intrigued crowd drew closer.

'Now I need you to listen to me for a moment longer as there are a few things I'd like to propose...' The Mayor took a deep breath. 'In recent discussions with the Headmaster I want to assure you that the woodland 'right to roam' – including the freedom of the Forest – will be protected for all...'

Astonished, the crowd grew quiet except for Gunnbjorn, his gun mates and the Wolf Men who started to grumble and growl at each other...

'For all...' repeated the Mayor emphatically. 'I'd also like you to consider a plan for the conservation of the ancient Forest and the restoration of the old Palace...'

The crowd murmured. 'A Palace?'

'Yes, the courtyards will be restored to their former glory and the large walled galleries will be opened to the public. I propose that the building and the grounds will be made into a Palace of the Fine Arts. Blossom Trees will be planted and sculptures, bronzes and statues will adorn the Palace grounds...'

Pleasantly surprised, the crowd listened on.

'Likewise, there will be new public gardens and playing fields to walk and play in, with stretches of sandy beaches for children to build sandcastles on. The Park's dilapidated bandstand will be repainted and will host the return of live music, whilst the refurbished Grand Pavilion will provide a covered space for afternoon tea dances, with light jazz for the late-night owls and lazy hounds. The cafeteria will re-open serving food and drink, with discounts for the poor and the aging, and a soup kitchen for the homeless opening at night…'

The crowd applauded, whilst in the air above, darting Zephyrs and Air Fairies sketched an image of an unchained Unicorn with their vapour trails. The sky-sign surprised and encouraged the Mayor for he somehow knew he was on the right track and did not want to hold back his newfound enthusiasm.

'Wednesday afternoons will be kept free for everyone to enjoy spontaneous weekday picnics, as well as for the pursuing of hobbies, interests and general relaxation. Sunday strolls and the walking of dogs, ferrets and ducks will be encouraged so people can meet and greet once more in the great outdoors to revive the art of conversation and camaraderie… A new conservation area will be created for the Zoological Gardens…'

Here the Mayor wondered if a certain silver-haired caretaker might fit the bill for leading such an enterprising scheme…

'Rowan horses, reindeer, and exotic creatures of the Lapp Forests and snow plains of the Far North, within safety and reason, will be allowed to roam free once more….'

The crowd murmured appreciatively, conceding that his proposals did sound rather splendid, albeit long overdue. Yet here reality intervened, piercing the Mayor's golden epiphany with a loud crunching sound, a throat-clearing cough and a pertinent question,

'Hh…hhm!' went Granny Goat Gruff's loud, leathery voice next to him. 'And where exactly are we to find the funds for all this?'

Granny Goat Gruff was not going to let the Mayor get away with any more stupidity. The other Grandmothers of Awe concurred. The Mayor was momentarily dumbfounded when another voice, lilting and gentle, interrupted to amaze them all.

'Oh!' said the golden-haired singer walking back onto the stage where the Mayor now stood. 'I believe I can help there. If I am not mistaken, you've been holding my father's Palace estate for me?'

'Why! Of all the love-a-ducks and strange deuces,' thought the Mayor. 'It must be her. Who else would dare?'

'Indeed, I have,' the Mayor lied aloud to the intrigued crowd as he regained his composure on this strangest of days.

Smiling, the Beltane Belter stared suspiciously at the Mayor. A recently lost lawyer stood at her side, waving some deeds of provenance the Mayor recognised from his most secret of cabinets. The wandering Princess had found the flabbergasted, browbeaten, bottom-sore lawyer at the foot of Fang Ridge Mountains muttering about Air Fairies, Trolls, and an untrustworthy Mayor called 'Bear'. The crowd seemed somewhat bemused by the lawyer's tall tale and the singer's claim of royal heritage, however enchanting and sincere the Princess appeared. Yet there was one amongst their number who understood the situation completely…

'My dear,' said Silly Tilly stepping forward from out of the crowd of gathered grandmothers. Then, to the amazement of all, Waltzing Matilda began to gently glide toward the centre of the stage in her crystalline slippers.

'Fairy Godmother?' asked the surprised, but delighted Princess. 'Is that really you?' After all the many centuries at last they were re-united. 'But your wings?'

'Clipped by a brick in the War of the Witches, I'm afraid,' Matilda replied sadly. 'But your wishes... the thousand fortunate wishes I bequeathed at your birth. Do you still have them?'

'Of course,' said the suddenly comprehending Princess. 'That explains why I've experienced so much wondrous good fortune...'

Matilda beamed. 'I am so pleased... for that is what I intended.'

'And I wish your wings well for it, Fairy Godmother...' and as the Princess spoke so Matilda's wings were mended, all gossamer and shiny and new.

In this act of generosity and kindness the crowd were stunned and won-over as Matilda began to rise, hovering over their heads. And as she began to fly about, she sprinkled the onlookers with golden fairy dust.

'Well I never,' chorused the Grandmothers of Awe momentarily feeling young again.

'Blow me down,' exclaimed Granny Goat Gruff to Matilda. 'Look at the splendour of you.'

Matilda smiled. 'Thank you all so much for your help.'

As the Princess seemed so magnanimous and fair, the Mayor straightened his hat and mayoral chain and pulled himself together with some quick thinking. Pushing out his chest, he cleared his throat and turned to address the bewildered crowd once more.

'Yes, I have been waiting for just such a day as this to increase all our bliss.' Seizing the moment and the Princess's shoulders, he ushered her forward. 'Please let me welcome Awe's long-lost singing Princess...'

Some half-hearted clapping rippled through the onlookers. Now what was the old fool up to?

'Thank you,' said the Princess giggling. 'I wish you well for it.' And so the Mayor's miraculous recovery continued. The Princess then made an extraordinary announcement to the crowd, 'And in celebration of oncoming Summer we should start with a month of Sundays.'

A loud cheer rang out, as yet another of the Princess's lucky thousand wishes became everyone's fortunate command. Unfolding events simply marched on to the melody of her happier tunes. She had been having such a wonderful time ever since she had left the easterly turret and now she understood the reason why. She certainly was enjoying herself – even the troubling years of her imprisonment were now viewed with wise distance and good humour.

Meanwhile, standing in the presence of the Princess, the people of Town's extraordinary fortune continued. Encompassed by her aura and Matilda's shimmering fairy dust, even the Mayor felt wonderfully refreshed. The Princess was truly captivating. He did not realise that he was ensorcelled. In her recent sojourn at Sky City, with the help of the Mountain Monks, the Princess had cast a 'Long Song of Summer Spell' across the whole of the Land of Awe, which was now awakening and responding to her Godmother's magically bequeathed wishes.

Aided by the Zephyrs, the enchantment of the Sky Monk's 'One Dream' rolled down from the mountains, and the sound of birds, bees and bells was carried across the land on an uplifting tonal breeze. As one, the Forest birds rose up with beating wings as though a gunshot had gone off. The earth thundered and the wood shook itself free from the malaise of the evil Witch Queen's ancient grasp. The poisoned plants sighed and the tainted trees breathed, casting a misty sickness up into the air to be dispersed in the gusts of darting Zephyrs.

The stagnant water in the Well of Tears and Good Wishes rippled as purification began to spring and wash away any remains of the Witch. The fountain of the Forest of Thirst was flowing again and the surrounding rose bushes were beginning to grow and bloom. The spire doors now unlocked from the inside. The few remaining dancing figurines in the Old Palace courtyard crumbled to dust as the souls of trapped courtiers were finally freed from the Witch Queen's curse. As statues tumbled, her spells of shadow and fear fell away.

'Thank you,' said the unfettered Palace spirits departing upwards where Snow Rose greeted them in her floating cloud kingdom above. In fond recognition, the ghosts of gaolers waved at the singing Princess who generously waved back. Then they too were gone.

'Now the Forest truly heralds the Summer's dawn,' whispered the Philosopher-Prince to his friend the Swallow Chief.

Soon it would come to pass that there would be extra sunlight, longer and warmer Summers, and more puffy white clouds in the azure-blue sky through which the Swallows could dive and wheel. Rain, within reason, would be restricted mainly to evenings and the Winter months would have lighter interludes of ice and snow. Sunrises and sunsets, with their fascinating displays of dappled colour and interspersing shadow and light, would be prolonged to allow more daily appreciation.

At this point, the Sun beamed down and the Westerly Wind blew strong. In a sweeping gesture of surrender the Mayor dipped his creaking knee and knelt down in a grand bow before them. Doffing his hat and removing his wig, he bent his balding head in salutation to the Sun, the Wind and the elemental spirits of old.

'Well done,' said the Sun.

'Welcome home,' said the Wind.

On standing, the Mayor threw his 'Hat-of-Good-Fortune' into the air, not caring where it landed. As the hat fell from the sky it alighted on the Statue's outreached hand. In the fortuitous sharing of providence and the chance miracle of the moment, the Statue's broken heart fused back together. Once more the Philosopher-Prince was smiling and carefree, and in his newfound joy he took hold of the hat, bowed to thank the Mayor, and placed it firmly upon his head. The Statue's happiness flowed like a fountain cascading upon the good people below. The Swallow Chief fluttered his wings and chirruped, whilst the Princess laughed joyously. The Lone Wolf Men, tiring of it all, sat astride their bikes and revved their engines. Some Nans up for further shenanigans climbed on behind.

Janus and the Headmaster were not present to witness the events taking place on the stage. Janus was still walking about the fete, whilst the Headmaster was sitting in his office discussing longcase pendulum technicalities and lantern movement with his good friend Jakob the Clockmaker. For a long time, Miss Beret's classroom clock had been stuck on 'Fair-Weather' whether the weather be fair or not. The Headmaster suspected the Goblins of interference and foul play, but the mending of such intricate things was rather complicated – particularly when you did not know what you were doing!

As the Headmaster gingerly tapped at the broken clock face with his wand, the Sun and the Westerly Wind sent a kindly beam and a light warm breeze through the open window. Knowing the Mayor's opening Rose heart to be sincere, the elemental friends pecked the Headmaster boldly on his cheeks to congratulate him on a job well done. And that is how he learnt that the School had been saved. Delighted, Jakob laughed and the Headmaster danced, and some passing judging birds were pleased to declare that the day's hat removal competition had resulted in a friendly draw.

The Headmaster leant out of the window and signalled to Janus that they had been successful by flickering his Star-Compass pocket-watch in the sunlight. Janus, still engrossed in conversation with Raoulf, Miss Beret and Mr Littlesøn, allowed himself a half-smile. Jakob and the Headmaster then decided they would re-join the crowd for late afternoon tea and a generous slice of Grinny Gran's rather delightful Danish Dream Cake – the one drenched in delicious sun-kissed rum. The Headmaster also had his fingers crossed for a nice win on the tombola. So far, according to his Far Sight, a ninety percent probability of a clean sweep was in the offing.

As Jakob left the room, the Headmaster turned back to his desk and rummaged through a pile of stacked up letters and papers. He was still waiting for a response from Miss Beret regarding a certain opportunity arising at the School, but so far he had received no word. Looking into his Mystic Mirror he hoped that her future wedding, motherhood and the happy fate of fairy tales would not interfere too much with her career prospects as the new potential Headmistress. Then the visage of a roaring Dragon filled the rippling glass. Somewhat intrigued, somewhat startled, the Headmaster quickly left the room.

My, oh my! What a cacophony of whooping, cheering and clapping greeted the Headmaster as he stepped outside. Now somewhat unemployed, the birds from Black Nest flew off skyward to return to the First Forest where Well waters ran fresh and changes of heart needed reconsideration. The Swallows soared into the sky as all the Song Birds and Turtle Doves of Town cooed and called out. A sudden, warm, southerly breeze tipped the spire bells once more in joyous celebration and it was just like a lovely wedding day in June. Not a moment too soon.

Standing tall upon the stage, Mayor Bear roared. Mayor Bear growled. Mayor Bear did a little laughing jig without his hat and lopsided wig. In his humbling collapse he had been caught as bare as he dare; he really had been seen parading in the ceremonial pomp of his all-togethers. So that was the act of heart opening of which Janus had forewarned him – the overwhelming threat of shame, shock and shadow. The Mayor sincerely hoped it was over. He had held love at a distance for far too long and he was none too keen to go through all that again!

Meanwhile, the Philosopher-Prince stood upon his plinth, inwardly rejoicing but quietly forgotten, whilst the Mayor's Tricorn hat still perched upon his head. All the Statue's gems, and gold and silver-leaf, were still in the possession of Town's elderly women. They might have few teeth left to bare, but they had daring, gnashing, political gums and lungs enough to huff and puff and blow an old fool's house down. Purse lipped, handbags gripped tight, elbows raised and at the ready, they knew how to eat politics and Mayor-ocracies alongside the slicing of cake and the taking of honey, whiskey and tea.

So it was that the Nanny Goats and Glamorous Grans saved the day in an old-fashioned way, simply sitting doing their knitting, talking to each other and not being afraid to converse with the birds. And that was how – through the principle of listening and sharing –

the avenging, great Goat caper by Grandmothers was achieved and the fortune of the Land of Awe restored.

'Bravo, sonny!' said Ninny Nanny slapping the Mayor hard upon his back.

Reeling, the Mayor sputtered.

'Odin bless you!' added a Huff pinching his ruddy red cheek.

'Good luck in all that you do!' cheered one of the Puffs blowing a large amount of cigarette smoke into his face.

'Thank you,' spluttered the Mayor, coughing and wheezing.

'Now, don't make us come back and sort you out again,' said a less than sympathetic Granny Goat Gruff who still had a kick or two left for any foolish man if need be.

Yet at last she felt satisfied that the Mayor had somehow turned out all right. The spirit of her old man, Joseph, stood behind her laughing. Granny Goat Gruff did not know it, but at last she was ready to give up the ghost. Well, almost, perhaps after a few more swigs and jigs to celebrate back at the Hazy Days Care Home. Along with all the other Ninnying Nans, Grinning Grans and the rest of the Huffing Puff Gruffs, that is. As the Grandmothers of Town turned to leave the stage they each in turn reached out to heartily shake the Mayor's hand.

Then Grinny Granny coughed loudly as they congregated together. Silently, they reached deep into their handbags and purses and took out the gold and silver-leaf and the remains of their takings. They stuffed it all into Granny Goat Gruff's great big glad-bag and nodded in accord as she now turned and placed the whole lot into the Mayor's sweaty hands. As treasurer, Grinny Granny was rather reluctant to release the large red ruby and two sapphires of brightest blue from her purse. Yet with an encouraging nudge from Mable Fable, a shake of her head and a slightly sad 'Aha!' she handed them over to the silly-old-sod, but duffer-done-good in the end. The Mayor grinned with delight at all the good fortune he was receiving. He felt his exuberance rising like a beam on his face. Why, it seemed they still had trust in him after all, and that was something worth smiling about.

'Use this to smarten up that Statue whilst you're about it,' said Granny Goat Gruff brusquely nodding at the Philosopher-Prince and poking at the Mayor with her cane, 'eyes and all. The birds will be checking your progress.'

'Yes,' said the Mayor stunned to see his triangular 'Good Fortune' hat sitting triumphantly upon the Statue's head. 'You're right, I will.'

But here the singing Princess and Matilda intervened.

'Why wait,' said the Princess handing the handbag over to her Fairy Godmother who fluttered graciously above the Statue. Matilda took hold of the Mayor's 'Good Fortune' Tricorn hat, emptied the contents of the handbag into it, and then tipped the treasure over the Philosopher-Prince.

'Whilst the Statue stands true,' sang Matilda floating overhead, 'Providence will reign over you…'

And so Town and the denizens of Awe came to be joyously blessed by a magical Fairy Godmother. The Sun's laughing light danced and twinkled in the sapphires of brightest blue, whilst the afternoon's colourful closing rays warmed the flaming ruby. The Swallow Chief and the Philosopher-Prince rejoiced. Events had certainly turned – the School had been saved and Town's guardian

Statue had been returned to its golden glory. The Sky Monks, the birds and the Philosopher-Prince had all got their timing right, and that was how peace was restored to the Jutted Land.

Next day, Mr Littlesøn drove to collect Miss Beret and Raoulf after School. Crossing the playground on their way out they bumped into Mr Woolfe leaving the Headmaster's office. Raoulf took his father to look at the freshly gilded Statue as a Robin chirped his feathery greetings from the Statue's outstretched hand.

'Good news about the School,' said Miss Beret cheerfully.

'Yes,' replied Mr Woolfe, 'although I won't be coming back after the Summer holiday. I was just informing the Headmaster that I've another job lined up… at the Zoological Gardens of all places.'

'No different than here then,' she joked.

Janus laughed. 'I'm hoping for a bit more peace and quiet.'

Miss Beret looked at Janus quizzically. She wanted to ask him how he had come to possess her father's talisman, the one he had given to Raoulf and which the boy always wore. To Raoulf it was like having a re-assuring spirit totem to believe in, like Saint Fork Beard or King Blue Tooth. He naively trusted that he was now safe from malevolent forces and could skip merrily along The Way unhindered. And it was true, as the protective spirit of the Huntingsman watched over him; watched over them all. Yet Miss Beret believed there to be some missing connection, some missing piece of information, which would complete her knowledge of her father and help her understand the troubling past.

As Miss Beret regarded Janus it was as though she knew his features by a feeling in her heart. She wanted to trace the outline of his weathered face with her fingers, because through such simple touch she could sense all manner of hidden thoughts and feelings. One touch would be all that it would take to unlock a mystery that still bothered her. Who was this silver-haired man and why had he helped Raoulf, and consequently her, so much?

For a moment, Miss Beret saw her father's spectral face shimmering before her, but really it was only Janus smiling back. Yet gazing into the caretaker's piercing, husky-blue eyes, she fleetingly glimpsed intriguing fragments… a gang of marauders, images of a ferocious Witch War, and three snow-blurred figures trekking South journeying down the icy slopes. Was one of them her father? Had Janus and the Headmaster known him from a time before she had been born? Then she saw no more in Janus's reflecting eyes of ice as he slowly blinked, unfreezing like a statue before her. Miss Beret's vision quickly faded.

Janus knew what Miss Beret was doing and he was almost willing to let her scry his memories, but not here, not today. He was not quite ready to tell his version of "Goat's Beard" to her yet. Things always changed when you did. At that moment Raoulf and Mr Littlesøn returned as the Robin hopped off back to the allotments in search of flies, worms and bugs for supper. Janus raised his eyes to watch a curious white cloud drift through the bright blue sky up above before returning his attention to his niece and the family standing before him.

'I hear you might be taking over from the Headmaster now the School is saved?' Janus politely enquired.

Miss Beret half-smiled and shrugged her shoulders.

'I think the Townsfolk would like that…' Janus said kindly. 'You know, with things in your hands the old ways will be remembered and passed on – things both fairy and fur, so to speak.'

Shaking herself free from her reverie Miss Beret replied, 'Thank you, Janus. I'm considering it, but it'll be quite the challenge.'

Janus nodded.

'Yes, thank you,' interjected Mr Littlesøn appreciatively patting his friend upon the back. 'For everything…'

'Get your moonshine sorted,' Janus said softly. 'You'll be all right.'

'But you and the Headmaster have done so much to help the folk of Town,' Miss Beret re-joined. 'I only wish they knew how grateful they should be to you both.'

'No!' Janus replied shaking his head vigorously. 'It's nothing really, only survival. For better or worse. That's what I said to the Headmaster when we first arrived here. The far Northern Slopes can get cold and lonely… Survival in some of those ice-blasted places was getting hard for me. The Dark Wars left a lot of Shape Shifters roaming around, splinter groups and factions, but they're all out of time and place in the New World. And I'm rather long in the tooth, you might say, to be dealing with the likes of them. Your father was one of the last true hunters…'

Janus trailed off looking at Miss Beret. He was stumbling over secrets he did not wish to reveal. Whatever 'Truth Revealing Charm' of hers was at work, he had said too much already. Her subtle Rose power, combining with Raoulf's Banshee blood, was greater than he realised, but Lone Silver Wolf was stronger than all that.

'Anyhow,' Janus continued, changing tack, 'the New Way is in the hands of the Mathmagicians now… There's only a few left in the world, but the Headmaster's been a true friend. He's been kind and good to me when a lot of folk would have been cruel in their prejudice and lack of understanding…'

Janus paused.

It was not all quite true, but his explanation would have to suffice for now. He could see Miss Beret searching for more detail, for something more personal to hold onto, but at present the revelations surrounding his brother's life and death still lay too deep for him to reveal. There were childhood secrets and past events that would hurt her and he did not wish that.

'This Jutted Land has been a special home for me,' Janus confided to Miss Beret, as he turned away to look at Raoulf and Mr Littlesøn heading towards the School gates. 'Some places are just like that. I'm grateful that the Headmaster chose here.'

'For both of us,' replied Miss Beret quietly. 'Although a place not without its share of difficulties too, eh?' She hesitated. 'Janus? I've been meaning to ask…' but at that point Raoulf ran back and interrupted their conversation.

'Mr Woolfe?' piped in Raoulf, 'can I come see you at the zoo?'

'Anytime, little fellow,' Janus replied laughing. 'I've lots of exciting tales about animals in me somewhere I reckon.'

'And courage and love I expect too,' added Miss Beret genially beaming down at Raoulf.

'Oh, I don't know about that,' Janus winked at Raoulf. 'Love was never really my thing.'

Sitting outside the notorious 'Peg Leg and Hook' tavern, Anders the Bard looked up from his writing as he heard the soft, reverberating beat of wings combine with a nearby bleat of happiness. It was the late returning Barn Swallows and his goat, Little Milk, merrily eating the buttercups and daisies. Anders smiled as at last he lay his quills down. Laughing once more, he strolled over and stroked his companion's butting white head. Up above, a drifting cloud was gathering holding the promise of a twinkling twilight star. The Bard untethered the goat and set off to find a bed of straw in the stable at the back of the tavern.

Lying contentedly in the crook of the Bard's arm, Little Milk chewed gently upon her master's fingers insisting on some final comforting words to conclude the bedtime tale. So Anders tugged upon the goat's magical beard in an attempt to Far See and complete "The Chronicle of Ages". Listening to faint cloud voices and the fluttering of Swallow wings in the stable eaves, the Bard finished with a flourish what distant Time and events had somehow begun…

…For in the end Miss Beret and Mr Littlesøn announced their engagement, helped each other to heal and then, in time, were happily married. Raoulf grew up being loved by two very different mothers, a father, a silver-haired wolf-man, and a retired Headmaster who kept constantly disappearing on marvellous Dragon adventures – all of whom showed him the winding ways of tangled woods and transforming mystery. Thus, under the silvery light of the Moon and the Stars and the bright golden Sun, Raoulf came to know and accept all of their stories and the fairy blood of their true inner natures. And so it was that…

'…They all lived happily there, then and in the ever, ever after…'

ABOUT THE AUTHOR

Keith Brazil was born in Broadstairs, Kent, England. He trained in Dance Theatre at Laban Trinity Conservatoire, London, and was a founder member of 'Adventures In Motion Pictures' Dance Company. He has worked as a freelance professional dancer, choreographer, teacher, and dance lecturer. Keith has also trained as a complementary therapist in spiritual healing and reflexology. He gained a degree in English Studies and is currently engaged in writing a collection of metaphysical and fictional stories, essays, poetry and novels. He lives and works in London.

www.ingramcontent.com/pod-product-compliance
Lightning Source LLC
Chambersburg PA
CBHW050021180626
46810CB00002B/516